AKAIRYA
First half of The Fractured Soul

ABRIANNA LEAMING

DEDICATION

Akairya is dedicated to every single person who has encouraged me to follow my heart and write. My parents, my family, my friends, my professors...you are all amazing. Thank you.

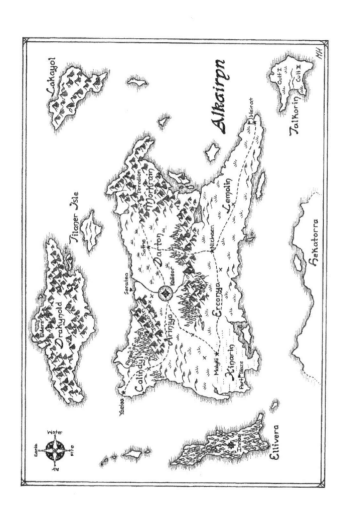

ACKNOWLEDGMENTS

I would like to acknowledge John Carroll, one of my professors from the University of the Fraser Valley. Without your advice and guidance, *Akairya* would not be the book it is without you. You helped me mature as a writer who could effectively tell a decent story. Also, huge thank you to Kayla Schulz, who painted my beautiful book cover, and Mara Haggquist, who drew such a wonderful map for me to add to the book.

CHAPTER ONE

Akairya lifted a hand, the skin coated with grime from her day's work in the dark corners of the city, and rubbed at her temple. Exhaustion had set deep into her bones. The lone candle on her table flickered. Its light helped illuminate the one room that made up the half elf's home. A rusted tub, currently void of water, sat near the pile of blankets she curled into each night. The only true furniture she owned was the table and the frail wooden chair she was sitting on. A single window allowed some light to fall into the hovel, highlighting its meager contents.

Her violet gaze barely took in the dirt floor and wooden walls, walls that were set flush against other hovels that made up the poor neighborhood of Yaeloa. Surprisingly enough, the poor of the city were quite honest, and did honest work each day to put food on the table. Akairya was the poorest of the lot, and she was finding jobs more and more difficult to find. Not everyone needed small errands done, and especially not by an orphaned half elf who had no true purpose in her life.

Akairya picked at the small loaf of bread she had managed to purchase for dinner. She had lucked out; the baker had been kind enough to sell her a loaf with bits of hard cheese dotted throughout the crust. Not every day was she blessed to eat such a thing, and she forced herself to eat slowly so as to enjoy the sharp flavor of aged cheese.

The floor of her hovel abruptly shook, and her candle sputtered in protest. She blinked as a shower of dust fell from the ceiling. The floor trembled again, and then screams began to rip through the formerly silent neighborhood.

Before Akairya could leap up, a great roar broke over the screams, and the heavy beat of wings shuddered through the air. She had just stood and snatched up her dagger when one wall of her home went up in flames.

Choking on smoke, she ran out onto the street.

Her eyes reflected the fire and ice that pelted her city from every direction. The cold glint of dragon scales flashed in the smoke choked sky as she stared at the chaos surrounding her. Her mind had trouble processing what she was seeing.

A dragon twisted through the ashy air some yards away, its flat black scales unheard of in the powerful creatures.

She watched the dragon land on the city's temple of elements and breathe flames onto fleeing citizens. An icy feeling of foreboding crept up her spine. The smell of burning flesh and charred wood clogged her nose, and it was all she could do to stop from gagging.

Her burgundy hair swept across her face from a sudden bout of wind, and she whipped around to see a massive dragon land on the burning remains of her hovel. Its eyes, bleached a hollow white, locked onto hers, and terror coursed through her. There was pure malevolence in that gaze; none of the wisdom and kindness that Akairya had come to connect with dragons could be found in those evil eyes.

Shuddering, she stumbled away as the dragon opened its mouth and let loose a torrent of freezing water. The spot where Akairya had been standing a split second before was slicked over with a sheet of ice. Its cold strength immediately broke the cobbles that had made up part of the road.

Swearing, Akairya looked desperately around for an escape. She caught sight of a thin alley nearby. Water dragons had the annoying ability to create ice…or boiling water if the mood struck them. She wasn't about to stay and find out how this Water dragon was going to attack her next.

The dragon roared in frustration as she pelted down the alley, her ragged clothing stiff from the icy blast.

You think running will get you anywhere, elf girl? Think again!

Akairya flinched as the dragon's voice stabbed into her consciousness. Instead of being musical and rich like the dragon voices she had experienced before, this dragon's voice was brutal and painful. It sliced into her thoughts like a dull blade, and even after it faded away it left a throbbing headache in its place.

The alley she had chosen was long and it wound behind many small buildings, most of which were now in flames, covered in ice, or torn apart by an Air dragon's power. The dragon who had attacked Akairya had taken flight and was looking for her from up above. Its filmy eyes darted all over the alley. As it fought to find her between the destroyed buildings, Akairya realized something wonderful.

It was partially blind.

When the eyes had been taken over by the horrible white, the dragon must have lost its naturally keen sight. Elated, Akairya slipped into a connecting alley and made sure to stay in the darkest areas.

The pursuing dragon became increasingly frustrated. It growled and circled the first alley, its jaw partially open, flecks of ice showering the ground below.

I will find you! The Shadow gave me strength that will not fail me!

Its voice was softer now; still painful, yet not as agonizing as before. Akairya continued to follow the second alley away from her attacker. Its words sunk in as she got farther away, and she slowed to a walk as she thought about what the dragon had said.

The Shadow that had plagued the world for the last fifty years had spread to its oldest race; dragons. Horrified understanding dawned on her as she visualized all of the colorless dragons that were attacking Yaeloa. *No*, she thought. *It couldn't be.*

The Shadow's power stemmed from an unknown source, and it was unimaginably evil. From its depths a terrifying race had been born; the Roraks.

Roraks were generally human in frame, yet their lithe bodies were twisted and splotched with discolorations similar to bruises. They had narrow, beetle black eyes and were faster and stronger than the average person. Roraks were known for their cruelty, and wherever a group of them went, chaos followed.

It was a tragedy like no other, the fact that dragons were now being poisoned and turned into colorless monsters who were just as evil as the Roraks.

Akairya fought to keep calm as she walked down the alley, its shadows lengthening as evening drew over the wreck of Yaeloa. She could hear the screams of the city's panicked inhabitants; there would be too many dead come tomorrow morning.

Just as she was about to pass through the alley's exit, a figure hurtled towards her, its face obscured by something dark. Caught off guard, Akairya jumped out of the way, violet eyes narrowed. As the person drew closer, the dying light illuminated its face.

Akairya choked back a scream.

She still could not tell if the person was female or male, since its face was plastered with a raw, oily substance that writhed and hissed in sinister joy. Blood dripped from the face, and a muffled gurgling could be heard from underneath the ebony mass.

Rorak vomit, Akairya thought to herself as her stomach churned in disgust and pity. Whoever it was, they would be in unimaginable agony. One of a Rorak's deadliest weapons was their bile. If they desired a victim to die slowly and painfully, they regurgitated on them and left them alone. Rorak vomit was strangely alive; it wasn't the normal acidic liquid one thought vomit to be. It was like rotting cream, thick and almost solid, and its craving for flesh was never sated until its meal was wholly consumed.

There would be no way to pry the vomit off the person's face, so Akairya did the only thing she could do.

Her jaw set, she drew a dagger from her belt and buried it into the person's heart. Their body jerked and slumped to the ground. The Rorak vomit hissed in annoyance at its ruined meal, for it could only consume living flesh. Now that the person was dead, the vomit hardened and then shattered into a fine dust that coated the cobbled ground.

Akairya turned away from the body before she could see the mangled face. She did not have time to give the person a proper burial; a Shadow dragon or a Rorak would most likely be close by.

Although she had no family and had been alienated from the citizens of Yaeloa throughout most of her life, she still felt a deep sadness for the beautiful city. It had been a prospering place set on the very edge of the province of Calindyl, with great stone buildings and a large keep that had been built on the cliff looking over the Western Sea. Calindyl was one of the most flourishing of the seven provinces of Alkairyn, with its rich soil and fishing industry. Now Akairya feared that the Shadow dragons and Roraks had destroyed the beautiful province like they had destroyed its proud city.

A great roar sounded behind her, and she flinched as a searing hot flame licked at her hair. Whipping around, she came face to face with a Shadow dragon whose mouth was full of hungry fire.

Time to die, elf girl.

Akairya's eyes flashed. Today was not her day to die.

As the dragon opened its mouth to release a fresh torrent of searing flame, Akairya sprang into action. She leaped onto the dragon's right forearm, and before the beast knew what was happening, she had jumped onto its neck. Her deep red hair bounced as she clambered up to its head, its black scales cold against her skin.

With a roar of frustration, the dragon shook its head violently, yet Akairya clung to its neck with a strength born from her Elvish heritage.

You do not have the power to slay me, girl. The dragon snarled. Akairya blanched as its words sliced into her consciousness, almost making her release her desperate hold. The moment passed quickly, and soon she had climbed to the dragon's head. With a grim smile, she whipped out her dagger and promptly stabbed the dragon in its milky eye.

CHAPTER TWO

The beast roared in anguish as the blade slipped into the area where its pupil should have been. It convulsed, and Akairya slipped off its head and landed onto the cobbled road. The dragon shook and flapped its broad wings, flinging oily blood. Akairya hissed in pain as a bit of it landed on her hand and burned her flesh.

Before the dragon had time to recover, Akairya had darted towards the city's open gates. The deep light of sunset bathed the path that led out of the wreckage of Yaeloa and into the green fields of Calindyl, where the once prospering farms were also being destroyed by poisoned dragons and merciless Roraks. The sea shone a mellow gold to her right, its calm surface contrasting horribly with the destruction happening on land. Her heart in her throat, Akairya dashed towards the city's main stable.

The stalls where the horses were kept were left untouched. Although the creatures were frightened and lathered in sweat, Akairya was able to grab a bright bay and bridle her. She didn't bother with a saddle; instead she simply boosted herself onto the mare's broad back and asked her to gallop for her life

The mare ran as fast as she could from the destruction of the city. Akairya's hair streamed behind her, the strands twisting with the smoke and stench of death and blood as her mount galloped.

When the elf girl looked over her shoulder, she saw the city's keep bathed in flames, with dark dragons circling its towers. Screams rent the air, and Akairya closed her eyes against a sudden onslaught of tears as great chunks of the keep's white stones fell into the waiting sea.

Surrounding horse and rider were others who were trying to escape, on foot or mounted. A woman, who was ushering forward two children, spotted something ahead and shrieked.

Akairya followed her gaze and went cold.

A large group of Roraks was stretched out across the main road, their slim bodies covered in sickly gray armor that accentuated the discoloration of their skin. Every one of them held a jagged blade, and Akairya could see the cold glint of their eyes as her mare drew closer to the horde.

She pulled her horse up, but it was too late. Their mouths twisted with cruelty, the evil spawn of the Shadow moved quickly towards the escapees.

Their blades cut through whoever they came across; women, children, elderly. Fresh blood soaked into the ground, and gleeful laughter echoed over the burning fields of Yaeloa's farms. Dragons flew over to join the Roraks as many escapees fell under the ferocity of the Shadowspawn. Some dragons breathed flame while others opened their mouths to release torrents of chilling ice. Powerful winds created small tornados, born from the power of Air dragons lost to the Shadow. There were even some dark Earth dragons, who were responsible for the sudden earthquakes and fissures that tore apart the fields.

Akairya's mount panicked as the ground trembled violently; she reared, rid herself of her rider, then promptly fled. Breath whooshed out of Akairya's lungs when she landed on the hard ground. The Roraks were also affected by the earthquakes; many of them had lost their footing or dropped their weapons. They screamed in frustration at the dragons, who roared back. The shaking of the ground stopped, and Akairya stood up.

A black stallion slid to a stop beside her, his muzzle frothy with foam and his neck drenched in an ivory layer of sweat. His rider was a pale young man, his brown eyes wide with fear.

"Get up behind me. Fury can get us out of here," he said breathlessly, one hand stretched out to help Akairya mount. She didn't bother to ask why he chose to help her; she just nodded and allowed him to help her up onto Fury's back.

They galloped east, away from the carnage that bled into the once vibrant ground of Calindyl. They left behind the Shadow dragons and Roraks, who were too busy fighting each other to really notice anything. They ran, leaving behind screams of terror as the evening finally gave way to a black night.

They rode all night. The stallion's breathing kept steady as he carried his two riders towards the neighboring province of Ariniya, keeping well away from the main road of stone that connected all the major cities of the country. Ariniya was the richest of the seven provinces, and it was home to High King Elric.

Akairya felt lost. She had no idea where she would go...her home was destroyed and she had no family to be taken in by. She quite literally had nothing, and she wasn't sure what her next step would be. Should she travel to the country's capital, Kalisor, and try her luck there?

She fought to stay awake as the horse cantered through fields of grass drenched in moonlight. The boy sat stiffly in the saddle, although Akairya could tell he was no warrior. He was fairly soft where she held him around his waist to stay balanced. She assumed he was a noble who had chosen to spend his life in the library, rather than learn the arts of war. Nobles had the luxury of choosing their life paths, and it seemed that this boy had decided to stay far from any sort of athleticism. Many nobles of Yaeloa had been scholars. The Ivory Keep, which had been home to the Duke of Yaeloa, had boasted a massive library that had been full of books no other library in the country had. As a result, the city's military had been mostly full of lower class soldiers who had wanted to escape the life of the country.

Now the city was gone.

Akairya shuddered as she remembered the screams and the blood that had coated the streets of the city. Although she had lived alone, practically shunned by society, Yaeloa had been her home. Her heart already pined for the life she had led there.

"What's your name?" the boy asked abruptly as Fury cantered into Calindyl's rolling hills. Eventually the grassy knolls would taper off into a thick wood known as the Forest of Souls, which was a part of Ariniya.

"Kairi. I was an orphan who lived alone in the city," Akairya replied. She gave him the nickname her father had called her. Her full name would have brought the boy alarm; it was the name of the first High Queen of Alkairyn, the elf woman who had created the seven provinces and who had begun the alliance with the dragons. Such a high name was generally not given to low born half elf girl.

Akairya's companion accepted the shortened version of her name with an unsuspecting nod.

"My name is Billith. I was studying in the Ivory Keep's library before…well….before *they* came." The boy whispered.

Akairya had been right; Billith was a noble scholar of Yaeloa.

"Thank you for helping me, Billith," Akairya said, her mind replaying the horrific images of Yaeloa's fall. If it wasn't for this soft scholar, she would most likely be dead.

The boy inclined his head in welcome.

They rode in silence for another few hours, the moon's pale light illuminating the rolling hills. As Billith slowed Fury down to a walk, a light breeze blew gently over the knolls and brushed at Akairya's hair. She breathed in the subtle scent of flowers. Not only were the hills of Calindyl blessed with lush, emerald grass, but also a variety of blooms. They were dotted throughout the grass, their many colours bright splashes against the backdrop of green. The mighty Kito river wound its path just a few yards away, its wide body glinting with moonlight. It was hard to believe that some hours west of such tranquility was tragedy.

Images of the person she had killed to save them from Rorak vomit flashed through Akairya's mind, alongside the screams of the citizens that were murdered by the Rorak and Shadow dragon hordes.

Shivering, she bit her lip and pushed the memories away. While she had no idea what the future held for her, she couldn't think about what she was leaving behind.

"What were you studying, Billith?" she asked, desperate for distraction.

"War," he replied flatly, "ironic, isn't it? I used to wish that our country wasn't so peaceful, that there were still wars going on that I could write about and become another famous scholar, like Haol, the scholar who had recorded the events of the War of Elves. Now that I've seen firsthand what it is like to be among such violence…I feel dirty for ever thinking I wanted war."

Akairya patted his shoulder awkwardly. The War of Elves had been a bloody series of battles between humans and elves, back before the dragons had shown their true intelligence. Years ago, everyone had believed the dragons to be great beasts that were no smarter than the common lizard. No one knew why they had kept their intelligence a secret, just that they had finally shown it to humans and elves when they had helped end the horrible war. High Queen Akairya had taken the chance to form an alliance with the dragons, and they had played a huge part in keeping the peace since. Until now.

As Fury tirelessly picked his way over the gentle slopes of the hills, the sound of wing beats reverberated through the night air. Billith and Akairya stiffened and Fury snorted in unease as the sound grew closer, bringing with it a sense of cold dread.

Before Billith had the chance to push Fury into a gallop, the dragon descended upon them in a cyclone of chilly wind.

Its black scales blocked out the moonlight, so the beast looked like a grim, dull creature of evil. Its hard ivory eyes were locked on the three of them, its great jaw open to reveal hungry flames.

Akairya pushed herself off the stallion just as the Shadow dragon blew its fiery breath. She cried out as her right arm and leg were engulfed in searing flame, the agony almost drowning out the screams of Billith and Fury. Desperate, she got up off the ground with some difficulty and dashed for the river.

She jumped into the water just as the dragon let loose another torrent of hot flame.

CHAPTER THREE

Birds chirped a cheerful melody, their sweet voices welcoming the bright sunshine. The gentle heat of the morning caressed Akairya's sore body as she regained consciousness.

She was half lying in the calm waters of the Kito, her head resting on the mossy bank. She blinked her eyes open and focused on the thick canopy of leaves above her.

The river had taken her straight into the depths of the Forest of Souls. She breathed a sigh of relief; she was in the province of Ariniya.

The death of her new friend and his tireless horse shot pain into her heart, and she shut her eyes. She could still hear their screams as the dragon's fire swallowed them.

Her right arm and leg complained with the pain of remembered fire. Groaning, she sat up and stretched her lower body farther into the river. The cool water soothed her leg, so she dipped in her injured arm as well.

Her burns weren't as bad as she had expected. The skin was bright pink and stinging. Did the river have healing powers?

As she mulled this over, a strange sensation whipped through her. She gasped and nearly fell face forward into the river as her entire body jerked in response.

It pulled her west, deeper into the forest. It yanked at her very being. She couldn't help but feel the need to follow the feeling into the thick swathe of trees ahead of her.

Intrigued, Akairya pushed herself out of the river and limped west. Her city was sacked and she had no clear idea of what to do. She felt little to no reluctance in seeing what was calling to her so powerfully.

The undergrowth of the forest was soft, and her footsteps were muted. Dappled sunlight shivered over the lush vegetation that grew under the thick canopy of trees. Many earthy fragrances perfumed the air. Akairya took a deep breath and thought sadly of Billith and Fury. She prayed that their deaths had been quick.

She walked for some time before she came across a large boulder with a perfectly flat top, its back nestled between two towering oaks. Moss clung to the stone, and strange markings were etched on it. The pulling sensation increased sharply as she stopped in front of the rock. The feeling was so powerful she nearly fell to her knees.

Breathing heavily, Akairya reached out and touched the stone with the palm of her hand, its height nearly level with her ribcage. The markings lit up like wildfire, and with an ear splitting boom the boulder cracked. She gasped and watched wide eyed as the two halves of the stone fell away to reveal a large egg.

It was a dragon's egg, she was sure of it. It was nearly as big as one of the halves of the boulder, and its shell was a beautiful ivory that glowed with an inner power. The pulling sensation strengthened until she had no choice but to step forward and pick it up.

Arms shaking with effort, she cradled the massive egg. As soon as she brought it to her chest, the sensation that had led her through the woods abated. Astounded, Akairya stood there and stared at the bright egg, its warmth radiating throughout her entire body.

Although she had witnessed the Shadow dragon's cruelty and savage strength, she felt no fear or anger towards the creature that was inside the egg. Instead she felt a powerful instinct to protect. The baby dragon that was inside was innocent; it had had no part of the evil that had ripped apart her home.

She placed the egg down gently at the base of one of the large oaks. She had no idea what she would do with it, but she wasn't going to leave it. Something had drawn her to it, and she was sure there had been a reason.

As soon as she took a few steps away from the egg, the pulling sensation flared up again. She chuckled and stopped at the broken stone.

She knelt beside one of the pieces and studied the markings that were etched into its surface. She could not read it, but she knew what it was – she had seen it before.

Dragonake.

The language of Riders, its sloping script was complicated and hugely different from the common tongue and Elvish, which made it easily recognizable for what it was.

Akairya went back to her egg and pondered the meanings of the markings. What could they possibly say?

Her musings were interrupted by the growling of her empty stomach. She rubbed her hip and smiled when she felt her dagger. It had stayed in its hilt through everything.

She patted her egg, whispered to it that she would be back, then walked a bit away from its resting place. She winced as the pulling sensation protested, and she couldn't help but wonder how she would be able to hunt while fighting the urge to run back to the egg. Her burns only added to her worry.

She settled into a particularly large bush, her lips pursed.

As time passed, the sensation calmed. It was still there, though softer, as if it knew that Akairya wasn't really going anywhere. She breathed a sigh of relief.

Nearly an hour passed before an animal strayed into her sight.

It was a plump rabbit, its large ears perked and its nose twitching in suspicion. Akairya quietly positioned herself and aimed with her dagger. With a calm exhale, she threw the blade and nearly jumped for joy when it found its mark.

Thanking her deceased father for his teachings, Akairya happily scooped up the rabbit before another predator caught its scent. As soon as she returned to the egg, warmth ran through her body like an internal embrace of welcome.

She quickly gathered some wood and started a small fire, again thanking her father for the skills he had taught her. He had been a hunter before a father, and he had known plenty about surviving alone in the wilds. He had always deemed it of utmost importance for his daughter to know the same.

Soon the rabbit was skinned and roasting over the fire. Akairya's stomach growled and she waited impatiently for the meat to cook. She turned her attention back to the luminous egg.

It was heavy and difficult to carry, which meant she would be moving slow. It was also a dragon egg, and Akairya was positive that the people of her country would not welcome such a thing. Not after the slaughter of Yaeloa.

Sighing, she took the rabbit off the fire and picked at the steaming meat.

"I am most definitely in a bad situation," she mumbled to herself as she stared gloomily into the flames.

A loud *crack* echoed throughout the forest, causing Akairya to jump and nearly drop her meal. She looked around in a panic, her imagination immediately conjuring up the worst possible scenario: a Shadow dragon or Rorak had found her.

Heart pounding, she went to put out her fire when another *crack* sounded. This time she was able to discern its location, and to her astonishment the noise had come from the egg.

Thin cracks had webbed across the shell's white surface, and the entire thing trembled. Dumbstruck, Akairya watched as a black scaled foot burst through the shell.

Its tiny black claws scrabbled at its prison, its efforts soon allowing its second foot to push through. After a few more seconds of struggling, a delicate snout poked out of the egg. Not long after that, a baby dragon was sitting among its shattered egg, its curious eyes blinking at Akairya.

Hello. A sweet, male voice floated through Akairya's mind, its rich tones healing the damage the Shadow dragons' voices had inflicted.

His scales were a lively ebony, far from the flat black that had taken over the Shadow dragons. Although he was no bigger than a medium dog, his body looked powerful. His head was angular, with a broad forehead, narrow muzzle and small tufted ears, reminiscent to that of a fox. Two pearly fangs poked out from underneath his upper lip, and thin black spikes ran from the tip of his tail, over his back, up his long, elegant neck and ended at the back of his head, where two small horns jutted out beside each ear. His furled wings were a deeper black than his body, each tip studded with a single sharp spike. His four legs were thick with muscle yet gracefully curved.

He was absolutely beautiful.

"H-hello," Akairya whispered. Entranced, she walked slowly over to the newly hatched dragon and stopped in front of him. He tilted his head and studied her with his bright black eyes.

You finally came, he said happily, his tail flicking back and forth. *I've been waiting ages.*

Akairya frowned. "What do you mean?"

My egg has been sealed in that stone for decades, back when the first Riders were gifted with their dragon partners. Your presence is why I finally woke inside my egg. I know nothing of what has transpired since I was sealed away; all I know is that I have been asleep for a long time, waiting for you.

Akairya stared. This dragon had been sealed away so he could wait for *her?* That made no sense. Dragon eggs were gifted to those who had proven themselves worthy of being a Rider. She had done nothing to deserve such an honor.

"Riders are given eggs when the Elders are convinced of their worth. I'm only an orphaned half elf who happened to survive the destruction of my city."

The dragon blinked and poked his pink tongue out. *What do you mean?*

Akairya told him the events of the past few days, and about the blight that was staining the world. The deeper into her tale she got, the angrier the dragon became.

*Those dragons are blemishes on my race. To embrace such darkness and act so evilly...*He snapped his teeth.

I knew when I was sealed away that when I awoke, I would have to take on some form of evil with my destined Rider. I never would have imagined that the evil would hold some of my brethren in its grasp.

Akairya watched as the dragon tried to walk, his limbs shaking with effort. Soft mewling sounds escaped from him as he shook off the remains of his egg and took a step forward.

"What do you mean, destined Rider?"

The dragon looked at her in surprise. *Do you not know?*

"No, I do not. I know absolutely nothing. Maybe the runes on the stone would tell me something, except they are written in Dragonake."

Huffing, the young dragon took another few steps and stopped, his body trembling.

I did not know that. Interesting. He noticed Akairya's curious expression and growled. *Although I*

*can speak and know some things, my body is young
and I am still fairly new to the physical world. It will
take me time to become accustomed to being out of
my egg.*

Fascinated, Akairya picked up the remains of her
rabbit and offered it to the dragon. He took it gently
in his mouth and chewed gratefully.

Thank you. He flicked his tail and devoured the
rabbit.

"So...what does the stone say?" Akairya pressed.
The dragon licked his lips and settled down to pick
the remaining bones clean.

*I do not know, since I was not aware of the
runes. My guess is that they describe you, my destined
Rider, and that you will be led to me by our
connection. Have you not noticed that our minds are
now blended?*

Akairya closed her eyes and felt around her mind,
using the mental skills her father had taught her when
he had bothered to teach her things unrelated to
hunting. Sure enough, she could sense the dragon's
mind thrumming with energy alongside hers. She
knew just by reaching out that he was calm and happy
to have finally been united with her.

Slightly overwhelmed, Akairya took a deep
breath. "Why me, though?"

Fate has her reasons, the dragon said softly, his
black eyes warm.

Akairya put a trembling hand to her forehead
and sat down near the fire as the dragon again
attempted to walk. This time he was able to move
forward a couple feet without swaying, and his eyes
shone.

I can already feel strength growing in my limbs, he said happily. He was soon walking steadily around the fire, his steps becoming surer. Eventually he flopped down beside Akairya, his pink tongue hanging out like a dog's. Akairya couldn't help but reach out and scratch him behind one of his small tufted ears.

That feels nice, he mumbled, his eyes fluttering closed.

Smiling, she continued to scratch him as she looked into the depths of the fire, its flames crackling merrily as it gave off welcome heat. She mulled over her situation and found herself accepting the dragon without reservation. It was if her heart had been empty and waiting for him, and now that they were united she was no longer incomplete.

It was strange; their union had been subtle. Her mind had opened effortlessly to embrace the dragon, so effortlessly that she had not noticed their connection until he had brought it up.

"Do you have a name yet?" Akairya asked, ashamed she hadn't thought to ask earlier.

I...do not have any name, no.

She chewed on her lip and studied the hatchling, her brow furrowed in thought.

"How about...Draykor?" she inquired, her face suddenly vulnerable. Curious, the dragon cocked his head.

I like this name. What made you think of it?

"It was the name my father wanted to give to his son...but instead he had me."

The dragon laid his head on his front legs.

I will humbly accept the name Draykor.

Akairya smiled shyly and nodded, her mind reaching for dusty memories of her dead father, a big brooding man with burgundy hair and black eyes. Although he had loved Akairya, she knew he had wished she had been born a male.

Back before her father had died, she had found a leather bag with the name *Draykor* stitched along the side. When she had asked her father about it, he had sighed and looked at her with intense eyes.

"I had it made for the son I had hoped to have. Then your mother gave me you, and I learned to love a girl who is just as strong as any son."

Not long after that the plague, which had been coughed into existence by the early stirrings of the blight, had swept into the city, and her father had fallen victim to its black grasp.

Wrenching herself away from such painful memories, Akairya leaned back against a tree. Draykor scooted closer and curled up against her hip. She let her head fall back and soon fell asleep.

CHAPTER FOUR

Screams ripped through Akairya's dream, the terrified cries numbing her heart. Blank terror was all she felt as she stumbled through the burning city, blood flooding through the cobbled streets. Fire and ice, two things that could never mix naturally, tore apart buildings and roads as evil creatures roared in glee. She wanted desperately to escape, but there was no way out of this terror and agony. The ground ripped apart and crumbled as screeching winds tore at the destroyed city, chunks of wood and stone flying precariously close to her face. More dying screams cut through her dream, and Akairya's soul went cold.

"What do we have here?" a deep voice asked as someone prodded Akairya in the side, tearing her from her nightmare. Soaked in sweat, she leaped up and looked wildly around.

A group of four men had surrounded her campfire, two of them holding down a distraught Draykor.

They came out of nowhere! I didn't have time to wake you up, he cried in despair. Akairya realized she had no chance of helping her dragon, not when the remaining two men were looking at her with a mixture of suspicion and curiosity. The one closest to her sighed and held out a hand.

"Name is Killian. Now..." He raised an eyebrow at her. "Who are you, exactly, and why are you in the company of a black dragon?" He had a pleasant voice, deep and subtly rough.

His tousled hair was a burnished gold that glinted in the flickering firelight, and his eyes were a piercing silver which hinted at turbulent secrets. His muscled body was clad in leather armor, and a deadly looking blade hung on one of his lean hips. Engraved on the scabbard was a crescent moon inside a sun; the symbol of the High King. Another insignia was carved on his left leather gauntlet. Perched on his left shoulder, amber eyes locked on Draykor in keen interest, was a falcon.

"You serve King Elric? Oh!" she exclaimed, relief flooding through her. "I don't know if the king has heard yet, but Yaeloa...has fallen."

Killian smirked. "We heard. We also heard that most of the damage done was by dragons...*black* dragons." He looked pointedly at Draykor.

Akairya frowned.

"I don't know if you're really that dim-witted, but all dragons are born black until their elemental power is awakened. Dray here is far from evil. In fact, he just hatched a few hours ago."

Killian's eyes had hardened to a stony flint. "We have no way of knowing if you are traitors or not." He replied stiffly. "As a result, we are going to take you to the High King himself and get him to decide what to do with you." He nodded to the man beside him and strode away.

His companion stepped forward and quickly looped a rope around her wrists, a sheepish smile on his lips. His brown eyes were friendly, and Akairya was glad for it. She was not in the mood to be handled roughly.

Draykor was given a rope collar and lead. The hatchling growled softly, but allowed the treatment.

I'm too weak to do anything other than bite them, and I don't want you punished.

Akairya opened her mouth to reply, but Draykor snapped his jaws and unfurled his wings. *You can reply to me through our mental connection. It will be strange at first, but this way they won't know what we are saying.*

The four men were looking at the dragon warily, their eyes narrowed. Akairya blew out a small breath and glanced at the man who had tied her wrists.

'Well, shall we?"

He shrugged and started walking, his grip tight on her rope. The man named Killian took charge of Draykor, face impassive. The young dragon's first few steps were a little shaky, but he gained strength after a few more strides.

"Why don't you send Itaye with a message to the king, Killian? Let him know who we found," the man in charge of Akairya suggested. Killian reached up and patted his falcon.

"Itaye hurt his wing earlier when we killed that Rorak sentry. He won't be able to fly for at least a few weeks."

"Rorak sentry? You mean there are some of those monsters in this forest?" Akairya cut in, horrified. Killian glanced at her.

"The woods are crawling with the creatures. You should count yourself lucky we found you before they did. Unless, of course, you are lying about your innocence and you are one of them."

Akairya glared at him and didn't reply.

Their small procession made its way slowly through the forest. After some time Killian found a faded path, and their direction turned east.

They walked in silence, their steps through the undergrowth the only noise they made. Birds chirruped as the morning grew late, Itaye occasionally calling in response to some of them. The sun soaked through the leaves of the forest's immense trees, and butterflies swarmed the bright flowers clustered at the base of the trees.

Akairya felt some hope as she followed her captors. They were taking her to the High King, the very man who had a strong connection with the country's current Dragon Riders. Surely he would give her a chance to speak before sentencing her.

By the time it was afternoon, the ground was starting to slope upwards. The Forest of Souls was nestled beside Ariniya's main colossal mountain range, the Jalkorin, Elvish for The Jaw. It was so named because it was made of two diagonal lines of mountains which stood side by side, separated only by a thin slice of grassland. Each line of mountains was many miles long, and each mountain in the range was massive.

"Are we climbing through the Jalkorin?" Akairya asked, her curiosity piqued as they continued to move towards the range.

"We're not going to clamber over a ton of mountains, no." Killian told her. "We are going to cut through the first line of the Jalkorin and then go southwest through the grasslands in the middle. That is much easier and quicker."

"I didn't realize it was passable. Last I heard there were a few groups of trolls terrorizing the grasslands." She replied, shuddering. Trolls were huge, lumbering creatures that either feasted on anything with a heartbeat or captured them and used them as slaves.

"Most of them were wiped out by High King Elric about a year ago. If the grasslands were still infested, we would backtrack to Calindyl and go around the mountains instead of over them. The mountains are huge; it would take many weeks of climbing before we made it out of the range."

"They're that big?" Akairya inquired, her voice small. The friendly man who held her rope smiled at her.

"Don't fret. The path we're following continues straight through the range into the grasslands. It'll only take us a few days."

Akairya smiled gratefully. "That's good to hear. My name is Kairi, by the way."

"Thoran."

At least one of them seems friendly, Draykor commented, his eyes on Thoran when they all halted for a quick break. *Although this Killian seems like a decent man…he's simply doing his duty.*

"The rest of our men and our supplies are just up ahead a little ways. Then we'll get some grub, eh?" Thoran said cheerfully, his face red with exertion. Akairya shuddered at how hot he must be, hiking in leather armor.

"What were you doing in the Forest of Souls?" she asked. Thoran sighed.

"King Elric asked us to comb the forest, in case any wounded from the attack on Yacloa had made it over the border. Of course, we weren't expecting to find anyone. Yaeloa is a good five days ride from here, and the attack happened nearly two days ago. How did you know about the attack? There is no way you could have traveled from the city to the forest in that time."

Grief welled in Akairya's chest as her thoughts turned to Billith. Shaking it away, she rolled up the sleeve of her right arm and showed Thoran the pink flesh there. Although her burns no longer bothered her (which was miraculous in itself) the signs of the Shadow dragon's flame were still there.

"I was fleeing the city on horseback when a Shadow dragon caught up and attacked. I was lucky and jumped into the Kito River before the beast could finish me off. It's strange though…my burns are healing remarkably fast." She kept the deaths of Billith and his brave stallion to herself; she didn't feel like sharing the tragedy of their loss.

Thoran inspected her arm and nodded.

"Yes, it's been speculated that the river has some magical properties. Sounds like the rumors are true." He then looked into her eyes. "It sounds like you've been through a lot, and have seen a lot of things. You were having nightmares, weren't you? When we found you."

Akairya looked away from Thoran's gaze. The emotional scars the destruction of her city had caused were fresh, and she felt even more fragile when someone noticed.

Killian strode over with Draykor still in hand, his silver eyes calculating.

"Careful, Thoran. We don't know if this girl and her dragon are of the Shadow or not. Don't be going and making friends."

Akairya fought the urge to punch him in his ridiculously handsome jaw.

"Look in Dray's eyes. They have black pupils. Shadow dragons have no pupils at all, only pure white eyes. That in itself should tell you the truth of things," she snapped. Thoran looked just as angry.

"Killian, I know you're my general and that makes you my superior, but you are also my good friend. You should know me well enough to realize I would never befriend someone that could possibly be acquainted with the Shadow. Kairi here seems quite free of the Shadow's stain."

Killian ran a hand through his hair, clearly frustrated. Just as he was about to speak, the sound of splitting twigs and disturbed foliage reached them. Itaye screeched a warning and Killian stiffened. He looked back the way they had all come and cursed.

"Roraks!"

CHAPTER FIVE

Akairya's heart sank as she followed Killian's gaze. She could just make out slim figures streaking towards them, their bruised limbs partially covered by their strange armor.

"There's about ten of them...if we're smart, we can defeat them," Killian snapped. His sword was already in hand. It was of simple make, yet the blade was perfectly forged and deadly. Itaye moved to take flight, but squawked as his wounded wing protested. The bird hopped off Killian's shoulder and stalked towards a nearby bush, feathers fluffed in irritation.

Three of Killian's men also prepared their weapons. Thoran whipped out a couple of sharp daggers, his eyes glittering. He used one of them to cut away Akairya's bonds.

"I know you have a dagger, may as well make yourself useful."

Draykor, his bonds also gone, moved closer to Akairya and bared his teeth at the upcoming Roraks.

Do you have enough strength? Akairya asked urgently. Her dragon snuffed.

My body is weary from our hike, but my teeth are still sharp..

Then suddenly, the Roraks were upon them.

They were cyclones of furious energy, their movements so quick it was almost impossible to gauge their attacks. Their sharp teeth were bared in dark

34

glee as they tore around with their swords. A haze of livid Shadow surrounded them as they fought, and it pressed down on Akairya as she dodged a fierce attack from a particularly small Rorak.

It hissed at her as she lashed out with her dagger, her mouth set in a grim line. She took a deep breath and focused on her father's training, her eyes never leaving the Rorak.

"You think you're good with that spindly blade?" the Rorak cackled, its voice gravelly and full of malice. "I could kill you with my back turned!"

Akairya stepped back as the creature swung its sword. Her foot caught on a thick root, and she fell against a tree. Sticky sap stuck to her shoulders and into her auburn hair, and she gasped as her skull smacked into the trunk.

"Got you," the Rorak grinned, its wide blade raised. Just as it was about to finish her off, a black blur leaped onto its narrow shoulders.

It screamed as Draykor bit into the flesh of its neck, his black snout even darker as the Rorak's poisoned blood stained the scales. Akairya watched in astonishment as her dragon snapped his jaws again and the Rorak's head toppled from its torn neck and its armored body slumped to the ground with a clang. A dense cloud of Shadow ripped away from the corpse, and rushed north.

Draykor stepped off the corpse and shook his head violently, sending hissing blood flying. Akairya winced as some landed on her cheek.

"You weren't joking when you said your teeth were sharp," she laughed weakly. Draykor's tongue lolled out as he looked at her in satisfaction.

I can tell you this much; Roraks taste absolutely disgusting.

What about the poison?

I believe I spat it all out. I'll wash out my mouth with some water, just to be sure.

As he walked to a narrow stream that cut through the earth nearby, Akairya stood up, slightly dizzy from hitting her head. Looking around, she saw that the other nine Roraks were also defeated. Most of them were dead, but Killian had one still alive. He had the tip of his sword at the creature's throat, his eyes cold.

"Who leads you?" he asked, voice dangerously soft. The Rorak's eyes bulged as Killian pressed his blade harder against its skin.

"The one who started it all," it spat out, its hatred strong in its discoloured face. "The Lord of the Shadow."

Akairya's bewilderment was echoed by Killian's expression. "The Lord of *what?*" he snapped with impatience. He pressed harder on the Rorak's jugular. A thin stream of blood trickled down its throat, but it just smiled, its teeth lethal points.

"Your ignorance of the Lord will be your downfall. My master is more powerful than any of you, and he created our strength. The Shadow is his child, and we his grandchildren."

With a blood chilling laugh, the Rorak leaned forward and slew itself on Killian's blade, its face one of pure devilish amusement. Akairya gasped softly; she had not expected that.

What sort of evil are we dealing with? She asked her dragon, disturbed. Draykor shuffled his wings, his eyes filled with a deep concern.

An evil that has no care for life, that's for certain.

Killian groaned in disgust and wiped his blade. Thoran kicked the Rorak corpse in frustration.

"Damnit. We almost had some useful information. I loathe these disgusting creatures," he spat, his hands still gripping his bloody daggers. "The Lord of Shadow? I've never heard of him."

Killian rubbed a hand down his face. "At least we know there is a leader, someone who controls the Shadow. The destruction of a city is the first major catastrophe led by the Roraks...I had a feeling there was a higher power commanding them. Shit."

He looked at Akairya with an unreadable expression. "I think I owe you an apology."

Taken aback, Akairya gaped at him. Thoran chuckled under his breath. Killian shot him a deadly glare.

"Why is that?" she asked.

"If you *were* an ally of the Shadow, you wouldn't have helped us fight them off. Jilk, take a look at her head. She took quite the hit." He turned on his heel and began inspecting the Rorak bodies.

Jilk, the third man in Killian's party, stepped forward with a stony expression. His sandy hair was crusted with dark Rorak blood, and he still held a broadsword in his hands. At his hip was a leather bag, which Akairya assumed was full of medical supplies.

"I still don't trust you, elf. You could just be playing games with us," he hissed. Akairya stiffened and raised an eyebrow. Draykor lowered his head and growled, his tail twitching. Jilk glanced at him warily.

"I'm half elf, thank you." She snorted in disgust. "Honestly, I don't care how you feel, since I know that I am not in league with the Shadow, and that's all the matters to me."

"Noble words, but they won't do you any good when you face the noose," Jilk sneered.

"That's enough, Jilk. I'll tend to the girl if you could go see Harrol. He was stabbed in the shoulder during the fight." Thoran stepped in, his exasperation clear. Jilk threw one last look of disgust at Akairya before walking stiffly away.

"Don't take it too personally; his entire family was wiped out by Roraks." Thoran sighed. "If he thinks someone has anything to do with the Shadow, he instantly hates them.

Akairya shrugged.

"I'll ignore him," she said. Thoran grinned before coming closer to inspect her head.

"You just have a slight bump; nothing serious. You'll probably have a headache for some time."

Akairya was about to reply when a shriek cut through the forest. Flinching, she first looked for her dragon and saw him staring at Jilk and Harrol, his tufted ears perked forward. She followed his gaze and her stomach churned.

Harrol, the fourth and final man of Killian's patrol, was writhing on the ground, his hands clutching at the moist earth of the forest. His back was arched in an unnatural angle, and his plain face was scrunched up in agony. Sweat dripped off him as he flailed, and when he rolled towards Akairya she caught a glimpse of his wounded shoulder.

The leather of his armor had been eaten away, revealing his bloody flesh. An oily substance oozed over where he had been stabbed, and the skin which surrounded the cut bubbled. A subtle black haze clouded over his shoulder and got darker as the flesh reached a boiling point. Harrol screamed as the remnants of the Shadow leeched into his wound, his face turning paler by the second.

"Shit, the Rorak blade was poisoned," Thoran cursed. Killian, who had been finishing his inspection of the Rorak corpses, hurried to Harrol's side. Jilk spoke a few words to his general, then pressed a shaking hand down on Harrol's good shoulder. Killian unsheathed his blade, his face carefully blank.

"You're just going to kill him? Without trying to make an antidote?" Thoran yelled over Harrol's moans. Killian sighed and shook his head.

"Thoran, even if we could find a way to drain the Shadow's poison from his system, he'll eventually turn into a sick, twisted imitation of himself. You know that. The Shadow's effects never truly leave; instead it will just slowly corrupt his mind and body."

Thoran's shoulders slumped, and Akairya felt truly horrified.

The Shadow's evil knows no boundaries, Draykor commented, his eyes hard. *It needs to be obliterated.*

I agree, Dray. But how? We don't even know where it came from.

Her dragon lowered his head and snuffed, his ears flat against his head. *I do not know.*

Akairya looked away as Killian lifted his sword and quickly thrust it into Harrol's heart. The sound of metal slicing through flesh and bone reverberated through her mind. Shivering, she walked to Draykor and laid a hand on his scaly back, beside his thin spikes. He looked at her sadly, his wings hanging loosely at his sides.

"Let's move on. The Kito isn't far from here; I'll place Harrol's body in her waters and catch up,"

Killian announced, his grip tight on the hilt of his sword. Harrol's blood still dripped off its brutal tip, and the dark crimson soaked into the thirsty earth of the woods.

Thoran stepped forward, expression incredulous. "What if there are more Roraks? We can't let you go off alone, Killian."

The general turned on his soldier, his silver eyes flashing with agonized grief. "We only have a few hours of daylight left. You have to catch up with the rest of our patrol before it gets dark, just in case more Roraks *do* appear. I'll be able to make it without you. Plus, I want to spend some time alone with Harrol. Say my goodbyes to a good solider."

Thoran had nothing to say to that. Unhappy, he turned away. A dark, tortured expression flitted across his face, but it was gone so quickly Akairya wasn't entirely sure she had really seen it.

Jilk stood above Harrol's prone body, his hands clenched into white-knuckled fists. Killian squeezed Jilk's shoulder before he bent down and lifted Harrol into his arms, the dead soldier's blood soaking his leather armor. Without another word, he turned and walked north towards the river.

"Let's go," Thoran sighed. Jilk shook himself and followed Thoran as he started back towards the Jalkorin mountain range. Draykor keened softly before he too began to follow. Akairya kept pace beside him, her violet eyes hard.

CHAPTER SIX

One week had passed, and they were still in the Jalkorin grasslands.

A brutal rain had picked up when Killian's patrol, Akairya, and Draykor had first stepped into the colossal valley, its unrelenting strength causing their progress to slow considerably. Although they were nearly two thirds of the way out of the grasslands, it should have only taken them four days to reach the southern end of the mountain range. They were now on their seventh day, and Killian was certain it was going to take another two before they reached the end of the range if the rain continued to pour.

The hike they had had to take to first reach the grasslands had been brutal. Although they had avoided scaling a full mountain – they had found a path that cut between two of the slopes – the shortcut had still been difficult. Akairya's limbs were sore from the steep climb, and the descent had been even worse. The mountainside facing the valley had been dotted with treacherous rock that had threatened to turn her ankle or cause her to lose her footing. She was still incredibly thankful that the rain had held out until after they had reached flat land.

Now she hated everything to do with the rain.

She wasn't used to such extreme weather. The rain came down in thick sheets of frigid water, which turned the grasslands into a mixture of slippery footing and hungry mud. A savage wind accompanied the rain, and it was constantly pushing at her, slowing her down.

The entire patrol, which now consisted of eleven armed men, was in low spirits. They had wanted to find shelter and wait out the weather, but Killian had taken one look at the dark gray sky and rejected the idea. He had known the rain would last.

The nights had been miserable. They had been unable to build any fires to ward off the chill and dry their sodden clothes, and the thin tents they were barely able to erect got soaked every time they set them up. It was a miracle no one had gotten severely ill yet.

Now, on the seventh day of cold discomfort, Akairya could only just keep up. Her entire body was numb and trembling with exhaustion, and she could barely remember the sensation of being dry. Draykor plodded along beside her, his black head hanging low and his tail dragging in the slick grass, flecks of mud spraying onto his scales.

Akairya marveled at the rate he was growing. He was just over a week old, and he had nearly doubled in size. When he stood beside her, his shoulder was aligned with her waist and his head was nearly the same height as hers. He had told her this morning that he felt like he'd be ready to attempt flight soon, which amazed her. She knew of no living thing that could grow as rapidly as a dragon; it just didn't seem possible. He didn't even eat that much. He would go out hunting once a day, catch a couple of rabbits, and be content until the following afternoon.

Akairya squinted through the gray rain at Killian. The young general was at the front of the group, his stride still strong and proud even though he must have been as miserable as everyone else. Itaye sat proudly on his shoulder, the falcon unaffected by the weather.

She felt a grudging respect as she thought of Killian; he led his men with a strict finality that was brushed with compassion. Although he had forced everyone to travel in the horrid rain, he did his best every night to make everyone as comfortable as possible. His men were wholly devoted to their general. They rarely questioned his orders, and many went to him for conversation and advice.

There was one elf in their company, a male with a narrow, shrewd face. His name was Yolor, and he refused to wear leather armor like the rest of his patrol; instead he was garbed in a black waterproof cloak over deep blue robes, which stated his affinity with the water element. Elves were not as blended with the elements as dragons, but they did hold some power. Most were born with control over a single element, and they devoted their entire lives to master it.

Yolor was young, and his power was limited. Although he had the ability to absorb most of the moisture in the soldiers' tents at night, he was not strong enough to completely dry them. The most he could do was make things a little more bearable.

Akairya had been astonished when she had first seen Yolor in the patrol. It had been her understanding that although elves were at peace with humans, they refused to have anything to do with the military and the politics of Alkairyn. When she had mentioned this to Thoran, he had shrugged.

"The Shadow has been getting stronger in the last few years. Although Yaeloa was the first major catastrophe, Rorak numbers have been steadily increasing in the island of Lakayol. King Elric was getting nervous, so he contacted the elves. A temporary contract was made, and now we have elves helping us with anything related to the blight. It's pretty convenient, especially since the only other magic users are warlocks and Dragon Riders. As you know, warlocks would never help the greater good, and we only have two Riders. Until you, of course."

Akairya had blanched at the mention of warlocks. Since humans were not able to control the flow of magic unless they were partnered with a dragon, the dragonless who desired power turned to other means: the demons. Demons were the bearers of darkness. They reigned over the abandoned places of the world, known as the Underearth, where light could not reach and burn them. There were demons of greed, lust, pain, misery, and countless others.

Demons had been a part of the world since it had welcomed the first rays of sunlight, and they had always lusted after the ability to walk in light without being crumbled to ash. As a result, they began to bond themselves with humans who desired control over magic. A warlock was a human who had accepted a demon into their very soul, a powerful being who had control over the darker magics of the world. However, even if the human had been good of heart before the bonding, the demon would take over.

Akairya shuddered as she thought of them. Children were told horror stories about warlocks when their parents wanted to scare them into behaving, and although warlocks were strictly forbidden in the cities of Alkairyn, there were a good number of them on the island of Talkorin, its barren wasteland divided into four territories the warlocks dubbed cults.

It only made sense to assume that warlocks had no interest in ending the Shadow; it was an entirely evil thing, and warlocks were purely dark beings.

Akairya sighed as she trudged on through the sodden valley, her heart as cold as the wet clothes she wore. Killian halted as the sky grew darker, his lips pursed as he studied a small copse of trees.

"This should do for camp. The lightning has stopped, so it should be safe enough near those trees."

Although the rain had faded to a light drizzle, everything was still frozen and soaking wet. Akairya dreamed about sunshine and warmth as she aided the patrol with setting up camp.

That night, while everyone sat around a fire that Yolor kept alive by driving the light rain away, Thoran successfully extracted the details of Akairya's and Draykor's bonding. He was just as bewildered as she about the entire situation, especially since Draykor only knew vague details about it.

"I wonder what you're supposed to do...wipe out the Shadow?" Thoran mused thoughtfully.

"If so, I have no idea how I'm supposed to do that. I only know enough about the use of weapons to catch dinner and fend off a single attacker. Plus, we have no idea what element Draykor will grow into."

"Didn't you say you were good with a bow?"

"Yes, but only for hunting."

Our path will be revealed the more we walk upon it, Draykor murmured, his angular head resting in Akairya's lap, eyes half closed. Thoran jumped; the young dragon had spoken in his mind as well as Akairya's.

"Hopefully it will be revealed soon," Akairya grumbled, her violet eyes uncertain as she scanned the sopping camp. The others were all huddled in their damp blankets, their faces pale from the watery chill. Itaye was sitting on a tree stump a few feet away, amber gaze looking out into the night. "I also hope this rain will stop soon. I'm surprised no one has fallen ill yet."

"No one will. Not if they continue to drink the potion Killian hands out each night," Thoran said.

"Potion? You mean the brandy that Killian gives us as soon as we make camp?"

Thoran burst into laughter, his entire body shaking with mirth as he stared at Akairya in disbelief.

"*Brandy?* That is some awful brandy we've been drinking, sweetheart. No, it's a special potion that wards off any sort of cold or flu, and it gives energy to the drinker." He chuckled again. "Every patrol is required to take some whenever they are on the road. Alchemist specialty. They make a fortune out of the damn liquid."

Akairya blinked in surprise. She never would have guessed that the stuff Killian made everyone sip from each night was an alchemist concoction. She gently rubbed behind Draykor's ears, and he nestled his head closer in response.

"Hey."

Thoran and Akairya looked up to see Killian standing a few feet away.

"Mind if I talk to you, Kairi? Alone?"

Taken aback, Akairya nodded. Draykor moved his head as she stood up, his dark eyes thoughtfully studying Killian as he walked away from camp.

I wonder what he wants.

Killian led her to a large tree a little bit away from the camp, and the cold hit her like a cruel slap to the face. She shivered as the light wind peppered her cheeks with water, the rain no longer driven away by Yolor's power.

"I'd like to ask you something, Kairi," Killian said quietly, his eyes downcast. "But first I'd like to apologize for keeping my distance. Thoran seems to be keeping you good company, and to be honest...I'm not too sure how to act around you."

Baffled, Akairya cocked her head. "Why would you not know how to act around me?"

"Do you not see how the men act around you? They respect you almost as much as they respect me, their general and commander. You have this aura of strength and confidence around you, Kairi. It's unsettling. Not to mention those eyes of yours. So full of the elemental power of Spirit, it's uncanny."

"I have no control over any element," she responded quickly, "not yet, anyway. Dray still has to come into his power." She frowned. "Also, I'm surprised your men respect me. People generally stay away from half elves."

He studied her. "Do you not know what violet eyes signify? It's very rare for an elf or half elf to be born with such eyes. Violet eyes mean you could one day control the most elusive element; Spirit. There have only been two elves to have the ability to wield spiritual power. One was the High Queen Akairya, the other an elf that has yet to leave this world. You may not know how to use your power, but it's there. Sleeping until you learn how to bring it to life…or maybe it won't come into itself until Dray matures. Who knows? All I know is that even if you had never become a Rider, you would have been a force to reckon with one day."

Akairya was speechless. Had her father known of her slumbering power? He couldn't have; he would have told her about it.

"I-I had no idea," she mumbled. Killian smiled.

"Clearly. However, it isn't too surprising. Not many actually know that violet eyes can mean such power."

The rain petered out, and when Akairya looked up she could discern a couple stars winking through the deep black of the wet night.

"Looks like we'll have a dry day tomorrow," she commented. Killian grunted, and Akairya looked back at him.

"You said you had a question for me, Killian. What is it?"

"When we fought off those Roraks that day in the forest…I noticed you had some skill with your dagger. Have you any experience with a sword?"

Akairya nodded, intrigued. "Yes. My father made a point of teaching me how to use different weapons. I've practiced with a bow, a sword, a dagger, and even a chakram…although I wasn't particularly good at wielding a chakram."

"Well, would you like to train with a blade? If the king decides you are no threat to the country, he will likely put you under the tutelage of one of the other Riders. I'd like to have a chance to see what you can do before that."

Nerves fluttered through her. Practice swordsmanship…with Killian? She saw how easily he carried his one-handed blade. He had skill, and she was almost positive he would make her look like a complete novice.

"You know how you said the men look at me with respect? That's going to change if they see you destroy me in a duel."

Killian laughed, his teeth glinting in the moonlight that had finally broken through the mass of rainclouds that had hung heavily over the grassland. "I'll go easy on you, don't worry."

Akairya followed Killian back to camp. Jilk, who was sitting away from the rest of the troop, glared at the pair as they neared the fire.

"I thought you were intelligent, Killian. Skipping off with the enemy and doing who knows what."

Killian tensed as the rest of the patrol stopped what they were doing and stared. Akairya blushed in embarrassment. Maybe the so-called respect everyone had for her was going to dissipate faster than she had expected.

"Keep your thoughts to yourself, Jilk," Killian ground out through clenched teeth, his eyes stormy. Jilk huffed but looked down.

"Just so everything is clear, Kairi and I were not doing anything other than making plans to work on her swordsmanship. If anyone is willing to help out, just say so," Killian looked at his men, his expression daring them to insult Akairya even further. Instead, a chorus of voices volunteered to help her become more skilled with a blade. Relief flooded through her, and she released the breath she had been holding.

Draykor ambled up to Akairya, his black scales reflecting the flames of the fire. He snapped his jaws as he passed Jilk, who flinched but didn't say a word. Akairya stifled a chuckle.

I don't like that man. He may have good reason to hate anything to do with the Shadow, but I still sense something cruel about him.

I agree, Dray. But there's nothing we can do about it, Akairya said in reply. He just snorted.

"Why don't we do some training tonight, Kairi?" Killian suggested. He slid his sword out of its scabbard. Thoran strode over with another blade in his hands.

"Sure, it will help keep me warm," She took the weapon from Thoran and tested its weight. It felt fairly balanced, and she swung it a few times to get accustomed to it.

Killian backed away a few steps and settled into a ready position, his feet apart and his knees slightly bent. He held his sword loosely at his side, but his eyes were locked on Akairya. The half elf laughed eagerly under her breath.

As soon as she moved into position, Killian quickly stepped forward and attacked with an overhead swing. His speed was startling, and Akairya was barely able to block it. She let out a gasp as she pushed his blade away and moved him backwards.

She released the pressure and swung to the right of his neck. He jerked his sword up and brushed her blade away as easily as if it were a feather.

"Looks like you need to work on your strength," Killian teased. The men had all gathered around the fighting pair in a large circle.

"She holds her own pretty well!" one of them called out. Killian nodded as Akairya deftly blocked another of his attacks. She grinned as he was forced back yet again by the ferocity of her attacks. Although she wasn't as strong, she had speed.

Killian set his jaw and doubled his efforts, which pushed Akairya back this time. Sweat beaded on her brow as he quickened the pace, his blade a silver blur. She was barely able to block his blows at this point, and her heart rate picked up. What if he actually wounded her?

Just as the thought crossed her mind, Killian twisted his blade and knocked Akairya's right out of her hand. Her wrist stung, and all she could do was blink in surprise. She had not expected that.

"You've got potential," Killian commented. He was breathing hard, which gave Akairya some satisfaction.

'That was the best duel I've seen in ages!" Thoran hooted, his eyes shining as he picked up Akairya's sword that lay near the fire. "Here, keep this. It's not the greatest piece of blacksmithing, but it should serve you well when you have need of it."

Akairya accepted the blade. She looked at the rest of the men who stood nearby, and was startled to see them all looking at her in awe.

"What?" She asked. Killian chuckled as he slipped his sword back into its scabbard.

"No one has been able to last that long in a duel with me since I was a boy. Let's just say you've gained even more respect around here."

The men all cheered. Akairya blushed and fiddled with her sword. Thoran handed her a leather belt that matched the leather armor she had been given the first night in the Jalkorin. A scabbard was attached, and Akairya quickly tied the belt on and slipped her blade into its home. She felt empowered by the weight on her hip, and proud she had done so well in the eyes of the patrol.

Draykor walked over, his black eyes bright with excitement. *You did wonderful, my Rider.*

CHAPTER SEVEN

The next morning was gloriously dry, with sunshine bathing the valley in a happy golden glow. Akairya stretched as she slipped out of her sleeping roll, her muscles deliciously sore after last night's duel with Killian. She hadn't had such a workout since before her father died, and she had forgotten how good it felt.

Feeling happier than she had in days, Akairya stepped out of her tent she shared with her dragon and walked over to the fire, where Jilk was spooning out warm oatmeal into wooden bowls.

"Good morning, Jilk," she beamed. Jilk narrowed his eyes at her, but didn't say anything. Instead he just handed her a bowl and looked away. Akairya shrugged and sat down near Thoran, who was already finished his breakfast and was leaning against a tree with his legs crossed.

"Where's your dragon?"

"Off hunting, I would think. He only got one rabbit yesterday. He must be starving."

Akairya leaned back against the tree and sighed as she basked in the sunlight that shone through the canopy of leaves above the camp. The ground was still slightly wet from the rain, but she didn't care. She was just relieved the sun had finally pushed its way through the gray.

What an excellent day of hunting. Draykor trotted over from the valley. Akairya could have sworn that he looked even bigger than he had yesterday.

How many rabbits did you catch today? She asked him, smiling before taking a bite of her oatmeal.

No rabbits. A deer.

Akairya choked on her food. Thoran thumped her on her back.

"Dray c-caught a d-deer today!" she choked out, her face red. Thoran laughed.

"Is that all? I was wondering when he would finally move up from tiny rabbits. He's bigger than a large wolf now."

Thoran's words rang true, and Akairya was struck again by how quickly Draykor was growing. It was astonishing. His angular head was nearly the size of a horse's, and his lithe body was growing stronger each day.

"Did you eat the *whole* deer?" she asked. Draykor huffed and plopped onto the ground, his muscled tail curled around his body like a cat. *Sure did. Bones and all.*

She had a sickening image of Draykor chomping down on a deer brain and fought not to gag. She put down her half eaten oatmeal and simply stared at her dragon, her face green.

"Wasn't your father a hunter, Kairi? Why are you so affected by this?" Thoran scooped up her breakfast and finished it.

"He always dealt with the...brains and all, when he needed the skulls. I never did." Akairya shuddered.

That's the best part! Draykor cried, his black eyes bright with humor. She ignored him and focused instead on calming her stomach.

It didn't take long to pack up the camp, and soon everybody was on the move. Akairya cursed the lack of horses, and hefted her share of the provisions onto her back. The wagon they had been using had finally broke, its wood worn from its many days of service. Now everyone had to carry some of the cargo. Even Draykor had a bag strapped to his back, his spikes surprisingly not piercing the fabric.

The heat from the sun caused the moisture to steam from the thick grass of the valley, creating a soupy humidity that was nearly as bad as the rain. The mountains that framed the Jalkorin were cloaked with a white mist, and Akairya couldn't help but feel worried. Something didn't feel right. Although the sun was shining, the air felt still and unnaturally cold.

The patrol walked on, their progress quicker with the lack of downpour. Killian estimated that they would be out of the Jalkorin and into the plains of Ariniya before nightfall, yet the end of the valley was still quite a distance away. Akairya dreamed of a warm, satisfying meal, a hot bath, and a soft bed. She hadn't had either since the sacking of Yaeloa.

As morning shifted into afternoon, the strange chill strengthened. Draykor was tense, his ears twitching to pick up the smallest sound. Itaye was also jumpy, his eyes darting around their surroundings.

Just as Akairya was about to say something to Thoran, a strong wind buffeted the entire patrol. Everyone cried out as the wind ripped around, tearing up grass and dirt. Itaye clacked his beak in anxiety, still too injured to take flight from Killian's shoulder.

Powerful wings thudded heavily, and a huge Shadow dragon broke free from the mist that covered the nearest mountain, its flat black scales draining the light around it. Thoran cursed. His face was pale as he watched the beast fly over and land in front of the patrol. Killian, who stood at the very front of his men, had his sword out and ready.

The ground shuddered as the great weight settled heavily on the earth; another bout of wind from its enormous wings pushed the soldiers back. It was easily ten times the size of Draykor. Its bulk cast a huge shadow over the entire patrol. Draykor growled deep in his throat as his kin folded its wings and looked at everyone with milky eyes.

I am not here to harm you, its evil voice ripped through the mental scars of Akairya's mind, its sharp touch giving her an immediate headache reminiscent of the pain the Shadow dragons from Yaeloa had inflicted. Everyone groaned and clasped their heads as they too experienced the dragon's voice.

Brother, the Shadow Dragon inclined its large angular head towards Draykor, who lifted his head and snarled.

I am no brother of yours, traitor, he snapped.

Very well. The dark dragon shifted its clouded gaze onto Akairya. *I am only here to relay a message from the Lord of the Shadow. There is no need for weapons to be raised.* Killian's sword stayed pointed towards the dragon's broad chest, his jaw set. The dragon snorted, and a plume of thick blackness coiled out of its nostrils.

Half elf, the Lord would like to extend an invitation to his palace. He is interested in partnering with you.

Astonishment at such a blunt request rocked Akairya, and she gasped. Draykor snapped his jaws angrily, and all the men in the patrol stared at her in disbelief.

He believes partnering with a Rider will be incredibly beneficial for him, and you will receive a great amount of power. If you choose to accept, travel to Tilaner Isle. The massive dragon flared out its wings and took off, the force of its departure knocking everyone off their feet. Itaye leaped nimbly from Killian's shoulder as the general fell hard onto his hip, cursing as he dropped his sword.

"I told you! I told you she was not to be trusted!" Jilk screeched. His eyes were wild as he scrambled back to his feet. "The Lord of the Shadow has called her to his side!"

"Don't be ridiculous, Jilk. Kairi was *asked* to join this 'lord.' If she was in cahoots with him the whole time, why would she be invited to his palace?" Thoran barked. Jilk pursed his lips, having no reply.

Akairya stood with one hand over her mouth, the other resting on Draykor. Her dragon was still growling, his eyes following the small speck that was the Shadow dragon.

"Right now, I'm more concerned with the news that this Lord of the Shadow has a palace built on Tilaner Isle. High King Elric believes that the isle is populated by unorganized Roraks. The fact that there is a palace and that there's some semblance of centralization is startling. Another attack could be imminent," Killian paced in a tight circle, his blade back in his hand, his falcon perched on his wrist. Yolor, his hands trembling, summoned some water into a small iron cup and handed it to the distraught general.

"Thank you, Yolor."

After a few tense minutes, Killian sheathed his sword and looked at Akairya.

"I'm not going to accuse you of anything, but we need to reach the High King even sooner than I had first thought," he broadened his gaze to include the entire patrol. "Time to pick up the pace. I want to reach the capital in four days maximum. There's an inn outside the valley; we'll buy as many horses as we can and ride the rest of the way."

"Yes sir!" his men chorused. Killian nodded, satisfied, then turned to continue the trek out of the Jalkorin.

Three days later found Akairya, Draykor, Killian, and Thoran a few hours away from Ariniya's capital, Kalisor. Draykor flew above the three horses that the Foxtail Inn had sold to them, his scaled body nearly the same size as the thick warhorse that Killian was astride. The young dragon had taught himself how to fly just two days before, to the astonishment of the others. He had said that the knowledge was buried deep in his instincts, and that all he had needed was the strength to take off. The whole situation gave Akairya a deep thrill; soon she would be able to fly with him. While excited, she was also fairly nervous about it. All of Draykor's landings had been anything but graceful.

The rest of the patrol had been forced to continue the journey on foot. The inn had only had the three horses available. Killian had apologized to his men profusely, but still abandoned them in order to reach the High King as fast as he could.

They were now riding up a wide grassy slope that rose up from the lush plains that made up most of the province, their mounts' hooves loud against the stone of the Onae Road, the main road of Alkairyn. Onae, which was Elvish for 'one true path,' connected all the capital cities of the country. Yaeloa, Kalisor, Terndion (the capital of the far eastern province Morkrain) and the other four major cities of Alkairyn could all be reached by the pale gray road.

While Yaeloa had been hilly and dotted with flowers, Ariniya was mainly flat, grassy, and windy, with a forest that took up most of its southern edge. The large hill the company was cresting at the moment was the first one they had come across since exiting the Jalkorin.

Akairya's gray mare enjoyed trotting up the hill. She snorted as she stretched out her stride, her tiny ears pricked forward as a light wind buffeted her mane.

"You'll get your first glimpse of the capital in a minute, Kairi," Thoran called from up ahead, his chestnut gelding already halted at the top of the hill. Killian had reined in his bright bay warhorse and was taking up the rear.

The only city Akairya had ever seen was Yaeloa, as she had been born and raised there. She knew the locations of other cities from her father's maps, but how they all looked had always been up to her imagination. Excitement flooded through her as her mare finally reached the top of the large hill, and what she saw below dazzled her.

The ground sloped down towards a massive, turquoise lake that was almost perfectly round except for where it broke into a river on its north and south shores. Kalisor was set right in the middle of its clear waters on a bright island of ivory stone and gold.

Many slim towers struck the sky with peaked roofs, their golden tops reflecting the late afternoon sun like burnished mirrors. A stark white bridge led from the western shore of the lake to the shimmering city, its immense width full of people bustling in and out with carts laden with precious cargo. A tall ivory wall encircled the city, and golden gates were situated at the end of the bridge. Far off to the east one could see the snowy peaks of Morkrain's mountains, and to the south was a dense forest that looked nearly black despite the shining afternoon sun.

"It's...beautiful," Akairya whispered. "Yaeloa was built with stone like that, yet Kalisor is more...pure."

"Different stones, Kairi. This city was built under the reign of the High Queen Akairya, and she built with stones that are only found in the dragon country, Drakynold." Thoran told her, his posture relaxed as he gazed at the city. Killian, who had ridden up while Akairya was staring in awe, clucked his tongue at his horse and rode down the slope.

"No use standing around and staring. I want to get to the king as quickly as possible. It may take us awhile to get across the bridge. It is nearly noon, and the market is in full swing. Farmers and people from neighboring towns will all be clustering in at this time."

Akairya followed him, her stomach tight with anxiety. The last few days had flown by, and now she was finally going to meet the High King. He was either going to declare her an enemy or help her figure out what was going on with her and Draykor.

Her dragon had landed before reaching the top of the hill, for fear of alarming the citizens and guards of the city. He now loped beside Akairya and her mare, his dark eyes giving the horse a quick once over.

I only have a little more growing to do before you can stop riding wingless creatures, he said matter-of-factly. Akairya chuckled as her honest mare picked her way down the hill.

When they reached the bridge, a group of guards came striding over through the thick throng of people. Each one of their armored chests bore the High King's insignia of a crescent moon inside of a sun.

"Welcome, General Killian. We expected you four days ago," the largest of the group said, his helmet visor open to reveal shrewd eyes, which were glued to Draykor. The men who flanked him all had their hands on the hilts of their swords. Suspicion emanated from them.

"I know. We hit a period of heavy rain coming out of the Jalkorin." He reached up and patted Itaye, who was impatiently kneading his shoulder with his claws. Not being able to stretch his wings was clearly agitating the proud creature. "Itaye hurt his wing and I was unable to send a message ahead of us. I am sure you have noticed, but we have a new Rider."

The guards gaped at her, their eyes roving down her body with no embarrassment. She flushed and shifted her weight. Killian noticed their perusing and moved his horse in front of her mare.

"I am very anxious to reach the king, so forgive us for rushing by."

He motioned Akairya, Draykor, and Thoran forward with his chin. They asked their horses to quicken their walk and were soon making their way across the bridge towards Kalisor's entrance, leaving the soldiers to stare after them.

"Are they always so bold with women?" Akairya asked. Thoran glanced at her and blushed.

"Only with lower class women and what people call 'half-breeds,'" he explained. Akairya sighed wearily.

"I should have known. It was the same in Yaeloa. Part of the reason why I kept to myself, even after my father died."

Killian, who was once again taking up the rear, rode up beside her and looked at her with serious silver eyes.

"I won't let anyone treat you badly here, Kairi. The fact you have both elf and human blood makes you special, not someone who is lower than full blooded humans."

Akairya smiled at him in response, her stomach doing chaotic flips as the word *special* sunk in. Although she barely knew Killian, the fact he thought she was special meant something to her. It was…odd.

Thoran stayed quiet as the group neared the golden gates, and Draykor watched Killian curiously.

Someone thinks highly of you all of a sudden. What happened to thinking you were a threat, hmm? He mused to Akairya.

His opinion changed in the Jalkorin. Didn't I tell you about the conversation we had before the sword fight?

Yes, you did. You told me he respected you and that he suspected you had a powerful affinity to spirit, not that he personally thought you were special.

Well, that's new to me too.

Draykor fell silent, and Akairya was left to ponder why Killian's opinion of her mattered so much.

Many people in the crowd that flooded in and out of the city stared at Draykor, their expressions ranging from horror and anger to wonder and awe. Children reached out to touch his scales before their parents stopped them, and most of the adults gave him a wide berth. That coupled with the frustration which stemmed from being forced to ride around countless carts full of goods for the market made the whole situation awkward and stifling.

They finally reached the shining gates just as the midday bell was rung. The brassy chimes echoed throughout the city and over the lake, and the horses flicked their ears to the ringing noise.

The two guards who stood at the gate simply nodded at Killian.

"Aren't they concerned that you're bringing in a dragon?" Akairya asked him, bewildered. Killian laughed and looked at her, and she was struck by how golden his hair was in the sunlight. *Stop it, Akairya. You're not some stupid girl who falls for the first handsome man she sees.*

"The guards here communicate with falcons. While we were riding across the bridge, the first group we talked to sent a message forward to let these two know that we are good to go."

"Oh. When we were at the inn a few days ago, why didn't you just ask to use one of their falcons to send a message ahead of us?"

"Falcons are used only by the higher classes and the military; anyone else make do with simple messengers. As a result, the inn didn't have any falcons I could use."

Makes sense, Akairya mused. *I never questioned why no one I knew in Yaeloa used falcons.*

Human society is complicated, I think. Draykor said in response.

The white stone floor of the bridge blended into a sandy brick that made up the city's roads. The wide paths wound around the many white and gold buildings that clustered together in chaotic organization. The expansive palace sat squarely in the center. All Akairya could see of the castle was its many reaching towers.

"It must be easy to get lost in this place," she commented as the three horses clopped past the gates, Draykor close behind them. His tufted ears were straining to catch the many noises that floated throughout the city: horse hooves on the brick roads, the clamor of talking citizens, and the distant sound of a falcon screeching as it flew to relay a message.

Killian, whose entire demeanor relaxed as soon as he had ridden into the city, patted his stallion on the neck. "I guess Kalisor would seem quite confusing to a newcomer. For those of us who were born here, we know the city like no other place. The market is in the eastern section of the city, beside the merchants' neighborhood and the slums. The Garden of Illumination is to the west beside the nobles' neighborhood, called the Shining Estates, and the middle class citizens live everywhere in between. The Mirror Inn, which is the best inn inside the city, is just outside of the market, and the palace, as you can see from the towers ahead of us, is in the middle of the island. Behind it is the Royal Gardens and Royal Army training grounds."

Akairya blinked as she tried to follow Killian's commentary.

"What's the Garden of Illumination?"

"Maybe I'll take you to see it once everything is smoothed over," he replied. His eyes were soft as he smiled at her. Thoran made a strange noise from Akairya's other side, and Killian shrugged at him before asking his stallion to trot.

More confused than ever, Akairya followed suit. Her mare quickened her pace happily, her head up in anticipation of a warm stall and oats.

It took a good while to reach the castle. The main road twisted and turned throughout the buildings as if its creator had been determined to make those who traveled on it view the entire city as they did so. Akairya caught glimpses of a colourful market that sent a cloud of delicious fragrances her way, a sparkling garden of reflective vegetation that made her blink in amazement, grand towered houses with golden roofs and sprawling courtyards, and many small shops that were not a part of the market. Alchemist stores, physician offices, dress shops, blacksmith shops, treasuries, and even some pubs were spread haphazardly throughout sections of the city that were devoted mainly to residences. Kalisor was a place of beautiful chaos that was painted in white and gold.

The only area that had any colour other than white and gold was the market, which made it even more bold and enticing. Akairya vowed to visit it as soon as she was able.

When the company reached the palace, its bulk jumped into their vision. One second they were passing a cluster of subtly elegant middle class estates, and the next they were entering the broad white courtyard that led to an arched bridge. The huge ivory and gold castle was surrounded by a wide moat. A line of guards stood in a line across the bridge, all standing at attention. On the other side of the moat, the palace was swathed in a vibrant garden of flowers that accented its ivory walls and golden roofs.

Killian dismounted from his stallion when they reached the bridge. Thoran motioned for Akairya to hop off too as he swung his leg off his mount.

"Good afternoon, general. The High King was worried about you," one of the bridge's guards said as he stepped forward, his steel armor reflecting the bright sun. "When a falcon came and gave me a message saying you had found a new Rider, I thought it was a joke. I see it was not."

Draykor twitched his tail in annoyance and spoke in the minds of everyone present. *Enough with the pleasantries. We need to see the High King.*

The guard raised an eyebrow at the impatient dragon but said nothing. He shrugged and moved aside, one hand on his sword. Killian, Akairya, and Thoran handed their horses over to the other guards. Killian also gave one of the men his falcon, sternly commanding him to make sure the bird was properly tended.

Head held high, Draykor walked beside Akairya as they crossed the bridge. Akairya patted his shoulder, which was almost level with her chin.

The sweet smell of flowers assailed their noses as they strode towards the castle's immense golden doors, the king's insignia plastered in white on the shining surface. Akairya was charmed by the large blooms, although she had no idea what species of flower they were. There were red, blue, purple, and yellow ones that were entwined in the deep green of the bushes and trees, the broad petals dusted with silvery bristles. White pebbled paths wound throughout the garden, golden benches placed at certain intervals throughout the vegetation. The castle was enfolded in the lushness of it and its bright doors reflected the strong midday sun.

The doors swung open as the company approached them, and the woman, dragon, and two men strode into the cool foyer of the king's home.

CHAPTER EIGHT

The castle was warmer than expected; the floor was a sandy marble flecked with gold, and the walls were paneled with glossed oak. Richly painted tapestries of the country's varied landscapes of prairies, marshes, forests, and mountains adorned the foyer's walls. The lofty ceiling was high enough to fit a dragon even larger than the Shadow dragon who had spoken with the company in the Jalkorin. Another set of large doors, this time made from a deep red wood, lay across the broad room. Two guards stood in front of them.

"What is the meaning of this, Killian?" One of them called. "You dare to bring an unknown dragon into the castle? How did you get past the guards on the bridge?" He drew his sword and pointed it at Killian's chest. Surprised, Akairya froze; she had expected these guards to know who they were like the others, but then she realized that falcon mail probably didn't extend to the inside of the palace.

"You dolt, we didn't sneak past. We were permitted entrance. I have brought this dragon and his Rider, Kairi, to speak with High King Elric. If it would make you feel better, send someone to ask the king if we could have an audience with him. We'll wait here until he responds," Killian purposely moved his hand away from the hilt of his sword as he spoke. The guard sheathed his blade and shrugged.

"Fair enough. Trov, go and do what General Killian suggests."

The second guard, who had been watching with a slack-jawed expression, jumped to obey. He nearly fell over as he heaved the wooden doors open and sped through them.

"I take it you came across no survivors of Yaeloa's fall?" the guard asked Killian and Thoran as he leaned against the wall. Draykor moved about the room, his eyes flicking from one tapestry to the next.

"I'm a survivor of Yaeloa," Akairya piped up. The guard looked at her in surprise.

"When did you come by this dragon?"

"We found each other in the heart of the Forest of Souls, after I was swept out of Calindyl by the Kito River. Draykor here was entombed in a large stone, and he had called to me when I awoke on the river's bank."

The guard blinked. "Is this true?" He demanded of Killian.

"It's what she says. I cannot say if it is true or not, Brant, since I was not there."

Before Brant could say anything else, the second soldier came bounding back through the wooden doors.

"High King Elric is in the throne room, ready to speak with Killian and his companions."

"Always the king's favorite, eh? He doesn't even hesitate to speak with you, even when you bring an unknown dragon into the castle." Brant sighed. "Very well. I'll take you to see him. Trov, keep your post here. I'll have someone relieve you soon." He stepped through the doors, and the others quickly followed.

They entered a corridor lit with many flickering torches, the floor made of the same sandy stone as the foyer. The walls were white marble, and as the company walked forward they passed many hallways that branched off the main corridor. Heavily armored guards were placed at each new hallway. Their eyes glittered as they caught sight of Draykor.

Akairya's chest was tight as she moved closer towards meeting the High King. She had never even met the Duke of the White Keep, the ruler of Yaeloa. She had been too lowly for such a meeting; her father had been a simple huntsman and she was not a full blood, human or elf. As a result, even the lowest ranking noble turned their nose from her. Now she was about to meet the High King, the man who ruled the entire *country*. The man who could quite possibly decide she was an enemy.

Sweat pooled in the small of her back, which itched underneath the leather armor. She bit her lip as the company passed hallway after hallway.

Relax, Akairya. The king will not think you are of the Shadow, Draykor soothed her, his soft eyes on her face as he fell into step beside her. Light from the fires of the torches flickered off his black scales and sharp spikes that lined his neck and back. She smiled at him.

You're right. He's bound to realize we are on the same side as him.

When they reached yet another set of massive doors made of the same red wood as those in the castle's foyer, Akairya was calm and ready to face the king. Brant strode up to the man who stood to the side of the doors. His stout figure was garbed in white and black robes, and he stood straight-backed and proud. He held a thick cane of oak, its bottom bulged yet flat where it rested on the floor.

He nodded to Brant after the guard muttered something to him, then turned and opened the doors. He swept into the adjoining room and Brant beckoned everyone to follow.

They walked into an immense throne room that seemed to blend into the outdoors. The stone floor was decorated with a rich velvet rug that stretched from the doors to the large golden thrones that stood opposite them. The marble walls of the corridor gave way to a single sheet of glass that wound around the entire room, which was situated at the back of the castle. Its glass walls allowed Akairya to see the Royal Gardens and Royal Army training grounds. The gardens were even more colourful than the one that flourished at the front of the palace; its flurry of reds, blues, yellows, purples, greens, and browns enveloped a large marble gazebo that stood on the top of a sloping hill. Lush fields of cropped grass surrounded a perfectly round pond, and Akairya could just see some soldiers sprinting around a dirt track on the right side of the gardens. A couple of low buildings sat nestled beside the large white wall that surrounded the entire city, and she assumed that was where the soldiers slept and ate.

All this she could see from where she was standing.

In the main throne sat a broad man, his bald head crowned with a circlet of gold and silver. He wore silver armor and a cape of thick white fur, his cuirass carved with the royal symbol. To his right were smaller golden thrones, which were occupied by two women, both of whom wore thin diadems of silver. They were white blonde and dressed in bright dresses of green and blue, their achingly beautiful faces curious. Seeing them reminded her that the king was married, and that he had a daughter close to her age. If he did have any reservations about her, maybe the fact he had a daughter would soften his punishment.

The robed man who had led everyone in slammed his cane on the stone floor, and Akairya understood why the end was so warped as it made a loud *crack* that resounded throughout the room.

"General Killian Theodin has returned from his travels, accompanied with Soldier Thoran Unnamed and a new female Dragon Rider and her dragon," the man announced, his voice carrying effortlessly to the king.

"Thoran Unnamed?" Akairya whispered, her eyebrow raised at Thoran.

"I'll explain later," he replied.

High King Elric stood and swept his arms out, his smile genuine as he took in the company clustered at the throne room doors.

"Ah, please, come closer. I am not that terrifying, I hope!"

Killian grinned easily and walked forward. Draykor went ahead as well. Flustered, Akairya fell in step behind her unruffled dragon, while Thoran bowed low.

"I am no longer needed, sire. By your leave, I would like to go so I can take a much needed rest," he called to the king, his brown eyes lowered. King Elric shrugged.

"If that is what you wish. Killian will tell me all I need to know, I suppose."

Thoran straightened and swept out of the room.

The king settled back into his throne as Killian, Akairya, and Draykor approached. His eyes were a clear blue, and he studied Akairya carefully.

Killian halted a few feet from the chair and bowed, his golden hair shining from the sunlight that streamed in through the glass walls.

"Greetings, my king. I am glad to see you well." He glanced at the two women. "It brings me joy to see Queen Leliana and Princess Theandi looking so beautiful," he said smoothly. The king chuckled.

"Your manners have improved while you've been gone."

The younger woman leaped out of her chair. Her green dress billowed behind her as she bounded to Killian and threw her arms around him. The queen sighed loudly and glanced at her husband, who looked amused.

"I am so glad you are back, Killian! Papa has been too busy to continue with my riding lessons, and I so want to learn how to jump in a side saddle! You must teach me!" the young woman cried. Killian coughed and carefully pulled her arms away from his neck.

"Ah, princess, I am sorry you have been without tutelage. If the king permits it, we can resume your lessons tomorrow."

A touch of jealousy pricked at Akairya as the king nodded. Draykor wound the tip of his tail around Akairya's calf, giving it a small squeeze as she fought to control the sudden strength of emotion.

You barely know him, my Rider. Do not fret. If it makes you feel any better, she is a princess while he is just a solider. She would never be permitted to

marry anyone but a son of one of the provincial
Dukes.

*I know. It shouldn't even matter... I don't
understand what has come over me.*

He gave her calf another squeeze and snuffed in
sympathy. The noise caught the attention of King
Elric, who then leaned forward and again fixed
Akairya with his keen eyes.

"So, a new Rider is among us, eh? You look no
older than twenty-five, elf girl. The youngest Rider
before you is thirty-seven, and he was partnered with
his dragon only five years ago after helping drive back
the warlock threat. How have you come by your
dragon, young one?"

She understood why he would ask, considering
Riders were only made who they were after proving
themselves worthy. She had done no such thing.

"It may seem impossible, my king, but Draykor
was waiting for me, in a large stone in the Forest of
Souls."

*It is true, High King Elric. My egg was sealed in
an enchanted boulder so I could await my destined
Rider, who turned out to be Akairya.*

"Akairya? No one has dared to be named after
the great High Queen, and yet here you stand, with a
dragon no Dragon Elder gave you."

Killian stared at Akairya, his mouth agape. The
princess, who had sat back down beside her mother
when the king addressed Akairya, looked at her with
interest.

"My father named me, sire. I had no say in the
matter. I have gone by the nickname Kairi for most of
my life, since I knew having such a grand name is

frowned upon. He said he had a reason to give me the High Queen's name, but I do not know what it is."

"Well, we will continue to call you Kairi. You do not seem tainted with the Shadow's stain, but the blight's touch has ways to conceal itself. I am going to send for someone who can confirm your innocence, and then we can go from there. Jervos, send for Yeilao."

The man who had announced the arrival of the company nodded and walked out of the room. Akairya nibbled on the corner of her thumbnail; what sort of test was the king going to put her through? Was it going to hurt?

Killian and King Elric spoke in low tones as they waited for Jervos to return. Akairya caught the words "organized," and "Shadow dragon," and assumed Killian was telling the king the news of Tilaner Isle being more than just a chaos of Roraks.

Five minutes sped by, then Jervos returned. He cracked his cane once more on the stone floor.

"Spirit elf Yeilao, your Majesty," he announced.

The elf who stepped in was ancient; deep lines cut through the pale skin of her round face, and her bright violet eyes were enfolded within wrinkled flesh. Her slender ears were nestled in a bush of ivory hair that snarled around her head and tousled down her stooped back, and her thick eyebrows were just as white. She was garbed in rich purple robes that pooled on the floor around her feet, making her even more hunched.

When her purple eyes, eerily similar to Akairya's, met the elf girl's, tears spilled down the old elf's cheeks. A soft 'oh," escaped out of her mouth, and she stumbled. Jervos steadied her, and she approached Akairya with a smile full of relief.

Akairya was astonished. She had never met anyone with the same eyes as hers. *Violet eyes mean you can control the most elusive element; Spirit. There have only been two elves to have the ability to wield spiritual power. One was the High Queen Akairya, the other an elf that has yet to leave this world...*so this was who Killian meant, that night in the Jalkorin plains.

"You are finally here," the old elf breathed as she took Akairya's hands in her own. Her flesh was soft, and Akairya smelled a subtle hint of lavender.

"Wh-what do you mean?" Akairya asked, unsettled. Yeilao shook her head and just smiled.

"Yeilao, I have sent for you to take a look at Kairi's spiritual self and see if you can see any of the blight's influence. She did not partner with her dragon in the known way, so I would like to know if she is...on our side," King Elric stepped down from his throne, his fur cape dragging on the floor. Yeilao nodded and took a breath, then closed her eyes. When she opened them again, Akairya gasped.

Her violet irises had gone ablaze; the colour was intense and it burned right through Akairya's flesh as the Spirit elf's gaze raked her from head to toe. The experience left the half elf strangely weak, and she had to lean on Draykor for balance.

"She is pure, sire."

The High King nodded and clapped his hands. "As I knew she would be! Very well, I will alert the kitchens to prepare for a large feast! Kairi, Killian, go and wash up. I will see you tonight."

Shaken from Yeilao's perusal and the king's sudden dismissal, Akairya simply stood where she was as the elf strode out of the room, Killian close behind her. He halted at the large doors and looked at Akairya.

Just as she was about to follow him, the bubbly princess scampered to Akairya's side.

"I'll take her and her dragon under my wing, Killian! Go and get yourself ready for tonight. It's not every night that my father's favorite general gets to dine with the royal family!"

Bemused, Killian nodded and left Akairya and Draykor with the princess, who looked positively delighted.

"Father never suspected you of anything, Kairi. He had to get Yeilao to check you, since if he hadn't, people would have called him insane and too naive and so forth. Oh, this is so *wonderful*. A Dragon Rider who is my age! The other two are so *old* and dreary. Well, Telectus isn't too bad, but he's still too old for me to really get along with…"

Akairya was pulled out of the room by Theandi as she talked, her blue eyes bright with excitement. She led her down a hallway that branched off the main corridor, then yanked her up a flight of steps to the next floor, talking all the while. Draykor stayed close behind, his eyes full of amusement. Akairya was amazed that he was able to move around so freely inside the castle; he was as large as the average horse, and he still had room to move about. The castle was enormous.

"…I'm going to have to get the maids to wash you three times to get rid of the travel filth! You're probably quite pretty underneath all that dirt. I have just the dress that will go wonderful with your hair. We must go for a walk in the gardens after dinner, just the two of us…well, three with your dragon! I want to get to know you as much as I can before you're whisked off to training. All new Riders have to go into training before their dragon matures into their element, you know. Just in case the sudden power is too much for the Rider."

Theandi's constant stream of one-sided conversation stopped when they reached a plain wooden door.

"Here's your room! It's the nicest we've got, next to mine and my parents'. I'll send up a few maids to help you clean up, and I'll dig up the dress I was talking about! See you soon!" The princess then bounded down the hall. Flabbergasted, Akairya shook her head and entered her room.

It was large, with a broad window covering most of the back wall. Sheer white curtains billowed from the window, and a low shelf covered in books stood underneath it. A plush crimson rug was laid out on the stone floor, and a fireplace roared on one end of the room. Across from the grate was a massive bed laden with thick white blankets and plump pillows, and near the door stood a tall wardrobe and a vanity.

This one room held more wealth and comfort in it than Akairya's small hovel in Yaeloa ever had.

Overcome, she walked slowly to the bed and sat on the edge. . Who would have thought that one day she would be a guest of the High King's? Especially as a Dragon Rider?

Draykor ambled over to her and placed his angular head in her lap. His black eyes studied her solemnly.

You're doing incredibly well, you know. Not many could handle so many changes and confusion in so short a time.

I'm barely handling it, that's for sure, she replied.

A knock at the door signaled the arrival of the promised maids.

"Come in."

Three young women in maid attire shuffled in, each of them hoisting large buckets of steaming water. Akairya leapt up in alarm.

"Those are *huge*. Do any of you need help?"

The maids placed their buckets on to the ground. Two of them swept back out of the room, and the one left behind put her hands on her hips.

"Milady, you will never be permitted to help any of us maids in anything. Only the royal family have higher status than you, being a Rider and all. It would be the utmost breach in regulation and rules to have you help us. Now, please sit and allow me to comb the knots out of your hair before you wash."

Akairya bit back a smile. She may not be allowed to help, but it seemed she was allowed to be bossed around. She obeyed and sat at the vanity.

The maid, whose name was Gretel, gently worked through the tangles in Akairya's hair as the other two maids returned with a large wooden tub. They poured the hot water into the tub, placed a couple different bottles of aromatic soaps on the bookshelf, a couple towels on the bed, and then promptly left.

A fine layer of dirt coated the comb that Gretel used in Akairya's hair. The elf girl was ashamed of her appearance; her hair was filthy and untidy, there were dark circles under her violet eyes, and dirt and dry sweat was caked on her skin. Her leather armor stank of travel and perspiration. To think, this was how the High King and his queen had seen her.

"Most of the knots are out, milady. I'll help you undress and then leave you to wash."

Akairya was soon soaking in the deliciously warm water of her bath, her armor taken away by Gretel to be cleaned and Draykor sound asleep beside the bed.

It took Akairya three washes with one of the soaps, which smelled of lavender, until she was satisfied with the cleanliness of her hair. She then selected another bottle of soap, which smelled like summer rain, and scrubbed her flesh until it was pink and raw. She then leaned back, inhaled the sharp fragrance of the soaps, and relaxed for the first time in days.

When Gretel returned, Akairya was just finished drying herself off and was sitting in front of the vanity in a plush robe she had found in the wardrobe.

"Perfect timing, miss. Princess Theandi has sent up one of her gowns. She would have come herself, except she is also getting ready for dinner."

The maid held up the dress, and Akairya gasped in both wonder and horror. Gretel walked over and signaled her to stand.

Before she put on the dress, Akairya was forced to slip on a soft chemise. She then stepped into the dress and sighed as Gretel pulled it into place around her, the material gliding on her skin like a caress.

The gown was made of shimmering, dark blue velvet that caught the light in a way she never thought velvet could. The scooped neckline was just low enough to hint at her curves, yet not too low that she felt uncomfortable. It hugged at her waist and billowed out from her hips. The neckline, edges of the wide bell sleeves, and the V across her hips were embroidered with a bright silver material that gave the dress an otherworldly feel. Akairya felt oddly restricted as she lifted her arm and watched the sleeve slip down her wrist.

"It's so…" she whispered as she picked up the skirt and rubbed the material with her thumb.

"Perfect," Gretel finished for her, smiling. The maid then maneuvered Akairya into the chair at the vanity and set to work on her hair.

"You will turn heads, Lady Rider. You can count on it," the maid said as she brushed Akairya's thick strands. She blushed at the compliment; she had never really thought of herself as pretty. Now, here she sat, in a dress made of a midnight struck sea. While she felt absolutely beautiful, she also felt out of place. She found herself missing her roughspun trousers that had served her well during her time living poorly in Yaeloa, trousers that had given her the freedom to move without restriction.

"There. My, you have wonderful hair, milady," Gretel said as she stepped back. Akairya looked in the mirror and she nearly clapped a hand to her mouth.

Her deep red hair fell in soft waves down her back, the strands that caught the firelight showing hints of dark purple. Gretel had placed a thin silver circlet studded with diamonds on top of her head. It was nowhere near as intricate as those the queen and princess wore, but it highlighted the silver that threaded through Akairya's dress and it brightened her violet eyes.

A knock sounded at the bedroom door, and one of the other maids poked her head in.

"Everyone is heading down, miss. Are you-oh my! You look wonderful, milady!"

The maid's eyes were round as saucers as Akairya stood. Draykor walked to her side and nuzzled her shoulder.

You smell better, at any rate, he said. Akairya hugged him around his ever-growing neck and turned to walk out of the room.

CHAPTER NINE

The dining hall was another room enveloped in glass. It was on the third floor, and the lake could be seen through the clear walls. Its calm waters were stained with hues of orange and red as the sun sank from the sky. The rich sunlight spilled into the dining room itself, so the glossy marble table was awash with darkening colour. On the table alongside polished plates, silver cutlery, and wine glasses were flickering candles, the many tiny flames cheery and beckoning.

The royal family was already seated in three of the twelve chairs by the time Akairya was led in by Jervos, whose nose was turned up importantly. He cracked his announcing stick, which Akairya had come to call it, soundly on the floor.

"Lady Rider Kairi, my lord and ladies," he cried. King Elric winced and shook his head.

"Good grief, man. There is no need to announce Kairi or anyone else during dinner unless we are in the middle of some sort of ball. Kindly show our newest Rider to her seat and then leave…*quietly.*"

Jervos, his squat face flushed, nearly shoved Akairya into a seat beside Princess Theandi before fleeing the room. Theandi giggled.

"He takes his job way too seriously," she whispered. She was wearing a dark red gown that draped off her shoulders and a delicate necklace of ivory pearls, her blonde hair swept up into an elegant bun. "Where's your dragon?"

"Draykor apologizes, but he is too tired to come to dinner. He isn't even a month old yet; the journey here took a lot out of him," Akairya replied as she stared in horror at the many forks and spoons that surrounded her plate. Theandi stifled a laugh at her expression.

"I'll talk you through the dinner, don't worry. Papa told me that you come from humble beginnings."

Akairya flushed. 'Humble beginnings' was a nice way to put living in a shack alone, alienated from society because of her 'half blood.' Having a bath had been a monthly luxury, simply because she had to bring in buckets of water from the well down the street and boil each bucket separately over her tiny fireplace. Most of the time her baths had been lukewarm, not steaming like the one she had had earlier this evening.

The dining room doors swung open again, and Jervos stepped inside.

"General Killian, my lord and ladies," he announced, a good deal quieter than before and without the loud *crack* of his walking stick. Killian strode in, his lean figure garbed in dark trousers and a white tunic, a black cloak billowing from his broad shoulders. Akairya noticed that the king had also traded in his steel armor for similar, albeit richer, clothing.

When Killian caught sight of Akairya, he stopped and gaped at her. She smiled uncomfortably – she still felt incredibly out of sorts in Theandi's dress.

"Kairi, you look…lovely! Who knew such beauty hid under all that travel filth?"

Queen Leliana gasped, her slanted green eyes turning on Killian with a look of motherly despair.

"Killian! You do not say such things to a lady! Especially one who has been bonded with a dragon."

"Sorry, milady," he said, smiling broadly. He winked at Akairya as he sat down across from her, to the right of King Elric.

"Finally, we're all here. Let's eat!" the king announced happily as he waved at a maid who hovered near the doors. She bobbed into a curtsy and darted out.

"Kairi, Telectus and Oren will be back from scouting Tilaner Isle in a couple days. You will then be put under their tuition. Meanwhile, I would like you to spend some time with Yeilao in the castle library. There is much you need to learn before your dragon embraces his elemental power."

Akairya nodded, her chest suddenly tight. Theandi squeezed her arm.

"Hey, don't worry! After you study with Yeilao tomorrow, I'll take you to the Royal Orchards. Perfect place to relax."

A line of butlers strode into the room carrying platters of steaming food, signaling the start of dinner.

Akairya couldn't get over the amount of food that was served. First came a rich, creamy soup that tasted like lamb and was dusted with finely grated cheese and onion. The soup was accompanied with toasted bread slathered in butter that had a hint of an herb she couldn't place. After the soup they tucked into large slabs of venison that had been seared to tender perfection and soaked in a seasoned sauce that tingled on her tongue. Alongside the meat were heaping mountains of mashed potatoes and gravy, peppered peas, honeyed carrots, more bread, and a sweet red wine that slid down her throat like the silk that trimmed her dress.

Throughout it all Theandi showed her the proper use of each utensil. It was quite confusing to Akairya, who had only ever used one fork or knife or spoon for any type of dish. She was entranced by how the two ladies consumed their meal. Each move was graceful, each bite like a smooth dance.

After her plate of venison was cleared away, she took a large drink of wine. Killian chuckled, and she blushed. Was she drinking too much for a lady?

She put her glass back down and nervously nibbled on her lip. In the back of her mind, she felt Draykor's soft presence. While they couldn't speak because of the distance between them, the more their bond strengthened, the farther they could go while still feeling each other's minds. Draykor was positive that soon they would be able to speak when they were apart. Now, however, Akairya just took comfort that no matter how awkward things became during this feast, her dragon was still with her.

She couldn't help but gasp as the butlers returned with a massive pie, its golden crust dusted with sugar.

"Full, Kairi? You're not going to want to turn this pie down; it's the best part of dinner!" Killian said. "However, if you have some you may not be able to practice your swordplay with me afterwards."

"Swordplay? After dinner? Really, Killian. This is Kairi's first day in the city! Why don't you practice with her tomorrow afternoon?" Queen Leliana dabbed her mouth with a napkin and took a sip from her wine glass, which was nearly empty. Akairya sighed inwardly; maybe it wasn't unladylike to enjoy wine.

"I'm sure she is dying to practice with a blade. We had no time for it on our way here," Killian answered his queen. Akairya smiled at Leliana and nodded her agreement.

"Killian is right. I'd love to do some swordplay after dinner."

A butler slipped a large slice of pie in front of her; the inside was stuffed with caramelized apples and sweet cherries.

"Excellent. I think I'll watch the two of you. There is no better entertainment than dancing with swords," Elric commented as he scooped up a hefty piece of pie, the filling giving off a fragrant steam.

"Oh, I'm not that good, your Majesty," Akairya mumbled, aghast. The king was going to watch? Maybe she *was* going to feel too full for practice. Killian gave her an encouraging smile.

"You're pretty talented, Kairi. You nearly beat me that night in camp. I think King Elric is going to be impressed; your father taught you well!"

The king raised an eyebrow. "Who was your father, Kairi? Killian tells me he was a hunter from Yaeloa, and that he was taken by the sickness that had rolled in from the blasted blight four years ago."

"His name was Alderon. He never told me his last name, just like he never told me my mother's name. I don't even know if she is still alive."

"Hm. I don't think I've ever met anyone named Alderon."

Akairya shrugged. "He was pretty secretive. He never told me anything about his life, only that he was a hunter. He taught me survival skills and kept me away from most people." That had been unnecessary; her impure blood had kept people away all on its own. She still found it amazing that everyone who had met her since she had bonded with Draykor were so unaffected by her half blood status. Apparently being a Dragon Rider made up for it.

Once the pie was finished and the plates cleared away, King Elric motioned to a butler.

"Get some extra hands and move the table and chairs to the side. Killian and Kairi will also need their blades; fetch them." The butler bowed and left to follow his king's bidding.

"We're going to practice in here, my king?" Killian's astonishment reflected Akairya's.

"I ate too much and I don't feel like walking to the training grounds. I respect the two of you for having enough energy to lift a sword; I find that venison sits in the stomach like a boulder when you eat too much."

Theandi giggled. "I agree, papa. I can barely lift a sword when I *have* energy!"

"Which is perfectly acceptable. Princesses are not meant to hold weapons," Queen Leliana sniffed. The king made a face.

"I think Theandi should take a couple fencing lessons from my men; it's good for anyone to know how to defend themselves."

The queen's reply was interrupted by the arrival of a stream of servants. Two of them handed Akairya and Killian their swords while the rest circled the table and lifted it. The marble was far from light; each of the servants strained to carry it to one side of the room, the thick tablecloth dragging on the ground.

When they lowered it back down, Akairya couldn't help but sigh in relief with them. She could only imagine how heavy it was.

Once the chairs were all moved over and the servants gone, Killian walked to one side of the room and brandished his blade. Akairya followed suit and moved opposite him, her stomach tight with nerves. She did *not* want the king thinking she was horrible with a sword.

"If you put a single rip in my dress, Killian, I will be very put out," Theandi called sweetly, her blue eyes twinkling. Akairya's heart dropped. She forgot that she was wearing such a beautiful gown.

"Maybe I should change first," she said nervously, plucking at the dress. Theandi laughed.

"I'm only making fun, Kairi. Dresses can be mended."

Killian swung his sword slowly as he shifted forward. "Enough talking; time to practice!"

Unlike last time, Akairya was the first to attack. She figured throwing herself into the duel would be the best way to forget that the king was watching, so she gripped the hilt of her blade and lunged, her skirts only slightly impeding her.

Killian deflected her swing easily and pushed her back with a flurry of attacks, his silver eyes bright. He had also had quite a bit of wine during dinner.

The wine in her system gave Akairya more courage; she stepped lightly and moved quickly, her ferocity slowly giving her the advantage. She barely noticed her full stomach. She was surprised by how easy it was for her to move in the dress; she had expected to trip over the hem at least once.

As the duel went on and she got warmer and warmer in her velvet gown, she noticed something. Killian didn't seem as on top of things as before; he was distracted. When his eyes dipped to her chest, she knew why.

Heat rushed to her cheeks, yet she pushed the advantage and grated her sword against his. With a flick of her wrist, she wrenched his blade away from him and it clattered to the ground.

King Elric roared with laughter. "Looks like Kairi *should* have changed, eh?" he chuckled. Killian blushed and avoided Akairya's gaze as he picked up his sword.

"Um, good job," he muttered. Akairya grinned.

The next morning, Akairya was shown the way to the castle's immense library. While not nearly as large as Yaeloa's library had been, this one was designed to appeal to the eye. The massive room was perfectly circular and stretched hundreds of feet up to the lofty ceiling. The bookshelves were made of the same red wood that made up the doors in the castle's foyer, and they were embedded in the library's walls. They were as high as the ceiling, the topmost shelves hidden from the light that came from fireplaces beside some of the bookshelves. The middle of the room was filled with plump couches, armchairs and wooden tables covered in parchment and writing utensils. A number of scholars were fervently working at the tables when Akairya walked in. The sandy floor was covered in plush crimson rugs that sank when Akairya stepped on them, and each fireplace was happily full of crackling flames. The light flickered throughout the room and gave off a welcome warmth.

"Akairya, child. Over here," Yeilao was nestled in a large armchair by one of the fires, her violet eyes reflecting the flames. Confused by the elf's use of her full name, Akairya joined her and sat in the armchair on the other side of the fireplace.

"The king wants me to be known as Kairi, not Akairya."

"I know, but I have my reasons for wanting to use your birth name. Those reasons will be known to you one day, dear. Not today, but soon."

Even more bewildered, Akairya simply looked at the old elf.

"The king has asked me to explain to you the fundamentals of elemental power. However, he does not seem to realize that this power has never been easily defined. Each element sustains the earth. Without one, the land would crumble and perish. Why do the dragons have sway over such an important part of our world? I do not know. How have elves, the ones independent from the partnership of a dragon, gained this strength when humans have not? I do not know that either. It just simply is. What I do know, however, is that one of the elements is the strongest of the five. Do you know which one that is?"

Akairya shook her head. Yeilao smiled and pointed at her own eyes.

"Spirit, child. Spirit is the strongest element. While Fire can refresh the land, Water nourish it, Air cleanse it, and Earth strengthen it, Spirit is the land's own soul. Do you know what that means, my dear?"

Again, Akairya was at a loss.

"It *means* that when Spirit has weakened, the earth is susceptible to disease. A disease such as the blight."

Akairya blinked and leaned forward. "Are you saying you know how the Shadow has come to be?" she whispered. Yeilao shook her head, her ivory hair orange from the fire.

"I do not know how the Shadow was born, but I know that the spread of its blemished touch was only possible because the land's spirit has weakened. When the High Queen disappeared, the element we call Spirit fractured. The land became hopelessly unprotected against darkness."

"You said that the High Queen…disappeared. Don't you mean died?"

"No, child. After the War of Elves, when the true intelligence of dragons became clear and the land was at peace, High Queen Akairya vanished. It was written that she had died, but the scholars lied. She had disappeared."

Akairya was almost positive that the Spirit elf was crazy. Why would the scholars from back then lie about such an important turn of events?

"I have a question about the High Queen and the War of Elves, Yeilao," Akairya said quietly. The elf dipped her chin in encouragement.

"The War of Elves was just that; a war between humans and elves. Yet wasn't the High Queen an elf? She had been a Spirit elf, just like you. Why would she go to war against her own kind? And how did she become queen over a human society in the first place? I know she had been responsible for creating the provinces of Alkairyn, but the fact that she was an elf against other elves baffles me."

"Ah, an excellent question. You see, Akairya was an orphan. She had been taken in by humans, and spent most of her life travelling across Alkairyn before it was so named. She was raised in a world of constant warfare, famine, and distrust among people simply because there was no order, no one to guide the people. The land at the time was wild and untamable; its spirit untapped. Then Akairya grew into her power, and she became the first Spirit elf. She discovered that she had the ability to rein in the spirit of the land, and thus she was encouraged to become the first High Queen, since she had made it possible for the people to build thriving farms, and build beautiful cities, and keep livestock healthy. The land finally accepted the humans who had lived against it for so many years, and all because its spirit flowed through Akairya.

"The elves grew jealous of her power. No one had ever harnessed Spirit before, except for a handful of dragons; its limits were unknown. She had the ability to snuff out someone's soul with the wave of her hand, and even had an elemental weapon that overpowered any of the others."

"Elemental weapon?" Akairya cut in, intrigued.

"Do you not know about the elemental weapons? If an elf or Rider succeeds in mastering their element fully, they discover the ability to conjure that element's weapon, which is made of the element's very essence. Fire is a sword, Water a whip, Earth a hammer, and Air, daggers. Spirit's weapon is a bow, with an unlimited amount of arrows that simply materialize when the wielder draws the bowstring. The elves soon discovered that a single Spirit arrow could dissolve any flame, drop of water, or boulder they threw, so they decided that such a power should not be possible. Thus, the War of Elves began, ten years after Akairya had created the seven provinces and began to build her capital cities."

Akairya sat back in her armchair and let out a deep breath. All she had known before was that the elements were just that; elements that could be harnessed by dragons and elves. She had no idea of the true extent of their power, or that they were so crucial to the health of the world.

"How does one truly harness an element?"

"That cannot be taught, I'm sad to say. In order to fully master an element, you must understand it and know every tiny intricate detail about it. I've been a Spirit elf for three hundred years, and I have not been able to conjure the Spirit bow."

"*Three hundred years?* Then you're old enough to have known the High Queen herself!"

The elf smiled knowingly. "I knew her well."

CHAPTER TEN

Akairya gaped at Yeilao. "I…didn't know that elves could live so long."

"Most do not. That I know of. Thousands of years ago, before Akairya and her kingdom and before history was preserved, elf life spans may have been more extensive. However, history has only been recorded since a hundred years before High Queen Akairya. I believe my long life has to do with my affinity for Spirit, but I may also just be lucky."

"Thousands of years ago…you'd think that Alkairyn would have been created long before Akairya. Why did it take so long for society to organize itself?"

"Oh, child. You are so young. Just because the history of the last four hundred years is all we have, doesn't mean there was never anything before it. I believe this land has been home to many kingdoms, all of them fallen for different reasons. Rebellion, plague…who knows? The dragons were here before us, and they have legends of ancient kingdoms. One legend has always been prominent, and it is the one the dragons tell of the Ryio Kingdom.

"In the tales, the Ryio Kingdom was grand and wealthy. Cities stretched across the land, and humans and elves flourished. Their king was wise and very kind, and things were wonderful for all races and classes. The legend even hints that the king also had control over the Spirit element. But then something happened; the king was murdered by his brother, and a great darkness cloaked the kingdom. In its grasp the people died and the cities crumbled. The darkness stayed until nothing was left of Ryio, and then it simply faded away, leaving no trace of the grandness that had once spread across the country. Dragons were left alone, since they lived in Drakynold, across the sea, away from the bulk of Ryio. Thus they were the only ones to remember such a kingdom had once existed…other than the demons of the Underearth." Yeilao drifted off, her violet eyes sad as she stared into the fire.

"If that's true, it sounds like the Shadow. I wonder how it ended?" Akairya mused.

"Well, once the land is broken and everything destroyed, the blight would have nothing left to feed off of. It would eventually die itself, which would give the land a chance to repair. My theory is that Akairya was born when the land had finished healing from the last blight, and that her ability to embrace Spirit finished the process. When she disappeared, it fractured Spirit and once again made the land vulnerable to a blight."

Akairya's head spun; she was finding the history lesson difficult to follow. Yeilao noted her expression and chuckled.

"I think that's enough for one day, child. Go and enjoy the rest of your day."

Relieved, Akairya bid the old elf farewell and left the warmth of the library. Who would have thought that the Spirit element was so crucial to the health of the land? She shivered as she realized that she may be able to wield the element one day. Killian believed so, or he never would have brought it up that night in the Jalkorin.

There you are! Draykor cried. Akairya jumped as her dragon bounded over from the top of a flight of stairs, his great weight shaking the floor. It was almost comical seeing him in the palace. *I was told you were in the library when I finally woke up, but I had no idea where it was, and I could just barely sense your presence...so I was wandering around the castle. Pretty sure I gave about ten maids heart failure.*

Akairya giggled. *Your fault for being such a sleepy head.*

Hey! I'm still a dragonling. Young dragons require rest.

The pair descended the flight of stone steps, oblivious to the figure who stalked behind them. When they reached the second floor, the person launched forward and tripped Akairya. Draykor roared in indignation and went to bite their attacker, but stopped just before his teeth sank into their neck.

It was Thoran, a huge grin on his face, although his eyes were wide from Draykor's near-bite.

"How do you two expect to save the world when you don't even notice a single stalker?"

You're lucky you still have your head, Thoran Unnamed.

Heart still pounding, Akairya looked at Thoran curiously. "That's right! You have no last name. Why?"

"Simple, really. No one knows who my parents were. I was found by an old fisherman when I was a few months old; he raised me until I was old enough to decide to be a soldier. Eventually I ended up here."

Sensing he was hiding something, Akairya just let it be. He barely knew her, what made her think he would open up and tell her all about his personal life?

"What are you up to?" she asked instead. Draykor huffed happily as Thoran reached up and scratched him behind one of his spikes, which were now thicker than Akairya's thumb. Thoran's smile faded.

"Just met with the king. He was hoping we had seen more of the Calindyl province before taking you here…he is worried that the Roraks not only destroyed Yaeloa, but poisoned the entire province."

Akairya felt sick at the mention of the beautiful plains dying. "I really hope not. It's bad enough the Roraks and Shadow dragons destroyed the capital city and surrounding farms…"

The three of them had made their way to the ground floor. They stood near a large redwood door much like the one in the library and foyer.

"This leads to the royal training grounds, barracks, gardens, orchard, and Rider quarters," Thoran told her.

"Rider quarters? I didn't see anything like that when I looked outside. Why aren't Dray and I sleeping there?"

"Probably because you're new to the city and the king doesn't want you outside of the castle, alone. You likely didn't notice the building because it's hidden in the deepest part of the royal gardens."

"Kairi! Done being lectured, I see!" Princess Theandi bounded over, her blond hair flying behind her and her blue eyes excited. "I can show you the orchard!"

"Oh, right. I forgot. I'd love to see it," Akairya smiled as the princess skidded to a halt in front of her. Draykor made a peculiar sound which Akairya thought was a dragon equivalent of a laugh. Thoran also looked amused.

"Mind if I join you? I don't have any guard duties or training sessions until tomorrow."

Theandi appraised him, her eyes narrowed. "I've never really talked to you…Thoran, right? But I know Killian thinks highly of you…so I guess so, if Akairya is okay with it."

"Of course I am."

The orchard was across the lush field from the barracks and training grounds, just before the sprawling gardens. Numerous strange looking trees were planted in straight lines that stretched to the edge of the wide moat that surrounded the castle. Akairya had never seen trees like the ones in the orchard; they had slim chocolate coloured trunks and branches, yet no leaves. In the place of leaves were thick vines that sprouted from the branches and the upper part of the trunks. Hanging from the vines were fruit that looked similar to apples. Some of them were purple, while others were a deep green.

"What kind of trees are these?" Akairya inquired. Draykor walked up to the nearest tree and stretched his neck up; he was just able to grasp one of the peculiar fruit with his teeth. He gently pulled it from its vine and walked back to Akairya. He dropped it in her outstretched hand, and she was surprised by its weight. It was just a little smaller than the average apple, yet quite heavy. Its skin was fragile; juice oozed from where Draykor's teeth had punctured it.

"We call them grapples," Theandi answered her. "An alchemist decided to fuse together the seeds of grapes and apples and plant them. These trees grew from the seeds. The fruit is really like a huge grape; they are incredibly juicy. Yet they have cores like apples and have a hint of an apple taste. The alchemist gifted the seeds to my grandpapa and the nobility loved them. They sell like wildfire and make awesome jam, or pie. Take a bite!"

Akairya lifted the grapple to her mouth and took a small nibble. Juice dripped down her chin, and the flavor that burst in her mouth was ten times a grape, with just a hint of apple. The flesh was a little harder than a regular grape's, yet its peel was just as delicate. It was delicious.

"Wow, Theandi. I see why you wanted to take me here."

"Oh, you trying out the fruit was just a bonus. The real reason why I wanted to take you out here was so you could try riding Draykor. He's bigger than the average horse, he could carry you no problem!"

Thoran, who had plucked a grapple for himself, choked on the piece he had just swallowed. "Are you *crazy*, princess? Dray has barely gotten used to flying alone! It would be suicide for Kairi to try flying already!"

I think it's a wonderful idea. I flew quite a bit before we reached the city; I am confident in my abilities.

Excitement fluttered in Akairya's chest as she studied her dragon. He *was* big enough, and there was a perfect place for her to sit where his neck met his back…the spikes were placed far enough away she could squeeze between them.

Will your scales cut me? She asked Draykor. He shook his angular head.

No. Have you ever cut yourself when you gave me a scratch? My scales may be hard, but they lay flat on me. There are no sharp edges for you to concern yourself with.

"What's the harm in trying? Draykor can fly low to the ground for the first bit…that way, if I lose my balance, it will be just like falling off a horse."

Thoran groaned. "People die falling off horses, you know. Watch, I'm going to be the one punished if you get hurt, Kairi."

"Not if I can help it! If Kairi *does* get hurt, I'll make sure everyone knows it was my idea," Theandi piped up, a huge grin on her pretty face.

Draykor unfurled his wings with a leathery *snap* and gave a huff. The membrane in his wings shone from the sun. Akairya's excitement grew as she stepped closer to her dragon.

Theandi giggled and pulled Thoran away from dragon and Rider so he wouldn't be buffeted by wings. He looked like he was going to be sick.

"Just…be careful. Please."

You're beginning to insult me, Thoran. I will not allow my Rider to be injured. Especially by me.

Thoran sighed and stayed silent. Draykor lowered his neck and bent his front legs, and Akairya jumped up with a laugh. Her elvish reflexes made it easy for her to clamber on, and she was soon perched on her dragon.

The view was much different than when she was astride a horse. Draykor's black scales glinted brightly, and his long neck blocked most of her vision when he lifted his head. She could feel his wings behind her, and she trembled with anticipation.

Ready? Her dragon asked.

Yes!

He turned away from the orchard and faced the castle, his small tufted ears perked. He took a few steps, then began to lope. Akairya was surprisingly comfortable, the spike behind her kept her in place while the one in front was the perfect handhold. Her legs were just behind his front legs, and she could feel the power as he picked up speed. He lifted his wings almost vertical from the ground, bunched up his muscles, and gave a powerful flap that propelled them up. He flew a few feet up then kept his wings straight so they could glide parallel with the ground.

I'm not yet strong enough to lift off from a stand still. Draykor apologized. Akairya patted his shoulder with happy enthusiasm.

I understand. This is great!

Want to go higher?

Do you really need to ask?

Draykor complied; with two great wing beats, they were soon a hundred feet up and climbing. Akairya was once again grateful for the spike behind her; while Draykor flew up, she would have slipped right off his back without it. The thought should have terrified her; instead, it made everything a whole lot more exciting.

When he finally leveled out, they were hundreds of feet up. She could see the glittering lake that surrounded Kalisor city and the distant forest in the south. When she looked west, she could see the peaks of the Jalkorin mountain range. To the east were the mountains of Morkrain.

When she looked back down towards the orchard, she could just see Theandi and Thoran standing near the trees. Akairya laughed, absolutely giddy.

Draykor flew in lazy circles while Akairya leaned back and lifted her face to the sky.

I may be confused as to why we are bonded, but I am so happy we are. She told Draykor.

Me too, my Rider.

They glided smoothly for a couple more minutes, until Draykor lifted his head and looked west. *Dragons!*

Fear clutched at her. Shadow dragons, here? Surely they wouldn't attack the capital city, not when the king had hundreds of soldiers at his disposal? She looked in the direction that Draykor had, and gasped.

The two dragons that were flying towards the castle weren't of the Shadow; they were clearly coloured. One was a bright ivory with faded blue wing membranes, the other was a deep crimson. Figures were astride them

The king's Riders! They're back! Akairya suddenly felt incredibly nervous. Those two had *earned* their status as Riders. The Dragon Elders had gifted them their dragons for some brave deed they had done. Would they look down on Akairya?

Relax. Draykor admonished her as he flew towards the dragons and their Riders. She tried desperately to follow his advice, but her heart began to pound as they grew closer.

The dragon in the lead was nearly as large as the Shadow dragon who had invited Akairya to Tilaner Isle. His great body was covered in pearly white scales that glittered coldly in the sun, and his spikes, claws, eyes, and wing membranes were a light blue. A wiry man with faded pepper hair was astride him, and Akairya was intrigued to see that he was using a small saddle that tied his legs securely to his dragon. She imagined such a thing helped keep a Rider on his dragon while they were in aerial combat.

The second dragon was a little smaller, although still much larger than Draykor. He was a dark red with orange eyes and spikes. His Rider, a slim elf with coal black eyes and hair, studied Draykor from head to tail as he flew up to them.

"Hail," the man mounted on the white and blue dragon greeted. All three dragons floated in a small circle above the western section of Kalisor's great wall, and a breeze picked up that tore at Akairya's burgundy hair. She wiped it away from her eyes impatiently, her heart still beating rapidly.

"Um, hi. I'm Kairi, I don't know if-"

"The new Rider. The High King sent a falcon to tell us about you. It is an honor to meet you, Akairya," the elf interrupted her solemnly, his dark eyes steady on her face.

"He told you my full name?" she said, surprised.

The man with the peppered hair chuckled, his sea green eyes crinkling at the corners. "He did not have to. We know who you are, and why you are bonded with your dragon. I am Telectus, and this is Oren. My dragon is named Saverign."

Greetings, young ones. The bright dragon inclined his head. The red dragon snuffed and blew out a thin trail of fire.

I am Xandior. It is a relief to know that the path paved for you has gone well, so far.

"It's…nice to meet you all. If you know why Draykor and I have bonded, will you tell me?" Akairya asked eagerly. This was news she had not been expecting.

"It is not our place to tell you, new Rider," Oren answered her, his deep voice soulful. "That is the task of the Elders."

"The *Elders?*"

"Yes. When it is time, you will have to travel to Drakynold and learn why things have come to be as they are. That time is yet to come, so please. Let's return to the castle. We have much to tell King Elric."

CHAPTER ELEVEN

Akairya sat in an oval room with stone walls that were covered in maps. There were a couple different maps of Alkairyn as a whole, some maps of the kingdom's singular provinces, maps of the dragon country Drakynold, the elf country Ellivera, the alchemist training island Lakayol (which was now overrun by Roraks), the warlock country Talkorin, and the island called Hekatorra, which was barely explored. There were rumors that there was more to the world than the great country of Alkairyn and the surrounding islands, but no one had been able to reach any new lands by boat or dragon. The distance was simply too far for a dragon to fly, and ships either ran out of provisions or never came back.

There was only one window in the room, and it was tiny. Barely any natural light came in from it, so a large number of candles were set out on the circular stone table that stood in the center of the room.

Akairya, Thoran, Killian, Telectus, Oren, Yeilao, and King Elric were all seated at the table, sipping at cups of steaming tea. The three dragons were in the Riders' quarters, deep in the Royal Gardens. Now that Telectus and Oren were back, Akairya would be sleeping there. Gretel, the handmaid who had helped Akairya get ready for the feast the night before, would be sleeping there with her.

"We have dark news, milord," Telectus began, his gray head bowed over his cup, fragrant steam curling towards his face.

"There are indeed massive amounts of Roraks on Tilaner Isle. They have spread from Lakayol and have built a castle made of black stone on the northern edge of the island. As you know, Tilaner used to be inhabited by a small population of fishermen. We saw no signs of these men and their families, so it is with heavy hearts that we suspect they are now dead.

"We tried to scout the island for more information, but a thick cloud of Shadow came from the castle when we got too close. We barely escaped its clutches, and we had no choice but to leave. Instead of heading straight home we headed towards Calindyl, in the hopes of finding any survivors of the sacking of Yaeloa.

"There is no town or farm left in the province. Every building we came across was burned or simply empty, and the land is dying. The once green hills are turning gray, and it even looks like the cliff that Yaeloa's carcass sits upon is threatening to crumble. I am sorry for not having anything good to say, King Elric...but it looks as if the Shadow is strengthening by the day."

"The Spirit of the land needs to be mended, and quickly," Yeilao cut in, her wrinkled face pale. "I can try to tap into the soul of the earth, but it is not meant for me to heal."

"Who is it meant for?" Akairya asked, her stomach churning from the news of Calindyl. Yeilao just looked at her, her violet eyes sad.

"We cannot weep about something we cannot fix, especially since we do not have the time to wait for those who have the ability." Oren said quietly. "Instead, we must strengthen our armies and prepare to fight back. The alchemists have concocted a poison against the Roraks, have they not? Anything tainted with the Shadow cannot bear the touch of this poison. We have that against them."

"The poison is deadly to them, yes Oren, but we do not have a large quantity. The alchemists are trying their best to make more, but they are unable to conjure the stuff out of thin air. You know how they work; they can only blend things or substitute certain things," Telectus said. The king sighed and rubbed his eyes.

"It saddens me to hear that my kingdom is dying, and I wish we had a means of repairing the land's Spirit, Yeilao, I truly do. But we have no such thing." He glanced at everyone in turn. "I agree with Oren though. We must strengthen the army and recruit more soldiers. I'll send falcons to each provincial Duke and tell them to ready themselves. We have no idea what this…Shadow Lord is going to do next. We are also going to be busy taking in the flood of refugees that will soon reach us from Calindyl." He got up and looked at the map of Tilaner Isle, a furrow in his brow. "We'll need more help from the elves.

"Kairi, I beg you, please dedicate yourself to the training Telectus and Oren are going to give you. Three Riders in this dark time is a blessing, and we will need you as prepared as you can be."

Akairya nodded, her heart pounding. A month ago, she never would have guessed she would be in this situation. Before the fall of Yaeloa, she had lived alone and had worked lowly jobs for barely any money. Now she was expected to help protect the entire country.

Killian, who had been speaking quietly with Thoran, looked at her closely.

"I know Draykor and Kairi were bonded differently than the traditional way…but why does everyone seem to think that they are so important to ending the blight? I don't mean that in a cruel way, Kairi, not at all," he gave her a small smile and continued, "but is there something I'm missing? I believe she may eventually gain power over the Spirit element, but that is just a meek belief."

"Ah, Killian. You may be the youngest general in the king's army, but that does not mean you get to know everything," Telectus chuckled, a twinkle in his eye. "You will know why Akairya is so important in due time."

"They won't even tell me what is so important, and I am the king!" Elric sighed.

"Why *can't* I know what you know?" Akairya asked, somewhat annoyed. "It affects Draykor and me quite a bit. You'd think we had a right to know as soon as possible."

"Child, we wish we could tell you. But it is not our right. Things need to be done as they are required, or else we could unknowingly change the path you are set on. You will travel to the Elders in time." Yeilao answered her. The ancient elf took a slow sip of her now cold tea, her eyes locked on Akairya's, violet on violet. "You are not yet ready for such a journey, both physically and mentally. What we are dealing with here is delicate, and much is at stake."

Even more confused, Akairya just shrugged. There was obviously no point in arguing when no one wanted to tell her what she wanted to know.

The next few weeks passed by in a blur. While the king had his army begin rigorous preparations for the coming war and immersed himself in dealings with the elves and the arrival of Calindyl's shaken refugees, Akairya was submerged into a heavy training program. When she wasn't training, she practiced flying with Draykor and spent time with Princess Theandi, who had adopted Akairya as a sort of sister.

"I've always wanted a sister, you know. Someone I can talk to about anything and everything," the princess gushed when the two of them were strolling through the city's colourful market. Draykor trailed behind them, eyes bright as he took in the many different stalls. They passed stalls that had piles of fabric, stalls with various foods and drink, stalls with herbs, jewelry stalls, cosmetic stalls, and even large stalls that held various animals. The market was a hive of activity, and people jostled everywhere. Many still gave Draykor a wide berth, but the news that he and Akairya were not of the Shadow had spread, and people were growing braver. Many even shook Akairya's hand. She wasn't used to such interaction with people, but she handled the spike in attention smoothly. She had to, especially since King Elric had announced that he was going to throw a ball in a week, to introduce her to the local nobility. She was terrified.

"Since I am determined for us to talk about anything, let's go straight to personal matters. Do you think Killian is handsome?" Theandi asked brightly as she slipped a shiny bracelet she had just bought onto her slim wrist. Akairya blanched.

"Uh...um...I don't know...I mean..."she stammered. Theandi giggled and looped her arm with Akairya's.

"Come on, out with it! If you're worried that he doesn't like how you are a half blood, don't be so silly. You are a Rider now! Practically royalty! Plus you are absolutely *lovely* and really good with a sword and even a bow, or that's what Papa was telling me the other day, because he watched you train with a bow with Oren..."

"It's not that!" Akairya cut in, blushing. She knew perfectly well Killian found her attractive; the first night they had arrived in the city and had had their duel in the dining room told her that. "I just thought...you might like him."

Theandi stared at her, her blue eyes wide in surprise. Her expression softened and she gave Akairya a tight hug. "You really *are* like a sister! Concerned with my feelings, and not wanting to find someone handsome simply because you think I may have a claim. Oh, goodness, Kairi. I grew up with Killian! He's like my brother. He taught me how to ride a horse, how to clean a sword, how to string a bow, and how to climb a tree, but I would never think of him as a potential *lover*. Sure, he is absolutely lovely with his golden hair and silver eyes, and his physique is quite appealing, but I say all that in a sort of...objective view."

Akairya couldn't help but giggle as Theandi skipped towards a stall that sold rich chocolate coffee. She bought a cup from the seller, who kept bowing at her, and handed it to Akairya to try.

"Isn't that delicious? I could drink a whole tub if it wasn't so rich. Anyways, I guess your concern sort of answers my question! You *do* think he is handsome!"

Akairya blushed. Theandi whooped and did a little skip. "I knew it! Don't fret, sister. I'll teach you the wily ways of women. You'll have that man in no time."

Draykor, who had finally caught up to them, snorted.

Females are so strange.

Akairya laughed, slightly embarrassed. She took another sip of the thick coffee, its sweet chocolate flavor smooth on her tongue. She allowed Theandi to steer her through the narrow market paths.

The girls and dragon soon found themselves on the edge of the market, and the colours of the stalls gave way to gold and ivory. However, the buildings that stretched down thin streets of chipped stone were more run down than Akairya was used to seeing in the city.

"Ah, the slums. I didn't realize we were so close," Theandi muttered. Her blue eyes studied the dirty walls of the houses, and a sadness came into her expression.

Akairya frowned as a girl wearing a tattered cloak stepped out of a nearby building, her strawberry blonde hair snarled into a bun.

"Fea?" She asked, astonished. The girl stopped in her tracks and stared at Akairya, her brown eyes wide. She took in the elf girl's rich clothing and Draykor, who stood at his Rider's shoulder.

"So it's true," she breathed. "The half blood has become a Rider. We all lost everything, and the poorest of us gained everything." There was no bitterness in her voice, only resignation. She shrugged thin shoulders. "I suppose you have come to gloat?"

Akairya blinked. "Why would I want to gloat? I lost my home, just as you."

"Oh, yes. The home where we all bullied you and only threw you scraps like a dog when we felt like being good people." Fea gave a high pitched laugh. "I suppose we deserve our fate."

"Don't talk like that. I hold no harsh feelings."

"I find that hard to believe."

"Believe as you wish, but I speak the truth. How many others survived?"

Fea dropped her eyes. "A good amount of the city's merchants. No lower class, save you, and no nobles. I think all of the refugees are from Yaeloa. I haven't met anyone from the outer villages or farms."

Her words cut Akairya like a knife. *So many dead.*

"May I see everyone else?"

Fea studied her carefully. After a moment she gave a slight nod. "As surprising as it is, it looks as if you are telling the truth about not harboring hard feelings." She twisted her lips. "If you wish to see the state of Calindyl's citizens, come with me. I'm warning you...you are in for a shock."

Theandi came as well, her grip tight on Akairya's arm as they wound their way through the slums. Tired people barely glanced at them as they passed, and dirty children peeked at them from cracked windows.

"It's so...sad here," Akairya said softly. "What do these people do?"

"They try to work, in the trades. But there are already so many people doing the same sort of thing. Sometimes they do well enough to move into the merchant's neighborhood, but not often."

"It's only gotten worse here now that we've all arrived," Fea added glumly. "The slums was the only area with enough room for two hundred refugees."

Two hundred out of thousands of citizens. The blight absolutely slaughtered them.

Which is why we need to figure out a way to help the king stop it, Draykor answered.

Fea stopped at the mouth of another street, this one even more dilapidated than the rest.

"Here is where the king has housed us, in the hall at the end of the street. Apparently the place was once used as a gathering area for meetings. But ever since things have gotten so much worse, what with the Shadow and all, the people here have given up any semblance of hope."

Unsure of how to respond, Akairya stayed quiet and followed Fea to the large building at the end of the road. Its golden roof shone in the sunlight.

"I'm surprised no one takes apart the roofs, seeing as they are made out of gold," Akairya commented.

Theandi laughed, her smile kind. "The roofs of the city aren't made of true gold, dear Kairi. If they were, the poor would have torn apart their buildings even more than they already have." She shook her head. "No, the roofs are made of golden marble that have been polished by alchemist power."

"Oh," Akairya said, defeated. Fea opened the large doors of the hall and strode inside.

The interior was dimly lit, but the few lanterns burning let off enough light for Akairya to see the cracked marble flooring and many bedrolls thrown haphazardly throughout the hall. People milled about, talking amongst themselves. Each person wore expressions of deep weariness, and an air of desolation permeated the hall. When Akairya appeared with Draykor, all talking ceased.

"I'm sure many of you remember our resident half blood," Fea announced her, not unkindly. "The rumors are true; she is our newest Rider. She has asked to come see everyone."

"A new Rider…" an older woman said in awe. She walked slowly over to Akairya, her filthy green dress many sizes too big. Akairya didn't recognize her.

"You will avenge our home, will you not?" the woman asked, a bright fervor in her watery eyes. Akairya looked around the room, and only saw a handful of people she vaguely remembered from Calindyl. It looked as if most of the citizens she had known had perished in the sacking of their city.

"I will avenge the loss of our province and your families. I promise." She replied, her voice carrying clearly throughout the hall. Everyone stared at her, and she was struck by the difference in their gazes. Just a short time ago they had looked down on her, and now they were looking at her with respect and hope, something she had never thought she'd experience. "I may not know most of you personally, but Calindyl and the city Yaeloa was my home just as much as it was yours.

"The Shadow will pay."

Later, the two girls were sitting in the dining hall, sipping tea and talking about their childhoods, something Theandi had begun in hopes of distracting Akairya from thinking about earlier. Draykor had gone to stretch his wings with Saverign and Xandior. The massive lake that surrounded the island could be seen through the room's glass walls, and the water glittered in the late morning sun. The sky was a deep blue unmarked by clouds and Akairya could just see the three dragons flying high above the castle grounds.

"I'll be the first to admit I was a very spoiled child," Theandi laughed as she dropped a couple more large cubes of sugar into her tea. She stirred it and grinned at Akairya. "I've always been father's little girl, and he sort of let me do whatever I wanted. Telectus told me that I even demanded to sit on the top of Saverign's head one day."

Akairya choked on her tea. "It's a good thing Saverign is so mellow," she chuckled. Akairya found it quite interesting that while Telectus was a very energetic man who loved a good laugh, his dragon was very calm and only spoke when necessary. The white and blue dragon was more like Oren, while Oren's dragon, Xandior, was just as passionate as Telectus.

"Yeah, Saverign apparently just sat there with this four year old me lying on his head, without a care in the world."

"My father would have loved all three of the dragons. He really liked meeting them. He met two unbonded ones before I was born, and he always told me stories of how they kept him company in the wilderness when he was out hunting."

Theandi looked at her curiously. "What was it like, growing up with a hunter for a father?"

"It was wonderful. I know how to survive alone practically anywhere because of him, and all of my weapon knowledge is because he took the time to train me. He thought it was very important. While we lived in Yaeloa, he took me out on every hunting trip he had to go on, since I had no mother and no one wanted to look after a half blood. So I got to see a lot from a young age. No other cities, though. Kalisor is the first city I have ever seen besides my home."

"It sounds lonely," Theandi said quietly, her blue eyes on her cup. "I mean, I always had loads of friends. The maids always brought their young ones to work, and the nobles in the city loved to bring their children to the castle to play with me. From what I heard today, it doesn't look as if you had many friends growing up."

Akairya sipped her tea thoughtfully. "I never thought myself as lonely until after my father passed away from the plague that hit Yaeloa. Then I got really lonely…no one wanted to interact with me, unless they asked me to do an errand for them. That's how I survived, making money on little jobs. Then the Shadow dragons and Roraks came a few weeks ago, and here I am."

"Well, you have no reason to feel lonely anymore!" Theandi said cheerfully. "You have Draykor, and me, and Thoran seems to really like your company. Killian too, even though he has been so busy training new recruits. Oren and Telectus are sort of your guardians now."

"I don't feel lonely at all, not anymore," Akairya agreed, smiling.

The rest of the week flew by for Akairya in a flurry of history and etiquette lessons, plus hours of training by the two older Riders. While it was crucial for her to learn how to properly take on the role of a Rider, she was also expected to act noble and be able to hold her own during the ball. She attempted to visit the refugees again, but each time she thought she had the chance, someone came to whisk her off into another lesson. When the day of her ball finally dawned, she was exhausted and terrified for the looming night. She had barely grasped the basic steps of the dances, and Queen Leliana had made a point to tell her that many noble families were officially attending. No one wanted to miss out on meeting the youngest Rider, who had come across her dragon by highly untraditional means.

Akairya was back in her room inside the castle that night, since traipsing through the gardens and lawns to the castle from the Rider quarters in her ball gown would have been illogical. A shimmering dress of smooth silver was laid across her bed, this time a gift from the queen herself. Akairya stood in a towel staring at the gown. She was supposed to make a grand entrance with Draykor, and she could just imagine herself falling down the wide flight of stairs.

A light knock sounded from her door. "Miss, are you done bathing?"

"Yes, Gretel. I finished a few minutes ago. You can come in."

The maid opened the door immediately, an excited smile brightening her expression. "I love this sort of thing! The king generally throws a ball once every few months, to keep the nobility happy. They are perfect for sons and daughters to be matched off, and the older generations love a good dance and opportunity to gossip." Gretel sighed dreamily. "There will be so many beautiful dresses, and eligible men who will be very interested in you, miss."

"Me? I'm just a half elf!"

"A half elf *Rider*. I told you before, the only people who are higher in class than you are the royals themselves. You would make a very fine wife for someone one day."

Disturbed by the thought of marriage, Akairya changed the subject. "Dray will be here soon. We should probably get started."

It only took a few minutes for them to get the dress on Akairya, and she was once again rendered speechless. The dress this time around was strapless, with thick lengths of silver fabric criss-crossing over her chest and blending into a flowing skirt that flared at the hips and fell in shimmering metallic waves to the floor. The bright dress was a shock against her dark red hair, and she felt like the physical embodiment of a streak of moonlight. Gretel clasped her hands together in excitement, and went to work on Akairya's mass of hair with gusto.

By the time Draykor walked into the room, black scales freshly polished, Akairya's hair was swept up into an intricate bun, her face framed by artfully placed curls.

You look enchanting, he said. She grinned at him, her nerves temporarily forgotten. She was reminded of them again by his next words. *I ran into Killian on my way up. Most of the nobility have arrived and are in the ballroom. It's almost time.*

When they reached the immense doors of the ballroom a short time later, which was situated a floor below the throne room, Akairya could barely feel her legs. Two smartly dressed guards stood at attention on either side of the doors. They nodded respectfully to her and Draykor before heaving the doors open and bowing the pair through.

"Walk straight down the hallway until you reach the archway, milady. Jervos will announce you."

Heart hammering against her chest, she walked through the doors on shaking legs, Draykor close to her side. They stepped into a slim corridor lit with flickering torches. The warm light illuminated smooth stone walls and marble flooring. The corridor was fairly short, and was open at the other end, a magnificent archway taking the place of doors. Akairya could see Jervos standing to one side, his back straight and his oak cane clutched in his hands. When the duo reached him, he gave them a small bow and ushered them into the ballroom.

The archway admitted them onto a balcony of white marble that overlooked a wide room completely walled in glass. Akairya glanced up and sighed in appreciation at the starry sky above, the glass ceiling so clear it was as if they were standing outside. Metal lantern posts carved to look like thick vines were dotted everywhere, washing the ballroom with a mellow buttery light. Small round tables were set up along the edges of the circular room, bordering an expansive dancefloor. Musicians played beneath the balcony, and the sweet notes of a violin rose up to greet Akairya as she stepped to the edge of the wide staircase that led to the floor. Jervos nodded to a butler who stood at the bottom of the stairs. The other man signaled the musicians to pause their music. Akairya blinked as the beautiful crowd below ceased their conversation and dancing to turn and look at her and Draykor, whose black scales glimmered from the lantern light.

Jervos knocked his cane loudly against the floor and shouted, with a strong voice that carried throughout the ballroom, "Lady Rider Kairi and her bonded dragon, Draykor."

Her legs still trembling, she began to descend the stairs, the hem of her silver dress spilling like stitched moonlight along the marble. She was so focused on not tripping that she didn't noticed Killian until she had reached the bottom.

He grinned rakishly at her. He had left his golden hair messy, but was dressed in dark pants and a collared white shirt that buttoned up to right below his chin, accentuating his strong jaw. An ebony cloak bordered with silver embroidery billowed from his broad shoulders, and his legs were encased in tall leather boots. He bowed deeply and offered her his hand.

"May I have the first dance, milady?" he asked her. He winked at her when she took his hand, and she smiled gratefully.

"Thank you. I was worried I would have to stand awkwardly by myself for awhile."

"Nonsense. Even if I hadn't of come up, someone else would have. You look riveting."

He led her to the dancefloor, leaving a bemused Draykor by the musician's stage. A few feet away from where the dragon stood were the thrones for the king and queen, which were currently empty.

Akairya watched as Theandi whirled by in the arms of a handsome nobleman, their steps perfectly in tune with the wild tangle of notes the violinist was playing. The princess's blonde hair bounced on her silk covered shoulders, and she grinned when she caught Akairya's eye. Akairya smiled back as Killian pulled her into middle of the dancing nobles. She felt hot as many pairs of eyes snuck quick looks at her. Cool judgement, curiosity, and even envy surrounded her, and she suddenly felt closed in. Killian must have felt her stiffen, since he put an arm around her waist and smoothly stepped into the dance.

"Don't let their stares get to you," he murmured. "They are noble. It's what they do; judge and whisper behind knowing backs."

"All of them?"

"Most."

The music slowed in tempo, and Akairya relaxed. Killian was an excellent dance partner, and she felt confident as he led her in the steps she had only just learned. The song ended sooner than she would have liked, and before she could say anything, a man she had never met before stepped up.

"May I have this dance, Lady Rider?" The stranger had a husky voice, one that didn't quite match his appearance. He was barely taller than Akairya, with thin hair and a lanky build. He was dressed quite similarly to Killian, but where Killian filled out his clothes, this man looked weak and improperly fitted.

"Ah, let me introduce you to Duke Gino, who hails from the winemaking city Nichaen, the capital of Erconya," Killian said.

"Not only do we make the best wine in the country, we also breed some of the best warhorses," Duke Gino bowed his head. "Enough of the pleasantries, however! May I have this dance?"

Akairya summoned back her brief etiquette lessons. She curtsied neatly and gave her hand to the Duke. "I accept this honor."

"The honor is all mine," the thin man responded. Killian gave her an encouraging smile before leaving the dancefloor. The music started up again, Gino's palms were sweaty, and his grip slipped as he attempted to lead her into a dance. She fought the urge to pull away and wipe her hands.

The conversation was stilted, and Akairya was positive her feet were stepped on every few seconds. She didn't wince once, however, but curtsied farewell to Gino in relief once the dance was over. Before she could escape from the floor, another nobleman asked for a dance.

The night passed quickly. Akairya's feet throbbed as she finally pulled free from her most recent dance partner and managed to walk gracefully to the nearest round table. She sat down with a sigh. Draykor appeared near her shoulder seconds later, eyes amused.

The noblemen sure speak nonsense, don't they? He said.

I can't get over it. The amount of Dukes and noble family heads and noble sons there are...and each one of them thinks they are the most important person here! Not to mention my neck and back are killing me. I've never curtsied this much in my life.

Theandi plopped into the chair across from Akairya. Her blue eyes twinkled as she took a big sip from a glass of wine she was holding. "Don't you just *love* this, Kairi? Dancing is one of my favorite things to do!"

A handsome young man had followed Theandi to her table. He nodded respectfully to Akairya before turning to the princess. "When you are ready, please seek me out for the next dance, milady." He kissed her hand before walking away.

"Kam is quite handsome, but that's all he is," Theandi sighed. "He is really quite ignorant and...well, simple. All he cares about is how much wealth he gets from his family and how beautiful his women are. He's fantastic to dance with, at least."

"I should hope so, I noticed he's the only partner you've had all night."

"Only because mother asked me to give him a chance. She fancies him. Thinks he'd make a lovely husband." She rolled her eyes. "I think he'd make one dud of a king."

"Good evening, Kairi," Thoran strode over, smiling. He was garbed in full leather armor, his two daggers hanging from his hips.

"Hello, Thoran. Why do you look ready for a fight?"

"I'm one of the guards on duty tonight. Which is too bad, I would have liked a dance with you."

"Father throws these balls often. I'm sure you'll get another chance," Theandi quipped. Thoran nodded before moving on, eyes on the crowd.

The music was once again fast paced and sharp. The dancing couples in the middle of the ballroom flew across the floor, gowns billowing and boots gleaming. Theandi took another great sip of her wine as she watched the dancing.

"Mother says you've been doing really well for your first time at a ball. Some of the noblemen you've danced with went up to her, surprised you had integrated so flawlessly…considering how you've grown up away from anything like this."

Akairya glanced at the now occupied thrones. The queen sat proudly, her hand currently being held by an older Duke. King Elric was laughing uproariously with a group of men, who Akairya recognized as the heads of the noble houses of Kalisor.

"I understand why all of Kalisor's nobility are here, but I'm surprised so many of the country's Dukes made it out. There wasn't a whole lot of notice for them."

"Oh, this ball was planned before your arrival. You just became the guest of honor, if you will. You had excellent timing. You've made a really good impression as well; the nobility are enamored of you already!"

Embarrassed but strangely happy, Akairya went back to watching the dancing. After a few songs, Theandi announced she was ready to continue her night and flounced off, likely in search of Kam. Draykor was still at Akairya's shoulder.

It's too bad Telectus and Oren weren't interested in coming tonight. I'm sure you would have appreciated their dragons' company.

Draykor flicked his tail. *I'm perfectly content. Watching the night unfold has proven mildly entertaining. Although no one has really…stayed to talk. I think I scare them, being ebony.*

They understand you're not of the Shadow, though…so if that's the case, they are incredibly dense.

Duke Gino wandered over with two glasses of wine. "Care for a drink, and maybe another dance?"

Akairya was saved from declining by Killian, who had also stepped up.

"Lady Kairi has already promised me the next dance, my good man. I hope you don't mind?" He said smoothly. Gino nodded, although he looked slightly crestfallen.

Relieved, Akairya stood and walked back towards the dancefloor with Killian. As they were about to step into the dance, a black arrow flew just past her cheek and hit the floor, breaking on impact. A few ladies nearby screamed, and the music crashed to a halt. Killian pulled Akairya off the dancefloor quickly, his grip on her arm tight. Uncertain of what was going on, she glanced behind her and gaped. Thoran was running through the panicked crowd, straight towards a man garbed in a black hooded cloak. The man turned and ran. He wasn't quick enough, however, and Thoran soon tackled him to the ground.

The king swept up to the struggling pair. "What is this! How *dare* you!"

Thoran soon gained the upper hand and stood, one of his daggers pressed firmly against the hooded man's throat. Elric stepped closer and pushed the hood down. Akairya didn't recognize the man, but many of the nobility did. Gasps of shock shuddered through the still crowd.

"*Father?*" an incredulous voice said from behind Akairya and Killian. She turned and saw Kam, who stood beside a pale Theandi.

"Lord Reinald?" The king was just as shocked as everyone else. He stared at the man, whose forehead was shining with sweat. Killian, still holding tightly to Akairya's arm, frowned.

"Lord Reinald is head of one of the most prestigious noble houses in the city. Why would he want you dead?"

He didn't have long to wait for an answer. The man spat and glared at Akairya. She blinked at the pure hatred that was in his small eyes.

"She is not of pure blood, your majesty. Not to mention I have heard she is likely in league with the blight itself! Look at her dragon! Black as can be, and yet you are foolish enough to allow them inside our city?"

King Elric went stiff. "How dare you say such things," he said coldly. "She may not be full elf or full human, but she is more than your equal. She is a *Rider*. And how dare you implicate that I did not make absolute sure she was free of the taint. Take him away, Thoran. I will take care of him in a moment."

Thoran nodded and dragged Reinald out of the ballroom, the older man struggling the entire time. His cries of, "blight spawn," and "half-breed," cut through the crowd like a poisoned blade, and Akairya tried to ignore the growing hostility that came from the rest of the nobility. The king strode to the center of the dance floor, his ivory cape billowing behind him. He glared at the room with hard blue eyes.

"Does anyone else share the same sentiments as Lord Reinald?" His voice rang clear, and some shuffled their feet uncomfortably. No one said a word. King Elric nodded.

"Do not allow fear to blind you of truth. Lady Rider Kairi has proven herself to me, and is determined to end this blight. Her dragon is black because he has yet to mature into his elemental power. Anyone who knows dragons knows that all young dragons are born without colour. The Shadow dragons are immensely different; I have not seen one myself but my men have given me detailed descriptions. Dragons who have given themselves to the blight are stained a black that dulls any light, and their scales refuse to shine. They also have dead white eyes. Does Draykor look like such a beast?"

Many turned to stare at Draykor, who had padded up to sit beside his Rider. Duke Gino caught Akairya's eye and gave her an encouraging smile as the king finished his speech.

"Now that we have that settled, it is time for us to end the night. I have some business to attend to." He walked briskly out of the ballroom, clearly headed to deal with Lord Reinald.

Killian let out a breath. "Are you okay?" He asked her. He was still holding her arm, and when she glanced at his hand, he grinned slightly before letting her go.

Akairya looked around as people began leaving the ballroom, most refusing to meet her eyes. "Physically, I'm fine. I'm not too sure about my reputation, though."

"Ah, the king gave the perfect speech. Anyone who still thinks you are in league with the blight are fools. I wouldn't worry too much, Kairi."

Later, in bed, Akairya turned over the night's events in her head. Overall it had been pleasant, but she was disturbed by the attempt on her life. The arrow had turned out to be poisoned, and she felt blindsided. Everyone had seemed so taken with her, but when Reinald had yelled his beliefs, many had turned to give her suspicious glances. She could only hope that the king's incensed speech had helped them see the truth.

After having a late lunch with Theandi and King Elric, Akairya ambled across the sloping fields towards the Royal Gardens, where the Rider quarters were. It was a large domed building set amongst a particularly dense part of the gardens. It was large enough to house the three dragons and their Riders, and it also had a big arena attached to it, where Telectus and Oren drilled her on dragon care and weapons. That was where she was to meet Oren for her next lesson.

Over the weeks she had learned how to care for a sprained wing or pulled tendon, how to check Draykor's teeth for any leftover bones (she made Draykor promise to eat carefully, since she did not enjoy sticking her head inside his maw), she learned how to put a light saddle made of leather on to him (which was only necessary for long journeys and battles) and how to fly with a weapon in her hands. She soon became quite balanced riding Draykor, and became fairly adept at brandishing a sword or bow while Draykor flew at high speeds or spun upside down. Telectus was particularly pleased.

"Your father taught you well, Akairya. You have such a natural skill with any weapon we ask you to try, and your elvish reflexes only help with your flying ability. It took me months of practice before I could draw a bow properly while Saverign twisted around."

Not only was her dragon riding improving, but so was her bond with Draykor. They were now able to speak when they were not in the same room, and the distance they could be apart and yet still converse was growing every day. This was on her mind as she walked into the arena, so she told Oren about it while he set up two targets. He nodded as he plopped one down, its white and red paint bright against the dimness of the sandy arena.

"Every bond between a dragon and their Rider can only grow stronger over time. Xandior and I can speak to each other even when we are miles apart."

Oren studied the target. He lifted a hand and snapped his fingers, and a small ball of flame appeared between his fingertips. While Akairya stared, he flicked the fireball straight into the center of the target, where it burst and burnt the entire thing to ash.

"Today you will not be able to practice what I am going to show you, simply because Draykor has yet to mature into his elemental power. Yeilao has told me that she has enlightened you about the true strength and mystery of the elements, which means you know about the elemental weapons; the Sword of Flame, the Whip of Water, the Hammer of Earth, the Daggers of Air, and the Bow of Spirit. In the past four hundred years, only six people have conjured the sword, eight the whip, twelve the hammer, six the daggers, and one the bow. As it turns out, I am one of the six who has discovered how to wield the Sword of Flame."

As he spoke, Oren held out his hand as if he was holding a sword. Akairya watched as his hand suddenly became enveloped in white flame. The fire then spread from his hand and stretched into the shape of a long one handed sword, its fiery blade crackling with heated power. Akairya sucked in a breath. Oren gave the sword a couple test swings, then charged the remaining target. When he reached it, he stopped the sword right before its flaming tip pierced the center. He gently poked the target, and it promptly burst into flames.

"As you can see, the fire that makes up this sword is more powerful than you could imagine," he said. He waved his hand. The sword and the fire that were eating up the target fluttered out. "I wanted to show you just a little of its strength; the flame that makes up the sword could eat through stone, but I didn't want to go that far.

"Can you guess why I showed you the Sword of Flame today?" His dark, penetrating gaze rooted Akairya to the spot.

She blinked. "To...give me a sense of caution?"

Oren gave her a dazzling smile and nodded. "Precisely. If you were to gain control over spirit, and somehow master it even when Yeilao could not...you would have the most powerful weapon in your grasp. Caution, indeed, is very important."

The door to the arena swung open, and Telectus rushed in. A ruffled falcon clung to his shoulder as he dashed to Oren and Akairya, the note it had delivered crushed in Telectus' hand.

"There's a Rorak outside the city."

CHAPTER TWELVE

Oren frowned. "Just one?"

"Yes. Holding a white flag. It wants to meet with the king," Telectus gasped. The falcon chirped and kneaded Telectus' shoulder. He waved it off, and it flew away with an indignant screech.

"That makes no sense. Why would a Rorak come here, alone?" Akairya wondered as the three of them ran out of the arena. Their dragons were waiting for them.

The castle halls are not large enough for us, we can only wait in the foyer. Shall we? Saverign asked as they all traipsed towards the castle.

Telectus shook his head. "No, you should all wait out here. If you're in the foyer it would take longer for us to fly if we need to."

So the Riders left their worried dragons outside, and they rushed into the castle.

They darted down the main corridor, their footsteps loud against the stone floor. They were just passing the doors to the throne room when an elf dressed in blue robes hailed them.

It was Yolor, and his blue eyes were wild as Akairya, Oren, and Telectus halted in front of him.

"Good, you are all here. The king just sent me to find you; the Rorak has been admitted inside the castle and it's speaking with High King Elric in the throne room," he told them, his voice strained. Telectus cursed.

"The king let the thing in? What is he thinking!?"

"Curiosity seems to have taken Elric's logic," Oren said slowly. He pursed his lips, shook his head, and walked over to the large throne room doors. There was no Jervos around to announce them, so he heaved the doors open and they all strode inside. Yolor wrung his hands with anxiety.

A sense of wrong instantly invaded Akairya's senses as she walked towards the throne, where the king sat in the armor he had worn when she had first met him. Beside him stood Killian, who was glaring at the twisted figure that stood kneeling in front of the throne, its bruised wrists manacled. Two guards flanked it.

Dray, the Rorak is inside the castle. Chained, but still inside.

What? Is the king mad? Her dragon responded, concern for her flooding through their connection. *Don't get too close; it could draw from the blight.*

Wary, Akairya followed the older Riders closer to the small group. What *was* the king thinking?

As if he heard her thoughts, King Elric looked up from studying the Rorak and gave his Riders a grim smile.

"Excellent, you are here. I know you must think me insane, but I wanted to know what this vermin wanted. He refused to speak until we brought him in."

Killian made a choked noise in the back of his throat. Elric ignored him.

"So, Rorak. You're in here. What is it you want?"

It was much larger than the average Rorak; its shoulders were broad and if it was able to stand, Akairya guessed it would be well over seven feet tall. Its face, though strangely elvish, was even more bruised and twisted than any other Rorak face she had set eyes on. It wore the same strange armor that all Roraks wore, except this one had dipped it into black paint that had chipped off in some places. When its black, empty eyes locked onto hers, it gave a smirk and hissed lightly. One of the guards knocked it in the back of its head with the hilt of his blade.

"Quit that. Answer the king."

"I'm here on business," it rasped, its eyes still on Akairya. Its gaze was almost hungry, and she shivered.

"What kind of business?" the king snapped. The Rorak hissed again and flicked its eyes back to the king.

"The Father wants to…*join* with you. He wishes to blend your authority, and control the land together."

Everyone stared at the Rorak, speechless. The king's face had gone a deep shade of red, and his eyes were flashing dangerously.

"How *dare* you come here, to ask such a *disgusting* thing?" he ground out between his teeth. A muscle twitched in his neck. Killian was palming the hilt of his sword, his handsome face scrunched up in anger.

"It was not meant to insult you, *milord.* But my Creator says that if you reject this opportunity, there will be consequences."

"There are consequences now!" the king roared. He jumped out of the throne and ripped his own sword out of its sheath. Its deadly blade shone from the sun that streamed in through the massive window encasing the throne room. Elric strode to the kneeling Rorak and swung the sword. The creature barely had time to hiss again before its head was toppling from its severed neck. Oily blood dripped onto the velvet carpet, and the guards stepped back from the body as it slumped forwards. The king, breathing heavily, just stood there as the Rorak's blood stained his steel boots.

As everyone recovered from their shock, a thick cloud of Shadow pulled itself out of the neck of the Rorak and swirled upwards. Telectus yelled and threw his hands up; a torrent of water appeared from nowhere and shot straight towards the writhing mass of black. The Shadow dodged the attack and streaked towards the doors, where it slipped through the cracks and vanished.

"Damn it," Telectus muttered. He glanced at the dead Rorak and waved his hands again. More water rushed around the body and the king's boots. With another motion, Telectus made the water and blood vanish. He then used his power over Air to lift the carcass up and took it out of the room.

Oren sighed and looked at Akairya. "That was rather unsettling."

"It was more than unsettling; it was terrifying!" Yolor squeaked from where he cowered behind Akairya. Killian stepped up to the king and placed a hand on his shoulder.

"Come, milord. Telectus is taking care of the body."

"I shouldn't have let that filth in here," the king said quietly. He looked up from his boots, which were now free of the dark Rorak blood. "I am sorry for making such a decision."

"Nothing truly bad happened, your majesty. There's just a stain in the carpet. This "Lord" of the Shadow would have waged war on us even if you had refused entrance to his Rorak. He's already destroyed Yaeloa and poisoned an entire province," Killian stated. Elric nodded and sighed, clearly exhausted now that his rage had subsided.

"Oren, I need to speak with you. The elves aren't quite convinced that things are as bad as they are, and I may need you to travel to your home country."

Oren let out a breath and followed the king out of the throne room. Yolor, still wringing his hands, scampered out behind them.

Killian and Akairya were left alone, and Akairya couldn't help but feel slightly awkward. He sighed and ran a hand through his hair, tousling the golden strands. He looked at her and gave her a small smile.

"Things are never boring here, that's for sure," he joked weakly. Akairya returned his smile.

Are you okay, Akairya? Saverign just left with Telectus to get rid of the corpse. Draykor asked, his mental voice tinged with anxiety.

I'm fine, Dray. Don't worry. Just a little shaken.

Okay. I'm going to scout the island with Xandior. Will you be okay without me for a bit?

Yes. I'm just with Killian right now.

Amusement flooded through their connection.

Has Theandi had a chance to teach you 'the wily ways of women?'

Akairya ignored him.

"How has your training been going?" Killian asked. He walked closer and stopped a few feet away from her. "I didn't think to ask you about it last night."

"Training has been going wonderfully; my bond with Dray strengthens by the day, and our flying is improving each session. I was able to shoot a grapple out of the air while Dray spun me."

"I think I saw you two practicing that. Looked impressive." His gray eyes were soft, and he shuffled his feet a little. "Look, I was wondering...well...I may not be able to do it for a while...but...would you like to-"

He was interrupted by the throne doors flying open, their bulk crashing into the little bit of marble wall that framed them. Thoran came rushing over, his face white.

"I just...heard...that...the king let...a Rorak in," he said breathlessly, one hand clutching his side, the other brandishing one of his favored daggers. Killian blinked, stared at the blade, and laughed.

"Were you going to charge in and slit the thing's throat, Thoran?" he chuckled, eyes twinkling. Thoran flushed and slid the dagger back into his belt.

"I...uh, wasn't thinking."

"Clearly."

"What were you two doing?" Thoran asked, looking between Akairya and Killian somewhat suspiciously.

"Just catching up. Kairi was telling me how her training was going."

"Ah. How *has* it been going, Kairi?"

While Akairya told Thoran, a hassled looking maid came bustling in.

"Lady Rider," she chirped. "Princess Theandi has requested to see you. She says it is highly important, and that I am to take you to her rooms immediately."

Killian raised an eyebrow. "I have never known Lady Theandi to be so bossy."

"She probably just heard about the Rorak and wants me to tell her all about it," Akairya told him. She waved goodbye to the two men and followed the maid out of the throne room and into the main corridor.

The maid led her up a couple flights of steps that took them to the base of one of the castle's many towers. The maid opened the golden doors and curtsied. Akairya, taking the hint, strode into the room.

"Kairi! Thank goodness!" Theandi squealed from where she was laying on a massive four-poster bed. She leaped up and dashed to Akairya, her blonde hair a snarled mess. "I heard about the Rorak, and how some of the Shadow escaped into the castle. The blight scares me, Kairi…and I was hoping you could sleep here tonight? Keep me company?" The princess's lower lip trembled, and it looked as if she was trying very hard not to burst into tears.

Surprised, Akairya nodded. "Of course, Theandi. I'll stay with you for tonight."

Relief flooded Theandi's face, and she hugged Akairya in gratitude. "Oh, thank goodness. I'll get my handmaid to fetch your sleeping things. Yana!" She called. The maid who had taken Akairya to Theandi popped her head in.

"Yes, miss?"

"Please inform Kairi's handmaid that she will not be sleeping in the Rider quarters tonight, and please fetch her night dress. She will be keeping me company."

"Yes, miss. I'll be back as quick as can be."

When the golden doors were closed, Theandi wandered to the large balcony doors that looked out onto a white stone porch and stepped outside. The sun had just sunk below the horizon, and the sky was painted hues of red and orange. Theandi's room faced the city, and Akairya could catch glimpses of the many white and gold buildings that made up Kalisor.

"I can't believe Papa let that thing in here," Theandi said quietly. She leaned against the steel railing that was twisted into the likeness of a tangle of vines and roses. "I mean, that thing could have thrown up its Rorak vomit onto anyone! Plus, I heard it was huge. We're lucky no one was injured."

"He killed it as soon as he realized its message was just an insult. Do you know what it asked your father?"

"Yes. It makes me sick, thinking that such evil is out there...and that it wants Papa to support it." The princess shivered. "I hope we can figure out how to end the Shadow soon."

"Me too."

The two girls fell silent as they watched the sky darken slowly into a velvety black studded with twinkling stars. After a while, Yana knocked and came into the room carrying Akairya's night dress and a tray of food.

"Queen Leliana sent this up, misses. She says that there will be no formal dinner."

Akairya took the tray from her and her mouth watered. Two bowls of creamy soup and a plate of buttered herb biscuits dotted with cheese sat on the tray. She took the food to the small wooden table beside the balcony and sat down. Theandi joined her, and they dug in to their dinner.

Later, when the two girls were lying in bed and listening to the soft sound of the lake, Theandi turned to look at Akairya. "Thanks again for staying with me tonight, Kairi. I know I should be mature enough to handle this fear on my own but you're the first girl I've ever truly connected with like a sister. I hope you understand?" She looked pleadingly at Akairya, her blue eyes shining silver in the moonlight that spilled from the balcony windows. Akairya smiled at her.

"I'm glad that you feel so close to me, Theandi. Really. I'm used to people avoiding me like the blight."

Theandi returned her smile shyly and sighed as she nestled into her blankets. "I'm so happy I finally have a sister," she yawned. "Goodnight."

"Goodnight, Theandi."

Screams and blood. Blood and screams. All she could see and all she could hear. Akairya trembled and fought to close her eyes. She tried her hardest to shut out all the terrible screaming, but she couldn't. Fire, ice, earth, and wind ripped through stone, marble, and wood. Her home was destroyed, defeated by the sheer power of the blight she was born to end...

"Kairi...wake up..." Theandi's voice broke through Akairya's heavy curtain of dreams. Blinking, Akairya sat up and rubbed her eyes.

The room was lit by the mellow orange of sunrise. Theandi was sitting up in bed, her eyes wide with fear and locked on the ceiling. Akairya followed her gaze and gasped.

The cloud of Shadow that had come from the dead Rorak earlier was floating above the bed. Smoky black wisps of nebulous poison stained the air around it.

"Why is it here, Kairi?" Theandi whispered, terror layered in her voice.

"I-I don't know," Akairya fumbled for her mental connection with Draykor and prodded her dragon's sleeping mind.

Wh-what? Draykor tiredly replied to her incessant mental pokes, his voice slow with sleep.

The Shadow that escaped is here, Dray, in Theandi's room.

I'll get help.

She grabbed Theandi's wrist. "Come on!" she commanded urgently. "We need to get out of this room!"

The princess didn't move; it looked as if she was frozen in fear.

"Your father insulted me, princess," a gritty voice cut through the bedroom, coming from the writhing cloud of Shadow. "As a result, I must punish him."

Before Akairya could move, before she could even blink, the Shadow coalesced into the shape of a spear and dove straight into Theandi's chest.

The princess screamed in agony as the Shadow bled itself into her skin, which faded into a sickly gray from its touch.

DRAY! Hurry! The Shadow threw itself into Theandi! Akairya roared to Draykor. She didn't catch his reply; she was too busy staring in horror at the princess.

Gray foam covered her lips, and her beautiful blue eyes were turning coal black. Oily tears slid down her ever-darkening cheeks, and she gurgled and convulsed as the Shadow spread throughout her body.

"No, no, no, no," Akairya moaned. She looked wildly around for something that could help…but what? There was nothing she could do.

Theandi's silky blonde hair looked dead, thin, and colourless and her entire body shook as more dark liquid spilled out of her eyes, mouth, and nose. With one final shudder, she fell out of the bed and went still as stone.

"Please, no…"Akairya sobbed. She fell to her knees and rolled Theandi onto her back. The princess's eyes were now completely dark, and they stared sightlessly ahead. Akairya pressed trembling fingers to her friend's neck, but didn't feel even the smallest flutter of a pulse.

Hot tears blurred her vision, and she found she couldn't breathe. Dry sobs racked her body, and she dimly heard the bedroom doors flying open. She barely registered a pale Thoran and a distraught King Elric, who howled in anger and grief.

Akairya suddenly felt trapped; with a strangled moan, she jumped to her feet and tore out of the room. Her burgundy hair flew behind her, and her light nightdress threatened to trip her as she ran down steps she could barely see through her tears.

Before she knew it, she was outside in the now blazing morning sunlight. Draykor landed heavily in front of her; he had flown to the king's chamber and bellowed for him to wake. Of course, he had been too late. The princess had died mere seconds after the Shadow tore into her.

Without thinking, Akairya leaped nimbly onto her dragon's back. He took off and flew towards the far northern shore of the great lake. Heavy grief gripped Akairya, and she was barely able to hold on as Draykor flapped his wings.

As they neared the shore, a strange sensation shivered through both dragon and elf girl. Trembling, Draykor fell to the ground, his hind legs splashing in the lake. Akairya toppled off him and barely missed the water.

Draykor shuddered and closed his eyes as his ebony scales began to blur. Akairya gasped as her heart clenched and she fell to her knees, the thick carpet of grass on the shore saving her from any pain. The sensation strengthened, and her vision went dark.

Still conscious, she breathed heavily as a searing heat engulfed her very soul. A flaming, angry power surged through her and branded her as its own.

Fire.

The heat faded and was replaced by the cool sensation of waves. A roaring filled her ears and drowned out all other thought but sorrow.

Water.

Then she felt like she was cocooned in a wild wind, its strength embracing her and lifting her heart to joyous heights.

Air.

Air was then replaced with an overpowering scent of dirt and torn grass, which was accompanied by the deep knowledge that she could easily tear through soil, uproot trees, and protect.

Earth.

Then suddenly her entire self leaped to attention, its spiritual awakening gifting her with powerful insight and the vision of a soul drenched in purity.

Spirit.

Just as quickly as it had left, Akairya's vision returned. Shaken, she glanced over at her dragon and gasped in astonishment.

Draykor was no longer black. Instead he was a deep gold, with sparkling silver claws, horns, and spikes, with metallic wing membranes that caught the light. His scales now reflected his and Akairya's power over all five of the elements.

He looked at her, and Akairya nearly wept with the wonder of it.

His eyes had become a pure, vibrant violet that matched perfectly with her own.

CHAPTER THIRTEEN

Akairya leaned against her dragon's now golden hip, eyes dry. The abrupt embrace of their elements had swept away the burning grief that had overtaken her, and now it simmered in her heart, feeding an anger that was determined to wipe out the blight.

A light breeze sifted through the grass that carpeted the shore, and the water lapped gently near Akairya's feet. The summer weather was gradually fading into autumn, and there was a subtle bite in the breeze that teased her hair. The sunlight brought out the violet hues in the red strands, and she studied the tips.

I wonder if there's a purple tinge in my hair because of the Spirit element, she mused. Draykor huffed as he nibbled at an itch near the base of one of his wings.

Could be just a coincidence.

Both of them avoided the subject of Theandi's death. While Draykor hadn't been as close to her as Akairya had been, he still felt sorrow. The princess had been what Akairya needed in this time of chaos, and now she was gone.

Akairya cupped her hands together and reached inside herself for the power of flame. She could feel it flickering weakly deep in her soul, but she couldn't grasp it.

Is it normal to have power over an element yet not know what to do? Being a Rider and all.

Yes. We just came into ourselves. It will take time for our souls to fully embrace our new strengths.

Akairya put her hands in her lap and sighed. She looked towards the distant castle, its shimmering marble towers somewhat hidden from view by the large wall that surrounded the city.

We should probably go back soon. Draykor told her, his violet eyes also on the castle. *It will look suspicious if we stay away for too long.*

When they moved to stand, a dragon flew over the wall. Its scales glittered white and its blue wings caught the sunshine; it was Saverign.

Akairya and Draykor watched silently as the dragon flew over. Telectus was sitting on his back, one hand up in a small wave.

Saverign alighted on the shore a few feet away from Draykor, his bulk shaking the ground. Telectus slid off and walked to Akairya, where he knelt and looked at her with serious emerald eyes.

"The king has requested your presence," he said softly. Akairya looked away and nodded. The prospect of facing King Elric brought her grief closer to the surface, and her eyes shone with tears.

"I see you and Draykor have finally embraced your elements," he said calmly. He gazed at Draykor and frowned slightly. "Which elements do you two have power over?"

"All five," Akairya muttered. Telectus went rigid.

"All...five? But...that's unheard of," he breathed. "There was never any mention..."

"Any mention of what?" Akairya asked sharply. Draykor looked at Telectus too, his nostrils wide.

"I-I'm sorry. I cannot say. But," he added hastily as Akairya opened her mouth furiously, "now that you two have embraced your elements, you are ready to travel to the Elders! This is what we've been waiting for."

Akairya blinked and suddenly found herself feeling nervous. The Elders were the oldest dragons in existence and were the most powerful wielders of the elements. Surely they were not going to be happy that she had somehow become a Rider without their blessing. However, it sounded like they had all the answers she sought.

"When can we leave?"

Telectus's discomfort was replaced with an expression of sorrow. "Not until Theandi is put to rest. Surely you'll want to be around for that?"

Once again tears threatened to make their appearance, and Akairya bit her lip. "Of course I do."

The funeral took place early that afternoon. King Elric, Queen Leliana, Akairya, Yeilao, Killian, Thoran, Telectus, Oren, many Kalisor citizens, and the few provincial Dukes who had yet to head for home after the ball stood on the eastern shore of the great lake. There was no trace of cheeriness in Elric's face now; his cheeks were pale and his blue eyes bloodshot. Queen Leliana looked as if she were made of stone, she stood so still. Draykor was a few yards away under a large oak, his head low and his wings drooping at his sides.

The men were all dressed in black trousers and shirts. The women wore sleek dark gowns. Everyone held a purple candle, the burning wicks giving off a powerful aroma of lavender. Yeilao stood closest to the shore, tears streaming down her aged face.

Theandi, her face wiped clean of the Shadow and her eyes closed, was placed on a bed of fresh flowers in a small boat. It was tied securely to a post driven into the earth of the shore. She had been changed out of her nightgown and was now garbed in a flowing white gown that rustled in the cool wind that skimmed the lake's surface. Her dead, thin hair was twisted into a frayed plait, and her pale hands held a bouquet of purple blooms.

Yeilao lifted her sputtering candle and closed her eyes. "Today we say goodbye to a lovely princess, whose soul was too pure for the Shadow to taint. As a result, she wilted inside and breathed her last breath as the blight blackened her eyes."

A soft cry came from beside Akairya, and she glanced over to see the queen biting her lip, her entire body trembling. King Elric gripped his wife's hand and took a breath. Stricken, Akairya turned back to Yeilao. Killian, who stood on Akairya's other side, placed a warm hand on her shoulder.

"The eyes, known as the body's windows into the soul, are precious to one's spiritual self. Princess Theandi's windows were shattered, and her soul flew from her physical body as a result. It is now searching for the path that will lead her to the Underearth. It is our duty to point her soul in the right direction, so please follow my lead."

Everyone watched closely as Yeilao stepped a few paces back from the bobbing boat and lifted the candle to her lips. She breathed lightly and whispered, *"we light your way with the essence of Spirit."* The flame fought against Yeilao's breath for a moment, and then sputtered out when she completed her sentence. A weak purple light, almost powdery in its dimness, fluttered up from where the flame once flickered.

Akairya lifted her candle closer to her face and replicated Yeilao's actions, as did everyone else. A soft chorus of *"we light your way with the essence of Spirit,"* whispered throughout the crowd, and many clouds of violet light drifted up from their candles and joined with the first.

Draykor looked up from under his tree and watched the cloud of light grow in strength, his golden scales reflecting the deep purple. Akairya felt a rush of power as Draykor called on the element of Spirit. His eyes flashed. The effect was instantaneous; the cloud of light multiplied then became charged with power. The hair on Akairya's neck rose as the spiritual energy washed over her, and every person on the shore gasped.

The now blinding purple light gathered itself and then struck the boat where Theandi's body lay. Her body, the flowers, and the wood of the boat promptly burst into purple flame. There was no smoke; just flickers of the light that lit the entire shore violet. The boat then collapsed, and Theandi slid into the lake, still cloaked in spiritual fire. A few seconds later she vanished.

"We have done all we can do for the princess's soul," Yeilao said heavily. She gazed down in the water where Theandi had disappeared and sighed. Her eyes were now devoid of any tears, yet there was a deep sadness etched in her ancient face.

Everyone except the Riders walked back towards the bridge that led into the city from the opposite side of the lake, sorrow weighing down their steps. Akairya watched them leave. Some of the nobles she had met during the ball had approached her after the ceremony to apologize for doubting her. Draykor's new colour and his help with Spirit had convinced them that the new Rider and dragon duo were no traitors.

Saverign and Xandior, who had been circling the lake while the funeral was taking place, landed beside their Riders. Draykor bent his head in greeting; he was still quite a bit smaller than them.

"Akairya, you are going to be leaving in under an hour," Oren informed her while he touched Xandior softly on the nose. The red dragon huffed and nuzzled Oren's shoulder. "We have to stay in the city, in case more Roraks come. King Elric has decided to send Killian with you."

"Wh-what about travelling supplies?" Akairya asked in alarm. Telectus gave her a small smile.

"We had the maids gather everything you need while we were saying goodbye to Theandi. You're already wearing your travel gear, and I'm going to give you Saverign's saddle. However, I advise you to ride your horse until you reach the sea. Draykor is still quite young, and having two people on his back will be tiring for him. The trip over the sea to Drakynold will be difficult enough without you two riding him all the way from here."

"What am I supposed to do once we reach the dragon country?"

"Just go straight to the Elders. They reside in the very center of the island, and they will know exactly who you are."

Oren walked over to her and took her hand, his serious eyes locked onto hers. "Practice wielding your elements as much as you can, Akairya. They will prove difficult to control at first, but the more you work with them, the easier wielding will become."

Akairya frowned and looked at Draykor. "How did Dray use the Spirit element? I haven't even felt a flicker of power, yet he was able to finish the funeral."

I can't even answer that, my Rider. Draykor answered her. *I just...sort of opened up to the element and it did everything without my guidance. I can't feel its power at all now.*

Oren nodded. "While Riders and dragons are bonded, there are still many inexplicable things that take place. It is possible that the element simply...found a body it could safely work through, encouraged by the presence of an adept wielder of Spirit. The fifth element is the most powerful and the most complex." He walked back to his dragon. Telectus, who had just slipped off the smooth leather saddle with its many loops off of Saverign's ivory back, strode over to Draykor. In minutes the younger dragon was saddled.

"One thing that is nice about dragons and their scales; they never get saddle sores like horses."

Doesn't mean they are comfortable, Draykor replied, his violet eyes narrowed. Xandior shook his head and growled softly. A thin plume of smoke unfurled from his nostrils. *Your Rider will be much more comfortable flying over the sea with that saddle. Or would you rather she fall into the churning waters if you are attacked by Shadow dragons?*

I didn't say I won't wear it, Draykor snapped. He shook his metallic wings irritably and went silent.

Somewhat amused, Akairya pulled her heavy black gown off. Now she understood why her handmaid had told her to slip on her riding pants and jerkin.

"I had the maids pack your cloak into the saddle bags that will be on your horse," Telectus told her as he took her discarded dress. "Mind you put it on before you leave, looks like a storm is brewing."

Sure enough, angry clouds were churning above the peaks of the Jalkorin mountains, and the wind was growing stronger. Akairya shivered. "Maybe it will hold off until we stop for the night."

"It may hit before you leave."

After the two older Riders left with their dragons, Akairya walked back towards the piece of shore where Theandi had been just a few minutes before. Grief still burdened her heart, but now that she had said goodbye she felt more accepting of the loss of her newfound friend. Rage trembled underneath her sorrow, and she was even more determined to figure out how to end the Shadow.

With a sigh, Akairya kissed her fingertips and dipped her hand into the cool water of the lake. She swirled her fingers and whispered another farewell before straightening and walking back towards the city.

Akairya leaned against the golden gates that led into Kalisor, her dark red hair plaited so it was out of the way. She shivered as a sharp wind, smelling heavily of rain, tore across the lake and over the island city. She glanced behind her to see if Killian was around; the guards who were on duty at the gates were staring, and she was beginning to feel uncomfortable. Why did she send Draykor ahead to scout the first bit of the journey?

"Hey love, want to talk?" the bigger of the two, who had a rather weak chin and thin, smirking lips, winked at her. He had taken off his steel helmet, and his greasy blonde hair barely fluttered in the strong wind.

"I'd rather not, thank you," she replied truthfully, her eyes cold.

"Oooh, chilly," the first guard's partner giggled. He was a spindly little man with a nose nearly as round as a button, with mean eyes that raked Akairya. She shivered, and this time not from the cold.

"Kairi!" Killian's voice cut through her discomfort, and she sighed in relief when she caught sight of him. He was weaving through the afternoon crowd that clogged the city streets, each hand holding the reins of a horse. Akairya recognized them as the two they had ridden here, and she smiled. The hardy gray mare was quite eager, and Akairya had grown fond of her when she rode her the three days to the city.

"Sorry I took so long, I asked the king's personal alchemist for some of the potion we drank when we were in the Jalkorin valley. Figured we may need some, considering we'll be…uh…*flying*," (At the mention of flying, Killian turned a faint shade of green,) "over the ocean to get to Drakynold." He barely noticed the two surly guards, who had immediately looked away when he had appeared.

"Don't worry, I wasn't waiting too long," Akairya assured him as she took her mare's reins from him. A brass nameplate was stitched onto the mare's saddle, and it read *Fedana*.

"I didn't notice that nameplate before," she said as she traced the metal with her finger. Fedana nuzzled her shoulder happily.

"The inn where we bought these two didn't name them," Killian answered while he checked his stallion's saddlebags. Akairya heard the sound of bottles clinking together while he rummaged. "So the royal horse handler gave them names. My stallion's name is Tridon."

At the mention of his name, the large golden bay swung his head and nickered. Akairya couldn't help but admire the stallion's beauty; his well-muscled body was clad in a coat of golden brown that shone, even with the sun shrouded by storm clouds. He stood a good two hands taller than Fedana, who was lazily nibbling at Akairya's jerkin.

"Where's Dray?" Killian asked. Akairya started and turned to look north, her mouth pursed.

"He went to scout ahead to the first town we'll reach. I didn't think it would take him this long, he's been gone nearly thirty minutes now."

"Well, the closest town in that direction is Durndel, and it's a six hour ride away. Would probably take him a bit to fly back and forth."

Akairya stared at Killian, then looked at the sky. "Six hours? That means we won't reach an inn until well into the night! I don't mind sleeping outside, but with the storm coming…"

Killian shrugged. "I mentioned that to Telectus, but he still thinks we should leave today. Ah, there's Dray."

Sure enough, Draykor's golden body could be seen flying towards them, his wings effortlessly cutting through the wind that was growing stronger by the minute.

There you are! Our connection isn't strong enough for us to communicate when we're apart more than a few miles, I guess. Akairya said to him, somewhat grumpily.

I noticed. I'm sure that will change as time goes on.

Yeah, hopefully. See anything interesting?

No. The town isn't that interesting either; just a small cluster of houses and a few shops, then the inn a little down from the main road.

"Dray says that there's nothing of interest on the way to Durndel," Akairya relayed to Killian. He nodded.

"I thought as much. We may as well get going, we're burning daylight."

He mounted Tridon swiftly and urged him into a quick trot. Akairya hurriedly jumped onto Fedana and followed Killian and his stallion across the bridge, the horses' hooves rapping smartly on the white stone.

Once they crossed the bridge, they turned right and followed the shore until they hit the Iolia River. There they turned left and began to follow the course of the river, which flowed towards the Northern Sea. According to both Killian and Draykor, the humble village of Durndel was situated right on the banks of the channel.

The first hour of the journey was uneventful; the wind roared louder than ever and the river crashed against its banks, but the rain held. When the storm finally began, it poured down with a vengeance, and the cold, merciless sheets of water brought back bitter memories of the journey through the Jalkorin's valley.

"Why does it always rain when we travel?" Akairya grumbled as she wrapped her cloak tighter around her, glad she had thought to dig it out of her saddlebag before the rain had started. The horses followed a dirt road that was quickly becoming mud; the main road of the country only connected the capital cities.

Draykor flew over the turbulent river, the tips of his scaled claws skimming the frothing water. His golden scales were slick from the rain, and they shone like burnished mirrors. Akairya still could not get over the rate he was growing; he was almost half the size of Saverign, whose wing span was thirty feet.

The dragon lowered his angular head and took a drink. He snorted as a wave crashed against his nose, and he looked at Akairya with an affronted look while she chuckled.

"So you've been gifted with all five elements, I hear," Killian called to Akairya from ahead. They had slowed their horses to a brisk walk because the ground had begun to slope unevenly towards the river, mud churning under the horses' hooves.

"Yes, but I haven't been able to properly wield any yet. Dray has already influenced Spirit, today at Theandi's funeral, but when I reach for it it's like trying to scale a stone wall with no footholds."

"Oren told me before I left that you will have some difficulty at first. I have strict orders to make sure you practice working at least one element a day." His tone was coloured with amusement; he was probably unaccustomed to taking orders from anyone other than the king.

They rode in silence for a while; the only sounds came from the storm and Draykor's heavy wing beats.

"Why did King Elric ask you to accompany me? Aren't you needed to train the Royal Army for the war?" Akairya asked.

"He thinks this journey is of utmost importance, and I'm the general he trusts the most. There are other generals who will do a fine job in preparing the army for war against this Shadow Lord. Plus," at this he glanced over his shoulder and winked, "I volunteered. Thought this would be an excellent chance to get to know you more and learn some valuable things about dragons."

Akairya was glad he then turned away; she blushed furiously when he mentioned that he wanted to get to know her some more. *What* was wrong with her? She had never been bothered to speak to the young men in Yaeloa before its fall. What was it about this young general that had her so flustered? Not to mention she had a lot on her plate already; she did not need to complicate things even more by fawning over the king's favored general.

"Where's your falcon, Itaye?" She asked, changing the subject.

"I left him behind – his wing is nearly better, but not completely. I don't want to push him too hard."

The treacherous ground sloped up into a stretch of flat plain, and the horses' snorted as they found that their hooves had stopped sinking hock-deep into the mud.

"We better pick up the pace, we don't want to reach Durndel after midnight," Killian commented. Akairya agreed, and the two of them asked their horses to pick up a canter, Draykor still gliding beside them above the river.

The storm abated some time later. A mellow sunset flooded over the prairie. The thick grass that stretched endlessly on both sides of the river glittered, and the air was heavy with the fragrance of rain.

I see something up ahead, Draykor said abruptly. He flew forward to inspect, and Akairya couldn't help but envision hundreds of Roraks popping out of nowhere.

It's a broken statue, her dragon told her from where he had stopped about a mile ahead. *I didn't notice it when I scouted earlier.*

"A statue?" She wondered aloud. Killian furrowed his brow and looked at her.

"It may be one of the ancient statues of the High Queen. There are a bunch of them placed throughout the country, but they haven't been repaired in years."

Intrigued, Akairya asked Fedana to pick up the pace.

Sure enough, Draykor had discovered a large marble statue that stood almost a hundred feet high. It was a depiction of a regal elf dressed in flowing robes, one delicate hand placed on her chest and the other clutching a slender bow. A thin diadem encircled her head, and her face was almost completely chipped off. Akairya saw that the statue was also missing a couple fingers.

Draykor had landed at the marble elf's feet and was snuffling at the hem of her robes. His tufted ears pricked and he reached out with one golden claw.

There was a terrified squeal as he scooped out a ragged looking man from behind the statue. Cowering in fright, the thin man scuttled away from Draykor, his feet tripping on his frayed robes and his wispy gray hair fluttering.

"Back, beast! I am not edible! I am a priest! My blood is divinely linked with the High Queen! I-" his high pitched voice stopped abruptly when he caught sight of Akairya and Killian. He squinted watery brown eyes at them, then glanced back at Draykor, who was watching him with polite interest.

"Hello," Akairya greeted the dirty man. He jumped at being spoken to and scuttled back towards the statue, as if it would protect him. Then he realized he had gone closer to Draykor, squealed again, and simply sat on the wet grass and clutched at his hair.

"Please, relax. We are not going to hurt you," Akairya said gently as she dismounted. Killian shook his head at the man and also hopped off his stallion.

The man was soaked from the rain, and his ragged robes bore many holes. Akairya was almost positive the man's trembling came from more than just fear. Killian, who had been thinking along the same lines, approached the so called priest with a small bottle of the alchemist concoction that protected the drinker against illness.

"Here, drink this. You won't get sick if you do. We'll build a fire for you too, warm you up."

The man squealed again and shot a thin hand out to grasp at Killian's cloak. "NO! No fire! *They* will see! They will come and investigate and kill us all!" he gasped and tore at his hair, beside himself with fear.

Who's they? Draykor asked, his head tilted slightly with confusion. *The only settlement nearby is Durndel, and it's populated with harmless villagers.*

"Not anymore! The beast is wrong! Those twisted creatures born from the blight have taken over! They killed the captain of the guard, and are now commanding the villagers to wait on them like slaves!"

"Twisted creatures…do you mean Roraks?" Killian asked in alarm. Akairya shared a look with Draykor, who had tensed at the mention of Roraks.

"Yes, those terrible, terrible beings who can kill with their very own bile…unnatural! Wrong! They have defiled Durndel, and so I have come to the Spirit Queen's statue, to pray! We need divine help!"

Anger bubbled up inside Akairya, and her hand clenched. As she did so, she felt a small flame flicker on her palm. Surprised, she opened her fingers just as a small ball of fire puffed into smoke.

Looks like anger helped you connect with the Fire element, Draykor mused.

Good, I'm angry enough to burn the Roraks to the ground.

"How many Roraks are there in the village?" Killian asked urgently as he paced near the statue, one hand on the hilt of his sword. The priest, who had guzzled the alchemist remedy, tucked the tiny bottle into the pocket of his robes, as if the small movement would help him gain control of his anxiety.

"Ten, I believe. Ten disgusting, vile, twisted-"

"Yes, we get it, thank you," Killian cut him off sternly. He glanced at Akairya.

"Should we help the village? We shouldn't waste the time, and it is dangerous, but I wouldn't feel right if we left them under the control of the Roraks."

Akairya gave him a small smile, her violet eyes blazing. "Let's kill every last one of the bastards."

Killian returned her smile and turned to the man.

"Tell us everything you know."

CHAPTER FOURTEEN

The night was perfect; the dark sky was clouded, so the stars and moon were veiled and gave off no light that could alert the Roraks to Akairya and Killian's presence. They were sitting behind a large boulder that sat on the river bank, outside the village of Durndel. As it was nearing midnight, the only building that had any light was the Ravenett Inn, which was also the village tavern. The priest, whose name was Boyde, had told them that the Roraks spent every night chugging back mead and devouring massive slabs of meat before stumbling to the river to drown one of the villagers. Every night they chose a random person to drag off and kill, so they could feed the Shadow hounds they had brought with them from Tilaner Isle. They had been there nearly three nights, which meant two people had already died.

Boyde had no idea why they wanted the small community of Durndel, but Akairya and Killian were determined to take it back from them.

"One thing that confuses me, though," Killian whispered beside Akairya, "Draykor didn't notice anything odd when he scouted ahead earlier. Also, you would think the Roraks would have noticed a golden and silver dragon flying above the village."

"Dray said he had kept his distance when he scouted, and that he had landed before being in view of the village. I'm guessing the Roraks weren't noticeable because they were all sleeping off the alcohol they had drank the night before," Akairya replied, her eyes on her sword. She was glad the maids of the castle had packed the sword she had used during both duels with Killian. She was familiar with its shape, which meant her attacks would be swift and sure. She didn't want to make any mistakes; an entire village counted on her.

She also wanted to kill the Roraks because of Theandi. The princess's death had been caused by a Rorak bringing the Shadow into the castle. Akairya would make the ones in Durndel pay for her lost friend.

Killian had come up with the plan, and it was simple; jump the group of Roraks when they came to drown the nightly villager. It was a rough plan, but Akairya liked it. She felt more in her element now that she was out of Kalisor. She had enjoyed the experience and glamour of being accepted into the royal castle, but she was a hunter's daughter. She felt much more at home outside, fending for herself.

Draykor had stayed at the statue with Boyde since he was too large to conceal.

Be careful, Draykor said softly through his and Akairya's connection. *I don't want to have to fly over there and burn the whole village because the Roraks beat you.*

They won't. Even if I slip up, Killian is an extraordinary soldier.

It was true. Although she had bested him in their second duel, she knew that if she had been a man instead, without the charm of womanly curves, her skill would not have been sufficient enough to beat him. His sword was like an extension of his arm, and he was quick. She had a feeling his skill with a blade was largely the reason he had scaled the ranks of the Royal Army at such a young age.

Gritty laughter cut through the cool night air, and Killian shot her a grin. His silver eyes flashed in the moonlight as he moved quietly, his sword held ready. Akairya followed suit and took a deep breath as the sound of many pairs of feet came closer to the boulder. The river chugged on in front of her, and she couldn't help but think of the two people that had drowned in its waters. She was going to help make sure there wouldn't be a third.

"Please, please…not me…my wife is pregnant with our second child…please…" a deep male voice pleaded, accompanied by the sound of something sliding along the dirt.

"Shut it," one of the Roraks rasped. "You have been selected, there is no replacing you. Get over it and stay quiet."

The other nine Roraks all chuckled in appreciation, and Akairya bristled with hate. Her grip on her sword tightened.

When it sounded like the creatures were right behind them, Killian nodded. They leaped out from behind their boulder and jumped into the group of ten Roraks, blades cutting madly.

Akairya sliced through the arm of the Rorak who had been dragging a thin, tall man. He gasped in amazement and simply laid there when he found he was free.

"Get up and run!" she hissed impatiently as the Rorak she had wounded howled in agony. Its discoloured face paled from the loss of sickly dark blood that pumped out of its severed arm, and it lurched towards her with a knife clutched in its remaining hand. Akairya raised an eyebrow at it and lopped off its head, her hate for the creature spurring her on.

The man took her advice and bolted, his shaggy black hair flying behind him.

Killian had already slain three of the Roraks; the remaining six had gotten over their surprise and were now attacking back with a fervor, their gravelly voices hissing insults.

"This is *our* village! You will not take it!"

"Scum! The Lord has favored us, we are his children! You cannot best us!"

Akairya silenced another Rorak with a solid stab into its chest. She couldn't believe that they weren't wearing their traditional armor; it made killing them so much easier.

A great heaving came from one Rorak as it opened its mouth wide and turned to face Killian, who was locked in combat with another of the cruel creatures.

"Killian, move!" Akairya bellowed. She dashed towards the heaving Rorak and kicked it hard in the gut; it choked on the vomit it had brought up and gasped as its own weapon turned against it. Akairya watched in fascination as the bile ate away at the Rorak, a gleeful gurgling coming from its quivering mass.

A rough looking dagger flew past Akairya's head, lopping off a strand of her hair that hissed from contact with the blade. She wrenched her attention away from the dying Rorak and faced the biggest of the lot. It was as thick as the Rorak that had come to the capital city, yet even taller. Its beefy, discoloured arms flexed as it spun another dagger in one of its thick hands. It smiled at her. Her hatred flared up even stronger than before at the sight of its grin, and she felt a sudden heat in her hands. When she looked down, she nearly dropped her sword in amazement.

The entire weapon was enveloped in flames that stretched from her fire blanketed hands. It wasn't the same as the Sword of Flame that Oren could conjure, but it was still magnificent. With a cry of fury, Akairya lifted the fiery sword and cut the large Rorak's head off as easily as if the skin and bone had been soft butter. She turned to the last two, who had been advancing on Killian, and simply lifted her hands and asked the element of Fire to burn them.

And burn them it did.

The two creatures went up in two identical twisters of flame that churned and crackled. Twin screams of agony erupted and suddenly ended when the fire strengthened and went white. When the two Roraks were burned to fine ash, the fire dissipated, leaving only smoke and a vague smell of burnt flesh.

Killian stood beside the last Rorak he had killed and gaped at the place where the twisters of fire had roared.

"I…think you have fire down all right," he said weakly. Akairya laughed and looked at her hands. She felt suddenly empty, and a little scared. Where had that come from?

Before she had the chance to gather her thoughts, a high pitched howl came from somewhere behind the inn, which stood down the dirt road that cut through the small cluster of houses and shops. Killian looked in that direction and gripped the hilt of his sword tightly.

"I believe we are about to meet the Shadow hounds that were fed the drowned villagers," he commented quietly. Horrified, Akairya stared in the direction of the inn.

After a couple seconds, another howl ripped through the night, followed by the padding of running paws. Three slim, dark dogs came bolting from behind the inn, their white eyes eerily clear in the dark.

As they pelted closer, Akairya readied her now semi-melted blade and tried not to balk at the size of the beasts. They were slim, but tall; it looked as if their heads would reach her chest. They had ebony coats that were slashed with trembling lines of bright red, and their fangs glittered in the moonlight. Their thin, whip-like tails were encircled with threads of pulsing Shadow.

Dray, we need your help.

I'll be right there.

Akairya barely had the chance to throw her sword in front of her to block the charge of the first hound. The other two made straight for Killian, and he grunted as he leaped out of their path.

The dogs snarled and nearly ran into the large boulder. Angry, Akairya lifted a hand and shot a jet of searing flame towards them, but it was simply absorbed into their skin.

"Kairi, I think those red lines mean they are somehow blended with the fire element. It's not going to help us here," Killian panted as he swung at the hound that was just about to pounce at Akairya again. He connected with its shoulder, and it yelped. Blood tinged with fire spilled from its wound, and Akairya blinked in shock.

"If only I could wield the water element," she groaned. The injured Shadow hound limped away, but Killian swung his sword into its muscled neck and severed its head from its body. More fiery blood spilled onto the ground and caused the grass to catch flame.

The other two hounds had been circling, gauging the fight. Their cold white eyes stayed locked on their enemies as they paced, deep growls coming from their throats. The fire from the dead hound's blood spread rapidly, steam from the water left from the storm earlier clouding the air.

Just as the Shadow hounds were about to leap again, heavy wing beats shuddered through the smoky air. Draykor had arrived, and the wind from his wings only made the fire bigger.

Dray! Land before you make the fire spread to the houses!

Her dragon obeyed instantly; he dropped to the ground with a snarl and nearly landed on one of the hounds. It yelped and tried to run from Draykor, but he simply swiped with one deadly claw and gored its belly. It gave one last howl before it died, hanging limply off the dragon's claws. Draykor impatiently shook it off and turned towards the last hound, but before he could advance, Killian had snuck up behind it and had run it through the heart with his sword.

The fire was now out of control. All three Shadow hound carcasses were bleeding profusely, feeding the flames that were growing taller by the second.

"We need to throw them in the river!" Killian yelled at Akairya. She nodded and ran to the carcass nearest to her. She yelped as some of its burning blood branded her hand, but she pushed back the pain and grabbed its now Shadow-free tail. She dragged its heavy body towards the river, which was thankfully not that far away. She was able to push it into the churning waters, the blood going out with a loud hiss.

We can put out the fire with our power, Draykor told her calmly as he shoved one of the other bodies into the water. Killian had also gotten his carcass into the river, and was now staring at the ravenous flames that were inching closer towards the thoroughly wooden village.

Do you know how? Akairya asked her dragon desperately.

Just call to the element and think about what you want it to do. That's how you burned the Roraks, isn't it?

Seeing the logic in his words, Akairya reached for the element of Fire. She wasn't quite sure how to truly call upon an element, but she recalled how she had simply drawn inside herself earlier when she had used Fire. She mentally focused on Fire and asked it to come to her.

Nothing happened.

Confused, she tried again. Still the element stayed asleep inside her. Frustrated, panicked the fire was going to reach the buildings, she angrily yanked on the subtle power that barely flickered insider her.

Finally it rushed into her veins, a warm sensation that embraced her. Holding on to it, she looked towards the large fire that had grown even more in the last few seconds and asked it to stop.

At first there was no visible change. The flames reached ever higher and the smoke thickened, choking her and making her eyes water. But then the fire slowly began to shrink away from the village. After a few minutes, even the smallest flame had died, leaving behind a film of ash on the ground.

Killian shook his head in wonder. "I doubt Oren would have guessed that you two could control Fire so well so quickly. I've heard how it took him months to just control a small flame."

We are far from mastering it like Oren and Xandior have, Draykor said as he walked towards his Rider. *We may be able to wield it already, but I think mastering it completely will still take quite some time. Akairya had difficulty calling it to her at first, as did I.*

Although fire had listened to them just now, Akairya found it strange how the element had been so difficult to use after she had wielded it so effectively during the fighting. What did that mean? Was that to be expected?

A few villagers were now peeking out of their doorways, their expressions ranging from fear to anger to relief. The man Akairya had freed approached them, close-set eyes wide.

"You're a Rider?" he asked her shakily. She nodded and Draykor lowered his head to study him. The man flinched but stood his ground.

"Your dragon's scales aren't black, so I take it you are not of the Shadow?"

Akairya looked at the man in amazement. "Why do you even need to ask that? We just saved your village! *And* you!"

He sputtered and looked away. A portly woman walked up and smacked him soundly on the shoulder.

"Jimo, she's right. She, this man, and this dragon freed all of us from the control of those disgusting creatures." She turned her brown eyes onto Akairya and gave her a warm smile. "Now, would you all like something to eat? The Roraks stuck mostly to meat, so I still have plenty of bread and vegetable soup left, plus a couple free beds."

Relieved, Akairya nodded. "That sounds wonderful, thank you so much."

Killian came to stand beside her and lowered his head to hers. "I'm going to go tell Boyde that the village is safe and retrieve the horses. Will you be okay alone for a little bit?"

She won't be alone, she'll be with me, Draykor said. Killian nodded and walked in the direction of the broken statue, where Boyde was likely still cowering.

"Dear, did he say that Boyde is out there?" The innkeep's wife asked Akairya.

"Yes, he told us he was a priest of the High Queen."

The woman snorted. "And I'm the daughter of a Duke. No, Boyde fancies himself as a priest, but really he is just a man obsessed with the idea of the High Queen. Turns out he has a small amount of elvish blood way back in his family, which automatically proved to him that he was divinely linked to the High Queen. He's harmless enough, and everyone here puts up with him fine and keeps him fed and clothed, but do not believe a word he says."

Amused, Akairya shook her head. "He did seem like an odd little fellow."

Akairya sat at a rough wooden table in the inn with a large bowl of soup set in front of her. The broth was rich and delicious, and she didn't hesitate to devour it. She was just wiping the bowl clean with a buttered slice of bread when Killian walked in, followed by a tall cloaked figure.

"I lost Boyde but found someone else," Killian said by way of greeting as he plopped into the chair across the table from Akairya. The cloaked person lowered their hood and grinned.

"Thoran! You missed all the fun!" Akairya exclaimed around a mouthful of bread.

He chuckled as he sat beside Killian. "So I heard! I was a little concerned when I reached the broken statue and found just the horses…your priest friend must have bolted as soon as Dray left him behind."

"Maybe he figured the villagers would tell us the truth about his priesthood and was embarrassed," Akairya suggested. The inn keep's wife bustled over with two more bowls of soup. Killian sighed appreciatively and tucked in.

"Not our problem," he said in between mouthfuls. "Where's your dragon?"

"Sleeping. He's still growing at quite the pace, and today's excitement tuckered him right out."

"Fighting with fire does that to you," Thoran commented, a smile playing at the corners of his mouth. Akairya couldn't help laugh.

"It's definitely exhilarating, having the power over such a destructive force…it terrifies me as well, though," she admitted. Killian looked at her, his silver eyes serious.

"I'd be concerned if you weren't scared, Akairya. The more respect you have for the elements, the more likely you will use them only for good."

She nodded and looked at Thoran curiously. "So, what brings you to Durndel?"

"The king asked me to scout around the northern edge of the province, see which towns have been affected by the blight. It worries me that the very first town I come to has been nearly taken over. If it wasn't for the three of you, Durndel would be in the Shadow's clutches."

Akairya bit her lip and frowned. "How will you be able to help the other towns if they are in the same predicament? Killian, Dray, and I had problems; I can't imagine what it would have been like alone. Even with elemental power behind me."

"I'm not supposed to help. I'm supposed to alert the king, and in turn he would have to send forces in to deal with the problem."

"But that could take forever! So many lives could be lost," Akairya fretted. She couldn't bear the thought of innocents being needlessly murdered by the Shadow's minions. It fed the rage that had sparked the day her city fell.

"The military is toughening up for war. The king doesn't want to waste manpower if the threat isn't even there. We don't know if other towns have been taken or anything yet. Most of the people who travel to Kalisor's market come from towns all over the province, Kairi. I'm sure they would have alerted the king if the blight was really spreading its poison," Killian soothed her. He had finished his soup and was now leaning back against his chair, arms crossed. She could tell that he was also worried about the people, just by the set of his jaw and the slight frown crinkling his forehead.

"Yes, don't worry about a thing! What's important right now, Kairi, is that you get you and your dragon to Drakynold and figure out your power

and position in this mess. Okay?" Thoran said.
Akairya sighed and nodded.

"I'm guessing he has sent other men to check on
the rest of the country?"

"Yes, he has sent falcons to every major city. The
Dukes will get back to him as soon as they receive his
letters.

"Now, enough of this talk. I want to see you play
with some fire!"

The three of them thanked the lady of the inn for
the food and assured her that they would be back to
sleep before heading outside. The night was slowly
fading into dawn, and birds were beginning to chirp.

"Let's not take too long with this, we need sleep
before we continue to travel," Killian said as he
yawned. Akairya agreed whole heartedly, so she
cupped her hands and reached for the fire element.

Nothing happened, just like before.

Akairya probed for the essence of Fire inside of
herself. She could feel its spark, but she couldn't wield
it.

"I can feel the power of Fire, but…it isn't
listening to me," she told the others. Killian raised an
eyebrow and Thoran simply looked at her with
interest.

"Were you feeling a particular emotion when you
used the element before?" he inquired.

"Yes…anger."

"Maybe try to remember that anger and try
again. The emotion might have helped you connect
with the element."

Akairya thought back to when she had burnt the
two Roraks in two cyclones of flame. She remembered
vividly the pure rage she had felt towards them. As she

remembered, the rage came back full force. The Fire element leaped to meet the rage, and she grasped its sudden eager strength and asked for it to create a sphere of flame in the palms of her hands. It responded happily, and she soon found herself holding a large, perfectly round ball of fire that crackled and snapped with heat.

Thoran whistled, and Killian took a step back from the sudden wave of heat that swept out from the ball.

Just as quickly as it came, the rage dwindled into pure exhaustion. The sphere puffed out with a sigh, and Akairya yawned.

"With that solved, it is definitely time for sleep," Killian stated. Akairya agreed wearily and followed him inside the inn, a thoughtful Thoran trailing in their wake.

CHAPTER FIFTEEN

The four of them left late morning, while the sun shone hotly on the wooden buildings of Durndel and glimmered against the black waste of land that sat beside the river. Akairya thanked the inn keep and his wife profusely; she was grateful for the hospitality that they had given after all they had been through.

Thoran mounted his bay gelding and waited for Killian and Akairya to hop on their horses before moving forward. Draykor had flown ahead to hunt, for there was no meat left in the village thanks to the late Roraks.

As they rode through the village towards the river, they passed a small forge where a thickset blacksmith and his apprentice were steadily working. The apprentice, a lean red head with a plump face, leered at Akairya with distaste.

"Don't come too close, half breed, or I'll have to brand you with this heated blade," he hissed. Killian and Thoran both reined their horses in, outrage clear on their faces. Before they could do anything, however, the blacksmith clouted his apprentice around the head.

"Quiet that tongue of yours, fool. If it wasn't for that girl and her powers, we would still be under the Roraks control!"

"Pah, her dragon and that soldier did all the fighting, I'm sure. She probably just cowered behind the boulder and whimpered," the apprentice retorted. Fury flamed inside Akairya's chest, and she lifted a hand. Without even thinking about it, she conjured a ball of fire the size of a small coin and flicked it at the younger man. It seared him right on the cheek, and he yelped in pain as his skin burned in response to the touch of the flame. The ball went out almost immediately, before any real damage could be done, but the apprentice's ego was sorely wounded.

"Think before you speak next time, you dolt," chuckled the blacksmith. He winked at Akairya and strode towards her horse. "I heard you ruined your blade last night, in the fight against those abominations."

Akairya nodded. "Yes, I wreathed it with flames that were too hot for it."

"I don't have anything of much value, but I can give you my best one handed sword...as thanks for your help in freeing my village."

"Oh, no, that's really..." her voice faded as the blacksmith ignored her and tramped back to his forge. Ignoring the incredulous look on his apprentice's face, he plucked a sword and a scabbard from his rack of finished weapons and came back over to Akairya. He handed the blade to her with a small bow of the head and a broad smile. "For you, miss, and many thanks."

Overcome with gratitude, she accepted the weapon and belted it to her hip. It felt quite light, much lighter than her old sword.

"We'd better get going, Kairi. Thank you, sir, for your gift. It will come in handy," Killian said. The blacksmith waved off the thanks and returned to his forge. Thoran nodded to him before clicking his tongue and setting off at a trot.

When the three of them were back by the river and a little away from Durndel, Thoran turned to Akairya.

"Is Draykor near?" he inquired. Akairya automatically felt along her connection with her dragon and only got a warm presence that told her all was well, but he was too far to communicate.

"No, I can't speak with him. He must have flown quite a distance for some game."

"I was going to ask if you and Killian would like to accompany me to the next village, which is only an hour's ride from here. Be nice to have some company, and it won't be that much out of your way…however, if Dray is still quite far, I'd understand if you would rather not."

Akairya considered it. "Well, if it's only an hour away from here, I don't see why not. He would be able to follow our connection to where I am if it's not too far. What do you think, Killian?"

Killian shrugged. "I have no qualms about it. We'll strike for Seratea City after and hopefully make it there in a week's time. Be prepared, there will be no beds to sleep in until then. It's wild country after Yokar, the village Thoran is going to."

Akairya smiled. "I'm used to sleeping outside. Perk of being a hunter's daughter."

Decision made, the trio pointed their horses northwest and left the banks of the coursing river and plunged into the grasslands that covered most of Ariniya.

After nearly an hour of riding, they came across a thick wall of trees. They grew so close together that their branches were interlocked and complexly woven into a dense web of wood and leaf.

"Yokar is just behind this copse, but we will have to go around; the horses won't be able to go through the trees," Thoran announced. He checked to make sure the other two were following before picking up a canter.

The copse, although thick, wasn't very large, and they soon rode around it and came in sight of Yokar.

An oily smoke hung over the village like a blanket soaked in poison. The stench of fear and death assailed the company, and the horses snorted with apprehension. Thoran, who was sitting stiffly in his saddle, glanced at Killian.

"We're too late," he said hoarsely. A cold chill descended over Akairya, and she shivered. She reluctantly followed the others in dismounting and hobbled her mare just outside the village. Its small buildings were cloaked with fog twisted with threads of Shadow.

Fedana snuffled Akairya's hair as she looked at Yokar.

"Will the Shadow poison us?" she asked quietly, loathing for the blight burning in her chest. The fire element perked up inside her, but settled when she took a controlling breath.

"No. It's more of a mark...a warning, really," Thoran answered her. Killian shot him a look.

"How do you know that? Looks like the normal deadly smog to me."

"Oren told me that Calindyl had the same thing all over the place after it was destroyed," Thoran replied quickly, a slight flush on his cheeks. Killian frowned at him for a few seconds before shrugging and turning towards the village.

They walked purposefully into the haphazard cluster of buildings that made up the small settlement of Yokar, their cloaks fluttering in the cool breeze that blew over the grasslands and through the village. It carried the smell of decay on its breath, and Akairya paled. She knew in her heart that they would find no living soul inside the village.

The first body they came across was sprawled in the middle of the single road that twisted through the village. Akairya stopped in her tracks and mentally reached for her dragon. The connection was there, but fuzzy; he was still too far for her to talk to.

Killian and Thoran had reached the corpse and were kneeling beside it, expressions grim. Akairya took a deep breath and walked forward. She was a Rider; she needed to be able to handle the evil in the world in order to conquer it.

Pain and sorrow lanced through her when she saw the body up close. It had been a middle-aged man, and his dead figure reminded her strongly of Theandi; the Shadow had also given him black eyes that swallowed all light, gray flesh, oily tracks running from eyes and nose, and crusty black spittle flecked over his lips.

"Oh, no…" she whispered sadly. While she felt sorrow for the man, the memory of Theandi's horrific death caused hot tears to sting her eyes.

Killian squeezed her arm in sympathy while Thoran stood and walked slowly into the nearest house, its front door shattered and strewn all over the entrance. Akairya trailed along behind him, leaving Killian kneeling by the dead man.

The house was just a single room that served as kitchen, bedroom, and bathroom. In one corner was a rickety bed that held two more dead, and beside it stood a rough crib.

Horror clutched at Akairya, but she forced herself to join Thoran, who stood staring at the crib.

He wept silently, with a bleakness in his eyes that spoke volumes. He gazed at the unmoving baby that lay nestled in its blankets, its face grotesquely covered in the residue of the Shadow's deadly poison.

The sorrow Akairya had felt earlier deepened the longer she stared at the babe. She gently touched the cold cheek. Her stomach tightened, and she wished with all her heart that she could at least wash off the evil that had stained such an innocent face.

She felt something jump to attention inside herself, and it took her a moment to recognize the essence of the Water element. Her sadness had given her the ability to use Water's cleansing power.

She cradled the babe's cheek while she willed the rippling element to flow gently from her fingertips. Its embrace of her mind was quite unlike fire; where fire was wild and passionate, water was soothing and subtly powerful. It coursed from her fingertips like a slow, meandering stream, and effortlessly washed away the ugliness of the Shadow. It could not take away the deathly gray of the skin, however, so Akairya stopped the flow of water with a sigh. At least now the baby only looked like a sculpture, instead of an abomination created by the blight.

Thoran was looking at her with an odd expression in his brown eyes. There was wonder, and some fear too.

"You never cease to amaze me, Kairi," he whispered. She blinked, unsure of how to reply. She was saved answering by a hoarse cry that came from outside.

"They're waking up!" Killian yelled, disbelief clear in his voice. Astonished, Akairya looked back down at the baby and recoiled.

Its black eyes were roving around the room with a chilly awareness. Thoran groaned and whipped out one of his daggers. Before she could stop him, he cut the babe's head off.

"*Thoran,* what-" she gasped. He shook his head and turned to the bed, where the bodies of the baby's parents were stirring.

"Show no mercy, Kairi. These things are only the poisoned shells of the people they used to be. They'll kill us without a thought."

Akairya lifted a hand to her mouth as the woman, her brown hair knotted and limp, rolled out of the bed and fell to the floor with a rasping growl. The man simply stood on the filthy mattress and turned his black eyes to Thoran, who now had both daggers out.

He grunted as he dodged the man, who had thrown himself off the bed with a snarl. With a flash of his blades, Thoran beheaded the poisoned man. He then quickly sliced the neck of the woman, who slumped to the ground and died for the second time. Billowing coils of Shadow ripped itself from the three broken bodies in the house and coalesced into one shifting cloud.

"Would Theandi had turned into one of these things too?" Akairya asked as she stared, wide eyed, at the two freshly killed corpses.

"Yes, but Yeilao saved her from this fate by cleansing her tainted body with the Spirit element. Remember Harrol, the soldier who was killed during the skirmish in the Forest of Souls?"

"Y-yes, I remember. Killian had stayed behind to take care of his body while the rest of us went ahead," Akairya answered. She flinched as the poisonous nebula rushed out of the hut, its dark aura heavy.

"Killian saved Harrol from turning into a Rorak by putting his body into the Kito River. Its waters are known to be threaded with the Spirit element."

Understanding dawned on Akairya, and she stared at the bodies with newfound horror. "You mean that these things would eventually turn into full-fledged Roraks?"

"Yes. In a way, they are only newborns."

A roar of fury interrupted their conversation, and Akairya suddenly remembered that Killian was outside, alone against an unknown number of newly risen Roraks. Panic rose inside her, and she ran out the door with Thoran close on her heels.

Killian stood in the middle of the road, beside a growing pile of beheaded Roraks. The cloud of Shadow that had grown inside the house was even thicker now, and it floated a few yards away from the furious Killian, who was slashing at the crowd of fresh Roraks surrounding him, all born from the corpses of the villagers.

A fear for Killian's life leaped inside Akairya's chest. Anger soon followed, and she suddenly found her hands gloved with flame. The heat spread to her arms, and with a cry of outrage she lifted her hands and pushed the space in front of her. The fire element reacted instantaneously; the many Roraks were enveloped in flames and burned to ashes in seconds. Killian lifted an arm to cover his eyes as the heat grew and then died as quickly as it had come. Panting from emotion, it was all Akairya could do to not fall to her knees.

The Shadow, which had gorged itself on the essence of darkness from each fallen Rorak, was now a colossal fog that churned ferociously over the roofs of the small village. Although it was still day, it was nearly as dark as deep night underneath the cover of the black cloud. Akairya shivered, her anger depleted.

"Ah, you have slaughtered my newborn children with considerable skill," a familiar, gritty voice addressed them. Akairya gasped; it was the voice that had spoken to Theandi before the Shadow had killed her. Newfound strength fueled her hatred, and she called on the fire element with murderous intention.

"Now, now, my feisty Rider. You are being quite rude," the voice spoke again, and as it spoke two thin tendrils of Shadow shot out from the cloud and grasped Akairya's wrists with startling accuracy. She screamed as the blight touched her skin, its strangely solid hold biting into her flesh and paralyzing her conscious hold on the Fire element. The heat inside her died, and she nearly wept from the loss of it.

"Kairi!" Killian yelled. He started to run to her, but more tendrils plunged out of the Shadow and wrapped around his waist. Agony flashed across his face, and he paled as the tendrils sapped his remaining strength.

"If you move, I will kill you. Now, let's have a civilized conversation," the rough voice grated on Akairya's senses, and she sobbed from the pain. She no longer felt like a Rider, or even a human. She felt like a shell, whose soul had been brutally ripped away.

"As I am sure you are aware, I have asked your weakling king to join forces with me. Since he has disobeyed, I have killed his only daughter and slaughtered one of his villages. I was hoping to add to my army, but you dispatched my young soldiers. Ah, well…I am willing to overlook this insult if you relay this message; *give me Alkairyn, or die for it.*" The last few words were laced with an evil power that pounded against their minds, and they flinched. After a few moments, the tendrils holding Akairya and Killian slipped off and returned to the large cloud, which gathered itself up and rushed upwards.

Daylight flooded back into Yokar as Killian and Akairya fell. Thoran, his face gray, darted to where the horses were tied and soon came back with the alchemic potion. Killian gulped down half the bottle and shuddered. He glanced over at Akairya, who lay curled in a fetal position.

Thoran pressed a hand on her quaking shoulder. "Kairi? Drink some of this, it will help."

She sat up, violet eyes wide, and took the drink without a word. After she emptied the bottle, she got to her feet. "I need to get away from here," she murmured. She began to walk weakly out of the village.

Killian slowly stood and rubbed his waist where the Shadow had clutched him. "That was not a good feeling," he rasped.

"I can't even imagine," Thoran replied. He looked in the direction Akairya had gone, sorrow and something else in his gaze. After a moment he turned back to Killian.

"I need to get back to the king and tell him what happened. Will you two be okay?"

"Yes, I believe so. I have more of the potion in Tridon's saddlebags. We'll head out shortly, before anything else comes along."

Thoran nodded and walked to his gelding. He glanced again in the direction Akairya took, hesitated, then mounted the horse and turned his head towards Durndel and the capital city. "Tell her I say farewell, and to take care."

Killian assured him he would, and Thoran galloped away.

Still weak from the Shadow's onslaught, Killian looked for Akairya. He found her leaning on a tree in the copse, her face still pale and eyes wide.

"How are you?" he asked. He knelt before her and took one of her cold hands in his own. A muscle twitched in his jaw when he saw the bruises circling her wrists.

"I've only felt that empty one other time," Akairya whispered, her voice ragged. "And I never thought I would feel that way again."

Killian rubbed her hand and stayed silent, silver eyes on hers, willing her to continue.

"It was when my father died. When he finally gave in to the plague, he left me alone in a city full of strangers I had grown up with. While they had never been truly cruel, they never accepted me because of my elven blood. When father passed away, I lost the only companion and guardian I had," she took a shaky breath and wiped a couple tears from her eyes. "I don't remember much of the weeks that followed his death…only emptiness. Not grief, or anger, or even confusion. Just emptiness.

"This time was worse. Before, I had fallen into the emptiness, as if I had slowly submerged myself into a tub of numbing water. Today, when the Shadow grabbed me, it ripped everything out of me and threw me into the emptiness. I lost all that I am in a split second, and was reminded of the time after my father's death. It didn't help that all of my power was cut off when the Shadow had its hold on me. I felt absolutely devoid of *everything*."

She fell silent and stared ahead at the empty village. Killian sighed heavily and shifted to sit beside her, his hand still holding on to hers.

"I understand partially what you went through, Kairi. While I had no elemental power to lose, the emptiness still took hold of me when the Shadow coiled around my waist."

Akairya shifted her gaze onto him, curious. He took a breath and quietly began.

"Most of my childhood I lived with my mother and younger sister, a bright girl of ten named Leala, on a small farm near the southern border of Ariniya. My father had been a solider of the Royal Army, so he would only come home for an occasional visit. One day we received a letter that he had been killed in a warlock ambush. This was before the blight was as strong as it is now, and before the Riders had driven the warlocks back to their home country across the sea.

"The king invited us to Kalisor to attend father's funeral. He had been a highly respected and loved general, and High King Elric wished to give him a funeral that befitted his reputation. He gave us a month to travel from our farm to Kalisor, a week longer than we needed for such a journey.

"Before we could leave, a small group of thieves attacked the farm. My younger sister and I huddled in the darkest corner of the house, terrified. We watched as the thieves cut down our mother for attempting to stop them from taking father's old set of armor, simply because they were more bloodthirsty than greedy." Killian cleared his throat and looked down, his expression haunted by the memories. Now it was Akairya's turn to comfort him, and she squeezed his hand in sympathy. Her eyes were now wide with sorrow, not fear. After a few moments, Killian continued.

"Leala was sobbing. Great, heaving sobs that ripped at my heart. All I could do was hold her and let her cry as the thieves tore apart our home and stepped on the body of our mother. Then *it* came in; a great big Rorak who had taken over the leadership of the gang. He sneered when he saw my dead mother. Then he caught sight of my weeping sister, my beautiful sister who had always lived in a fantasy world of light and beauty. His smirk turned into a dark leer, and I'll never forget the panic my eleven year old self felt when I realized what that look meant.

"Surprisingly, the thieves were disgusted when the Rorak advanced towards Leala, who continued to cry, ignorant of what was going on. They yelled that she was too young, that they should just steal our things and be done with it. Who would have thought that they could ever appear moral? Yet at that moment they did, and I remember feeling a rush of gratitude towards them, the men who had just slaughtered my mother and were now my sister's unlikely champions.

"Of course, the Rorak ignored them and snatched my weeping sister from my arms, who finally realized what was happening and screamed. I tried to leap to her defense, but the Rorak hit me on the head and I fainted.

"The scene I woke to will forever be burned into my memory. I opened my eyes to sunshine flooding in the house, the light beaming on my dead mother, whose mouth was crusted with dried blood and whose kind gray eyes were cloudy with death. Then I saw my beloved sister, her broken child's body sprawled on the floor of my home, her eyes covered in a black film and her once lovely blue dress torn and bloody. The Rorak had snapped her neck after he had finished with her, and all I felt was a yawning emptiness that swallowed my entire self. I left my farm that day, after burning my home with my mother and sister still inside it. I travelled to Kalisor, where the king took me in and gave me the option of enrolling in the army the day I turned twelve, five months after the death of my family." Killian tore a couple blades of grass from the earth and ripped them slowly apart.

"Once the emptiness faded, anger came. And now all I want is to wipe the blight from all of Alkairyn, before more innocent mothers and sisters are killed. Today's reminder of my emptiness only made me angrier."

Akairya brought his hand to her lips. "We have that goal in common," she whispered. He smiled weakly.

"I haven't let myself get too close to anyone since that day. I cared for Theandi, and felt the blow that her death brought, but I always stayed distant from people in fear that I would only lose them. Yet I can't help but be drawn to you." His eyes hardened, and he gripped Akairya's hand tightly. "I will do my utmost to protect you from further harm," he swore.

Akairya opened her mouth to reply, taken aback, but froze as Draykor suddenly brushed her consciousness.

Akairya, where are you!? I just arrived in Durndel, but your presence is nowhere near the town.

Oh Dray, finally! Killian and I are about an hour northwest from you, beside a ruined village called Yokar. A lot has happened since you went hunting.

Alarm flooded through their connection. *I'll be there as soon as possible.*

CHAPTER SIXTEEN

Dray was true to his word; he soon soared into view, his golden body bright against the blue sky. He landed beside Akairya and Killian, who were still sitting near the copse. Akairya had most of her colour back, but her eyes still held a haunted look. He walked over and she leaped up and threw her arms around his neck.

Oh, Dray…it was terrible. I never want you to feel the helplessness I felt.

She told him what had happened, and anger radiated from the young dragon.

We need to get to the Elders, fast. I want us to become strong enough to wipe this Shadow Lord from existence.

He had spoken in both Akairya and Killian's minds, so Killian nodded in agreement.

"Yes. We should get moving. I want to reach Seratea city in at least a week."

With grim determination, the trio moved on from Yokar and struck hard north, towards the fishing capital of Ariniya.

The first day they didn't make much progress; a heavy storm rolled in around evening. They were forced to make camp underneath the foliage of another copse of densely branched trees. Akairya reached for the water element to drive off the damp of the rain that managed to break through the shelter, but she found her way blocked. She could still sense her power, but a yawning chasm separated her from it. Troubled, she kept it to herself.

While she felt closer to Killian now that they gone through so much together, she was shaken by what had happened and withdrew into herself. If the Shadow only had to touch her to stop her powers, how was she to defeat it? The odds were set against her.

On the third day of riding, the flat plains grew more hilly and wild. Thick grasses that reached as high as Fedana's withers waved gently from the breeze that blew from the distant ocean, and large trees covered in moss were dotted haphazardly throughout, their branches sporting huge round leaves dyed deep red. Something about the trees spooked Akairya, and she mentioned it to Killian as they rode past a particularly huge one.

"These are Blood Trees, so it only makes sense that you get a strange feeling from them. If you were to slice a branch off one, it would scream a very human scream and then bleed from the stump. And when I say bleed, I mean bleed." He said seriously. "Not sap, or water, or anything else. Legitimate blood flows in these trees, and legend says that each tree houses a malignant soul of the dead, souls of past evil men who couldn't find peace in the realm of the Underearth."

"That…is really creepy," Akairya muttered. Goosebumps rose on her skin as Fedana took her past another Blood Tree. Its trunk wasn't overly thick, but its bark was a deep brown that looked crimson at a certain angle.

"Yes, it is very creepy," Killian chuckled. He patted his stallion's neck. "Horses feel it too, and we should be grateful these two haven't spooked and bolted yet. The only animals that reside in this part of Ariniya are bats. There is a myth that a Blood Hawk calls this place home, but there is no true evidence."

They pressed on through the rest of the day, Akairya shivering as the Blood Trees stretched on. When evening bled into night, Killian reluctantly called a halt underneath the largest tree yet.

"You aren't going to like this, but we need to stop and camp," he shrugged. "At least the night is clear and we can start a fire. That should help somewhat."

After trampling down a section of the thick grass and ripping some up to add to the tiny dead twigs they had found for fuel, they built a small fire that crackled in the pressing darkness. Akairya hugged herself tightly as Draykor and Killian settled down. The two horses were also unperturbed; they stood side by side with their heads drooping.

"I'll take first watch," she announced. "I won't be able to fall asleep right now anyway."

"Alright. Wake me if you get tired or need some company," Killian replied. She nodded and he rolled out his bedroll and promptly fell asleep. Draykor yawned before he also dozed off.

As the night continued, a light breeze rustled the grass that surrounded the camp. Shadows flitted through the firelight and set Akairya on edge; the aura of the tree behind her made her incredibly aware of her surroundings.

The beating of a pair of wings interrupted Akairya's careful study of the area, and she jumped.

Killian and Draykor slept on, and she sighed. Just a bat, she mused.

Before her heart could calm, a bird dropped out of the sky and landed a few feet from where Akairya sat on her bedroll, its red eyes gleaming in the firelight. She stared at the creature and went cold when she recognized it for what it was.

"You're the Blood Hawk, aren't you?" she asked softly. The bird cocked its head before it began to preen its black wings.

Yes, I am, a rich voice threaded with a dark strength spoke in her mind. It was different from the agonizing voice of the Shadow in that it inflicted no pain. Instead, it simply gave off a black aura that felt strangely pure.

Do not fret. I will not harm you. I only wish to tell you something.

Curious despite herself, Akairya held out a hand to the hawk. It blinked once before hopping onto her wrist. It was surprisingly heavy, and its ebony claws were icy against her skin.

As I'm sure you are aware, the Spirit of the earth is poisoned and slowly dying, it said matter-of-factly. Akairya nodded, her gaze locked with the bird's. There was something strangely hypnotic about its red eyes, which were shining with evil; waves of dark energy pulsed from the creature, but she wasn't afraid. Its flavor of evil was bewilderingly right.

I have a special interest in the earth's strength, so I desire to aid you as much as I can. When you cannot find answers to questions, not even from the Elder dragons, travel to the Twin Slabs. I will meet you there, no matter when you arrive.

Before Akairya could respond, the Blood Hawk took off from her wrist with a screech. Killian jumped to his feet, his golden hair in disarray but his silver eyes bright with awareness. Draykor hadn't moved, but his eyes shone in the light of the fire.

"It's alright," Akairya said. She rubbed her wrist to warm it and winced as she brushed the bruises she had received from the bout with the Shadow. "It's already gone."

Killian frowned at her and looked up at the sky, a black canvas studded with stars.

"What was it?"

She took a breath and strode over to Draykor. She nestled against his side, and he huffed softly before resting his head back on the ground. She looked up at Killian, who was still standing with his hand on the hilt of his sword.

"Everything is fine, Killian, really. I just had a short conversation with the Blood Hawk."

"The what!?" he yelped. "The Hawk is just a myth!"

"For a myth, it was quite heavy on my wrist," she replied drily. "It asked me to meet it at the Twin Slabs some day…wherever that is."

Killian stared at her. After a few minutes of silence, he rubbed his face and sat down. "I think I've heard of those. I don't remember where they are said to be though."

"Well, I doubt I'll ever take it up on its invitation." Unless I have to, she thought to herself. Draykor shifted slightly, and she wondered if he could sense her intentions. She yawned. Exhaustion had finally crept into her limbs. Killian studied her.

"Go to sleep," he said. "I'll watch for the rest of the night."

Akairya smiled gratefully before curling up against Draykor, where she fell asleep almost immediately.

The next morning, a thick fog threaded through the long blades of grass and red leaves of the Blood Trees. Akairya shivered and tightened her cloak around her as Killian stomped the remains of the fire. Soon they were back in the saddle and moving on, with Killian constantly glancing at Akairya and muttering about Blood Hawks.

The Blood Trees appeared less and less as the morning wore on, their crimson leaves dully reflecting the sunlight and waving in the gentle wind. The warm sun burned away the fog that curled around the grass, and Akairya found herself relaxing as the bulk of the trees were left behind; even Fedana was more at ease than before.

In time, the last Blood Tree came into view. Draykor, who had been gliding ahead to stretch his wings, was on the ground near the tree with his nose pointed to the base of the trunk.

What is it Dray? Akairya asked him.

Some sort of creature. It's terrified; I don't want to get too close.

Curious, she dismounted when Fedana reached the tree. Killian stayed astride Tridon close to the Tree, his hand on the hilt of his sword.

Cowering against the mossy trunk of the Tree and partially concealed by the tall grass was a tiny fox like creature. Its chestnut fur was bristling, and bloody scratches stretched from its neck to the base of its bushy tail, which was clamped against its body. It hissed as Akairya crept closer, and it flattened huge ears against its tiny head. Big brown eyes watched her fearfully and it bared sharp white fangs.

"That's a Squirlox," Killian said in astonishment. "One of the few creatures that can dip into the elemental power. I think they can use some of Earth's strength." The Squirolx snapped its teeth as Akairya inched closer.

"It's okay," she soothed. Its bright brown body was slender and curved like that of a squirrel, and its paws were tipped with sharp claws.

"It's hurt," she commented. Blood still dripped from its wounds, and while there was fear in its eyes, there was also pain and exhaustion. Akairya slowly knelt and held out a hand. It gave a small whimper before eventually stretching out its neck and sniffing her fingers.

Holding her breath, Akairya slowly moved and rubbed the Squirlox behind one of its huge ears. It blinked in surprise and then leaned into her touch, eyes half closed. When she pulled away, it made a noise similar to the meow of a cat and stumbled to its feet. It ambled forward on short legs and fell in front of Akairya, where it looked up at her with beseeching eyes.

"Looks like it was attacked by bats. The ones that live in this area are ferocious; they attack anything they deem weak." Killian commented.

Sympathetic to the hurt creature, Akairya gently picked it up and cradled it in her arms. It sighed and snuggled into her, ears flopped and eyes half closed. Akairya studied it curiously.

"Are you male or female?" she wondered. The creature widened its eyes and stared at her. She chuckled.

"Male?" It bared its teeth and growled softly. "Female, then."

The Squirlox wriggled happily in Akairya's arms and moved her head in a small nod.

"Well, aren't you a smart little thing," Akairya exclaimed. She grinned at Killian and Draykor. "I'm keeping her."

"She likes you," Killian said. He shook his head in disbelief. "Squirloxes generally hate people...but why am I surprised?"

Akairya strode to Fedana and dug in her saddlebags for a salve. Finding it, she patted the Squirlox.

"This is going to sting, but it will help you heal," she told her gently. The creature blinked woefully and sighed.

"I'll take that as permission."

Akairya carefully rubbed some of the ointment into the deep scratches, and the Squirlox yelped. She didn't try to escape, however; she just looked trustingly at Akairya.

"You should name her Jaxei. It means fierce in Elvish," Killian said as he watched. The Squirlox made an excited sound and nodded her head.

"Jaxei it is," Akairya laughed. "What do you think, Dray?"

A fitting name, her dragon declared.

The group soon moved on from the Tree. Jaxei was comfortable in the hood of Akairya's cloak, her wounds lathered with ointment and bandaged. She slept soundly as the horses trotted briskly out of the long grass and into hilly plains dotted with thick brush and sliced by thin streams of chilly mountain water. In the far west stood the massive lumps of the Jalkorin range, their peaks cloaked in steel clouds that threatened another storm. Draykor, who was gliding ahead of the horses, looked towards the looming clouds and shook his head.

I'm going to guess that we will be travelling through more rain in a few hours.

Akairya grumbled and glared at the mountains. *I'm really beginning to hate these autumn storms. Doesn't look like we will have dry shelter tonight, either. All I can see ahead of us are hills and brush.*

I'll scout ahead.

Akairya explained to Killian what Draykor was doing as the dragon increased his wing beats and shot higher into the air. In no time he was far ahead of them, golden scales flashing against the blue sky.

"If we are lucky, he will find the castle ruins," Killian mused. Akairya shot him a look.

"Ruins of what castle?"

"I don't know. No one does, really. I camped in them once before, many years ago. The ruins must have once been a magnificent castle, more so than the High King's palace in Kalisor, but very, very old. I think it must have been a king's residence before High Queen Akairya's time."

"That would be interesting to see," Akairya said, eyes searching the landscape for hints of the ruins. She contacted Draykor through their connection and asked him to look for the ruins. The dragon assured her he would keep an eye out and soon flew too far away for her to continue talking to him.

After about an hour of silence, Draykor soared back into view. *I found the ruins. They are about a half day's ride, and are a little farther west than the path we are currently following.*

Killian grinned. "Nicely done, Dray. We'll have a dry place to sleep tonight!"

CHAPTER SEVENTEEN

The rain broke over their heads long before they reached the ruins, the heavy curtain of water accompanied with deep rumbles of thunder and knives of lightning that cut through the grim sky. Jaxei chittered unhappily, her nap in Akairya's hood having been interrupted by the volume of the storm. Akairya and Killian sat hunched in their saddles, and their horses trotted with their heads lowered.

Draykor was the only one unaffected by the turn of the weather. He twisted in the air and rocketed far up into the belly of the dark clouds, only to flip and plummet back towards the sodden earth. He pulled up seconds before crashing, and levelled himself so he could land on all fours and walk without breaking stride.

"Someone's feeling good," Killian called from atop Tridon. The stallion's coat was soaked right through, and he stepped forward as proudly as he had done when the group had just left Kalisor.

Flying is exhilarating in a storm, Draykor stated simply. Akairya sighed.

Yes, until you get struck by lightning.

Her dragon looked at her, affronted. *I would not allow myself to get struck by lightning.*

I don't think anyone has ever meant to be hit by lightning, Akairya bounced back, amused. Draykor snorted and didn't reply.

Jaxei, bored with being in Akairya's hood, scrambled out and clambered onto the half elf's shoulder. The Squirlox pressed herself against Akairya's neck and gazed around with wide eyes, chestnut fur disheveled from her nap and the onslaught of the storm.

"Why, hello little one," Akairya greeted her, smiling. She reached up and scratched Jaxei behind an ear, and the creature closed her eyes in bliss.

The group continued forward as the storm raged on. In time they saw the shape of a large hill, its surface covered with thick bush and some trees.

The ruins sit against the other side of that hill, Draykor notified them. Relieved, Akairya unconsciously asked Fedana to speed up. The mare, sensing that the end of the day's travels was near, readily picked up the pace with her ears pricked. The company rode around the huge hill and finally came across the ruins.

They sat flush against the side of the hill. White marble pillars and golden tile covered in vegetation lay broken underneath tilted domed roofs that had been knocked off their foundation, all boasting cracked murals of rich landscapes. Statues of great men and women were scattered around the destroyed castle, each one either missing limbs or knocked completely over. Draykor walked up to one and sniffed it, violet eyes thoughtful.

This place is old, he said. Akairya nodded as she halted Fedana and dismounted. Jaxei stayed on her shoulder, her big ears twitching as she looked at the ruins with interest. Killian studied the ruins with a critical eye.

"There was nothing dangerous when I was here last, but that doesn't mean nothing has made the ruins its home since. I think I should scout the area first, just to be safe."

He was gone for roughly half an hour before returning to where the horses stood. Jaxei was now on the ground and was walking from statue to statue, her little nose twitching as she sniffed the broken remnants. While her movements were still strained from her wounds, she was definitely livelier than when Draykor had first spotted her cowering against the Blood Tree.

"I didn't see anything particularly dangerous," Killian told Akairya as he joined her in unsaddling the horses. "No creatures that can threaten us, and the ruins are surprisingly stable considering most of the roof is on the ground."

Soon they were settled underneath a large section of ceiling that was still mostly attached to the moss covered walls of the old castle. The spot was big enough to shelter everyone, including Draykor's increasingly large bulk and the two horses. A fire was crackling in a makeshift pit that Killian had dug, and four rabbits were spitted over the flames thanks to Akairya's hunting.

"Your father taught you well," Killian commented as he prodded one of the rabbits with a stick. "While I am a much better swordsman than you, I am all bumbling limbs when it comes to hunting. Especially during heavy rain."

"You aren't *that* much better with a sword than me," Akairya teased half-heartedly. She was still feeling quite out of sorts, and humor was like wading through a thick swamp. Killian didn't seem to notice and chuckled. Draykor, on the other hand, looked at her curiously.

Are you still unable to reach your powers? He asked her casually. Akairya winced.

I never told you that! Are you shoving into my thoughts without me realizing it?

The golden dragon rolled his eyes, clearly unimpressed. *No, I would never do such a thing. I can, however, sense your emotions. I felt your frustration when you couldn't reach the Water element when we camped under those trees. You are easy to read, Akairya. It's a wonder Killian hasn't noticed anything amiss.*

He better keep on not noticing, Akairya said. *I just need to figure this out on my own.*

Draykor gave a slight shake of his head and didn't reply. He shifted into a more comfortable position, and Jaxei, who had been napping on his back, mewed a complaint as his movements shifted her into the base of one of his wings. Affronted, the Squirlox inched back to her preferred spot and curled back into a ball.

"It's amazing how quickly Jaxei adapted to you two," Killian said. "She hasn't even come near me yet."

"Maybe because of your fearsome reputation with a blade," Akairya smiled. Killian frowned at her as Draykor huffed a laugh.

Akairya still felt melancholy the next morning, but she pushed her dark thoughts away and attempted to show a brighter visage for Killian's sake. Draykor kept his thoughts to himself.

The rain had ceased during the night, but the morning was gray and thick with mist. The horses' hooves squelched with each step, and their progress was excruciatingly slow. Draykor opted to glide above the ground, but he was repeatedly circling back because of the horses' slower pace. Jaxei was again in Akairya's hood, eyes watching the dragon with interest.

"I'm going to estimate that we will reach Seratea city in two days. Let's hope the weather dries up until then; we'll be lucky to find any shelter from here on out." Killian said.

"Why aren't there any inns around here?" Akairya asked him as she looked at the sky. There were still gray clouds, but they were lightening and drifting south.

"There aren't any inns between Durndel and Seratea because of the Blood Trees – there are too many superstitions surrounding the trees, so people refuse to build even remotely close to them. We won't see any farms until the very outskirts of the city; the people of Seratea tend to rely more heavily on fishing."

"I can't say I blame them," Akairya grumbled. She shivered as she recalled the dark aura that had surrounded the Blood Trees.

Luckily, the sky cleared of rainclouds and continued to stay clear for the last two days of their journey. Akairya felt drier than she had in days, and her spirit brightened considerably. Draykor, in preparation for the upcoming flight across the ocean to Drakynold, flew the rest of the way. He practiced the many exercises that Xandior and Saverign had taught him, and Killian's face grew increasingly green the more he watched the golden dragon twist in the air.

Seratea City was visible several hours before they reached it. The land leading up to the city was almost perfectly flat and only covered with coarse grass and bristly brush. The wide Iolia river coursed to their right, and to their left was more flat land and the distant lumps of the Jalkorin.

The mist they had woken up to at the ruins had stayed with them for the rest of their journey, occasionally thinning out but always present. Now it thickened with a vengeance and cloaked the nearby city like a pearly blanket. Akairya could barely discern the square stone buildings that were clustered together in organized blocks, and as they drew closer she wrinkled her nose; the strong scent of fish wafted up from the sea and assailed her with the assistance of the wind.

"Ugh, it stinks more than it did in Yaeloa, and it was right on the water as well."

Killian laughed. "Well, the fact that Yaeloa had been on a massive cliff probably helped matters. The fishing industry there was mainly outside the city; here, the fishing industry is in every nook and cranny."

Jaxei had perked up and was sniffing appreciatively at the air. Draykor, who had been flying low to the ground in increasingly smaller circles behind them, finally landed and walked beside Fedana. His golden scales were dotted with moisture that clung to the mist around them, and his violet eyes glowed from the recent exercise.

Feeling prepared for our flight to Drakynold? Akairya asked him as the horses skirted a clump of tangled brush. Draykor nodded his angular head and flashed a glance at Killian.

I feel as ready as I can be. Killian, on the other hand, turns a pretty interesting shade of green every time we mention it.

He'll be fine.

I may have some fun with him, Draykor said, snorting with amusement when Akairya shot him a glare.

Don't you dare! We need him to be mentally prepared for whatever is awaiting us in the dragon country.

Oh, I'm only kidding. Don't fret.

Akairya rolled her eyes and asked Fedana to pick up a trot. When she caught up to Tridon and Killian, she reined in her mare. Killian looked at her questioningly.

"Everything all right?"

She smiled brightly. "Yes, all is well."

Draykor gave another snort, which Akairya ignored.

The group soon reached Seratea City's main entrance, which was marked by two intricately sculpted statues of fish. One guard lounged against one of the statues, a pipe clenched between his teeth. He squinted at the two riders, Squirlox, and dragon suspiciously.

"Eh, what's this?" the guard asked gruffly. "A dragon! He aint black, so I am going to assume he aint going to try and destroy the city. Still, what you all want?" He puffed on his pipe while Killian reached into one of his saddlebags and took out a sealed roll of parchment. The seal was a wax replica of the High King's symbol. The guard's eyes took note of it and nodded without reaching for the roll.

"Eh, alright. I see kingly Elric's sign. That's all I need." He waved them on. As Draykor strode past him, he took out his pipe and waved it threateningly at the dragon. "Mind you don't break anything!" Draykor simply blinked at him before following the horses into the city.

"He didn't even read the king's letter!" Akairya said in astonishment as the horses followed a wide cobbled road that cut straight through the city. While Seratea was quite large and sprawled along the coast, it was strictly organized; each street was straight and no building was placed out of the square block system that made up the entire settlement. They passed inns and shops that sat facing the main road, and behind them were the private homes of citizens.

"The people here aren't particularly concerned about visitors. Keep close to me while we are here; rules aren't exactly followed, and with you being a...well..." Killian trailed off and looked uncomfortable.

"A half breed?" Akairya finished for him as a group of fishermen passed them and leered darkly at Draykor, who met their gazes indifferently.

"Um, well, yes." Killian shifted in his saddle and looked at her apologetically. "Elves aren't seen in this city often, and any half breeds are only given jobs no one else wants. The lifestyle here is quite...well, cold."

Akairya shrugged and watched as more knots of people passed by and stared at Draykor. No one, however, seemed to particularly care that there was a dragon in the city. She guessed that dragons were a fairly common occurrence, since this was the closest city to Drakynold.

"The guard didn't seem to care about Dray, either," she mentioned. Jaxei chittered before clambering onto Akairya's shoulder and leaping onto Draykor's back. The Squirlox nimbly darted to the top of Draykor's head, where she sat behind his foremost spike and looked regally out to the city.

"Young dragons who are exploring the lands outside of their home country generally come here first, before dragons were afflicted by the blight." Killian replied, confirming Akairya's suspicion. "Although I'm surprised he didn't question Dray's colour. There has been no mention of a golden dragon ever existing before Dray."

An infuriated yell echoed down the street. A plump woman stood outside the first alchemy shop Akairya had seen in the city so far, her hands on her hips and her frizzy blonde hair sticking up in all directions. She screamed angrily again and kicked a cauldron that had been knocked on its side, its spilled purple contents slowly oozing over the cobbles of the street. By the time the horses reached the shop, the concoction had hardened and darkened to a wine red.

"This is just perfect!" The woman growled. Akairya and Killian reined in the horses as a small boy darted out from behind the cauldron and fled into the blocks of homes behind the shop.

"Come back here, you useless bit of human flesh!" The woman roared. She made to give chase, but slipped on the solidified contents of the cauldron and landed on her hip. She cursed loudly and stayed there, stringing together harsh words that made Akairya wince. Killian, who was fighting valiantly to hold in his amusement, swung off Tridon and held a hand out to the woman. She took it and pulled herself back to her feet, her expression thunderous.

"Thank you, rare kind man. Now please excuse me, I have a young boy to murder."

Killian caught the woman's arm before she walked two steps. She bared her teeth and looked at Killian with such poison, Akairya was impressed he didn't quail. Instead he raised a brow and motioned to the mess on the ground, which was suddenly steaming.

"Why don't we help you clean up first?"

The woman made a noise in her throat and opened her mouth to speak, but then caught sight of Draykor and Jaxei.

"Is that a Squirlox?" she breathed. Her eyes shone as she stepped towards the dragon. Jaxei twitched her ears and twittered from atop Draykor's head, her large eyes on the woman as she came closer. Akairya moved towards her dragon and lifted an arm. Jaxei leaped from Draykor's head and onto Akairya's shoulder, her brown eyes still on the woman.

"Yes, this is Jaxei."

"M-may I *touch* her?" the woman whispered. Her hair grew even frizzier in her sudden reverence. Killian hid a smile behind his hand, silver eyes twinkling.

"If she lets you," Akairya replied, somewhat bewildered. She jumped as the cobbles underneath the steaming potion cracked. The woman ignored it and stretched a shaking hand towards Jaxei. The Squirlox met her fingers with her nose, ears perked. With a sudden motion, the woman placed her hand on Jaxei's shoulder and pulled away with a clump of hair. Jaxei yelped and snarled in surprise. Akairya gasped, but before she could move away the Squirlox lifted a tiny paw and smacked it on Akairya's shoulder.

A small fragment of cobble floated from the ground and pelted towards the woman, who laughed and ducked before it could make contact. Jaxei hissed. Draykor growled deep in his throat, and the Squirlox flattened her ears before curling herself into Akairya's hood.

"Sorry, I couldn't resist," the woman said happily as she examined the small clump of hair in her hand. "It's not often an alchemist can get their hands on some Squirlox fur. It has wonderful properties."

"It still wasn't very kind. I don't know if you have noticed, but she is currently injured. Hence the bandages," Akairya glared at the woman. Killian stepped to her side and squeezed her shoulder.

"Don't be so angry, Kairi. The woman is an alchemist. Their craft comes first, no matter who gets hurt," he told her. He glanced at the alchemist, who was carefully placing Jaxei's hair into a tiny bottle. "What's your name, anyway?"

"Mandolina E. Thrafter, or Mandy, if I like you enough."

Killian stared at her, looked at the sign above her shop, then laughed. "I should have guessed."

Confused, Akairya squinted at the sign. It was a simple wooden square with the initials M.E.T entwined in a nest of vines, thorns, and snakes, with a cauldron perched precariously on the topmost vine, its carved contents beginning to spill.

"Heard of me, have you?" Mandolina asked as she pulled on some gloves and dug out a flat steel tool out of a pouch on her hip. She bent to the solidified concoction and began to scrape it off the cobbles.

"You are pretty infamous among Kalisor's alchemists," Killian replied, smiling a little. Mandolina gave a feral grin as she worked, and Akairya couldn't help but think of the woman as a wild creature, with her messy hair and animal-like smirk.

"I should think so, considering I'm responsible for blowing up the main shop of the city. Damn Squirlox hair and dragon blood does *not* mix. I'll be sure not to repeat that mistake." She glanced speculatively at the bottle of Jaxei's hair in her pouch.

"Didn't you refine the current fatigue fighting potion? That stuff works almost too well – I drank a half-dose once and was wide awake for two days and a night."

"Yes, although the damned recipe has fallen into the hands of some of the most prominent alchemists, so I barely make any money from it. My royalty percentage is meager, to say the least."

Someone cleared their throat near the door of Mandolina's shop, and Killian, Akairya, and the alchemist turned. The small boy from before had returned, and he stood as if ready to take flight at the smallest hint of anger from the woman. Mandolina huffed and returned to scraping the solidified potion off the broken cobbles.

"Hello, Irk. Could you go inside and get my chalk, please? I need to fix these cobbles."

The boy bobbed his head and slipped inside the shop, only to return a few seconds later clutching a thick piece of gray chalk. Mandolina swept the now crumbled potion into the cauldron, pushed it upright, and took the chalk from the boy. She then bent to the broken cobbles and drew a few symbols around the area. Akairya craned her head to look, but couldn't decipher the symbols at all.

When she was done drawing, Mandolina placed her hands on the centermost cobble and closed her eyes. After a few seconds the symbols glowed a faint green and dissipated as the stones roughly merged together. When Mandolina stepped away, the cobbles were relatively fixed, although one could still discern where they had been previously broken.

"H-how did you do that?" Akairya stammered, surprised. Killian studied the cobbles curiously and answered her as he ran a finger down a remaining fracture.

"Alchemists, while mostly known for their potions, also devote time to studying the elements and how they interact with the world. They use Elvish symbols to draw some elemental power, although doing so is mentally taxing and slowly kills them if they are not born with the innate ability to wield elemental power. Mandolina probably lost a few months of her life by fixing these cobbles."

Mandolina shrugged as she motioned the boy back into the shop. "If I had left them broken, the guards would have fined me money I don't have."

"I still don't fully understand how the cobbles were repaired," Akairya said as she walked slowly around the cobbles, looking for any sign of the chalk symbols the alchemist had drawn.

"Mandolina-"

"Mandy, please. You two seem likeable. I hate my full name," the woman interrupted Killian pleasantly.

"Okay. *Mandy* simply drew the symbols for Earth and channeled her life force into the symbols and, correct me if I'm wrong, asked the element to repair the stone."

"That's it in very basic, almost insultingly ignorant, terms," Mandy chuckled. "I'll forgive you, however. Alchemy is for life – I've been studying it for nearly thirty years and can barely concentrate enough to fix a few measly rocks! Potion making, while less life-threatening, is also very complex. I won't go into any detail, I can see this young lady's eyes glazing over already."

"What? No! I-"

"It's quite alright, elf. Or girl. I don't know. You're both, so it's slightly confusing for me. Do you care if I call you elf?"

"Uh, either works…" Akairya replied, slightly thrown. She had no idea how to take this alchemist. Draykor, who had been sniffing the repaired cobbles, snorted. She shot him a look before glancing at the darkening sky.

"We should probably find an inn before it gets dark, Killian. I'm starving."

"Oh, I didn't tell you? We won't be staying in an inn, we'll be going up to the Duke of Seratea's estate. You are a Rider, after all. The estate is the only place where a dragon and their rider can get accommodations."

"I was going to ask about that," Mandy said. "How'd you become a Rider? I have never heard of you, and don't you need to be some stuck up hero to be gifted an egg? And what elements do you and your handsome young dragon have power over? I don't think I've ever heard of a gold dragon."

"It's…a long story," Akairya replied. She patted Draykor on the shoulder when he came to stand beside her. "We have power over all of the elements, although they are proving to be slippery to control."

Mandy gaped at them. "*All?*"

"My reaction was quite similar," Killian commented drily. Akairya shifted uncomfortably as Mandy continued to stare at her. The alchemist shook herself before pertly brushing imaginary crumbs off the front of her dress.

"That is quite intriguing. I won't keep you any longer, but please come by before you leave the city. I would love the opportunity to ask you more questions. Purely from a scholarly point of view, of course." Her eyes glittered with contained excitement. "Thank you for the Squirlox hair, as well. Seems like our chance meeting was purely beneficial for me!" She then swept into her shop and firmly closed the door.

Taken aback from the abrupt dismissal, Akairya and Killian swung back up onto their horses.

"She…was an interesting person," Akairya commented lightly as Fedana followed Tridon down the main street, which was nearly empty due to it being dinnertime.

"She most definitely is. Brilliant alchemist, albeit a little rough around the edges," Killian replied.

The sun, which was almost completely set, gave off a strong orange light that burnt away the remaining fog that curled around the buildings of the city. Akairya could just hear the familiar rush of the ocean and the pitched screeches of seagulls as they flocked around discarded pieces of fish, and she breathed in the damp sea air with a faint smile. While Seratea was more grim than her destroyed city, the fact that it was settled against the ocean put her at ease.

Killian guided Tridon down a street that branched off the main road. "The Duke's estate is a little out of the city, at the end of this road. The Duke and his Lady are...unique, so be prepared."

Akairya scratched Fedana on her withers and smiled. "I have seen a lot of unique things lately, I think I'll manage fine."

Chapter Eighteen

They followed the road through numerous blocks of residences, most of which were painted dull ivory and faded blue. Countless skinny dogs prowled the streets, and the dying sun created more shadow than light as the company made their way through the city. Grubby children played near their respective homes, but most of the citizens were inside enjoying their evening meal. Akairya's stomach growled when she caught the scent of roasting meat, and she realized they hadn't eaten since midday.

The sun was nearly set when they left the bulk of the city and turned onto a wide road, the rough cobbles of Seratea's streets replaced by smooth pale stone. A guard simply nodded at them as they rode past, his attention on a small piece of wood he was carving.

The horses' hooves echoed on the stone as they walked west, following the curves of the road which eventually led them to a sprawling estate that boasted an elegant manor. The large home had arched windows and broad oaken doors that complimented the rich beige walls. A massive sculpture of a fisherman with a haughty expression stood near the tall ivory gates, his right arm holding a fat fish aloft. Two guards stood at the gates, their eyes on the approaching company. Akairya immediately sensed a difference in these guards; they stood alert, and moved to block the company from coming closer.

"Halt. Who are you?" the taller of the guards demanded, his sharp eyes roaming over Draykor and flitting back and forth between Killian and Akairya.

"Killian Theodin of the King's Army and Lady Rider Kairi Unnamed." Killian glanced at Akairya. "I have to call you Unnamed, since that is the custom when introducing anyone without a known family name." Akairya shrugged, unperturbed. The guards studied their garb, their glances taking in the king's clasp that closed Killian's cloak.

"The Duke of Seratea is at sea for the remainder of the season, so only Lady Calipsi is here to greet you," one said. The second guard strode to the elegantly crafted gates and soon had them open, his face expressionless as his comrade led the company into the estate.

A pair of grooms appeared and motioned for Killian and Akairya to dismount. When they did so, the men led their horses towards a large stable located slightly behind the manor. Jaxei, who had been fast asleep in Akairya's hood, awoke and chittered curiously as she studied her new surroundings. Draykor stood near his Rider, violet eyes on the guard. The man closed the gates without returning the dragon's gaze.

"Do we just go to the front d-" Akairya was interrupted by the opening of the huge entrance doors, revealing a tall woman with a cascade of black hair. Shrewd blue eyes topped with arched eyebrows met Akairya's, and the elf girl couldn't help but stare at the woman's cold beauty.

The woman stepped lightly out of the threshold and walked with graceful steps to where the company stood, the draping skirts of her navy gown rustling with her movements. A thin silver circlet with a small pearl teardrop adorned her head, and a delicate necklace that carried a tiny golden shell rested on her bosom. Killian bent at the waist and dipped his chin, his golden hair richly illuminated by the last rays of the sinking sun. With his sharp, handsome features, he looked like a nobleman come to court his Lady, not a general accompanying a Rider.

"Greetings to you, Lady Calipsi. You are looking as lovely as ever."

The Lady smiled demurely and gave Killian a small curtsy. "Always wonderful to see the king's favorite general. To what do I owe the pleasure?" Her sharp eyes flicked to Akairya, cool curiosity clear in their azure depths.

"Lady Calipsi, this is Kairi, Alkairyn's newest Rider. She has been bonded to this dragon, named Draykor, by means none of us yet understand. We are currently journeying to Drakynold, and would humbly appreciate the pleasure of spending the night here, before we take flight to the dragon country in the morning."

"Ah, yes. King Elric sent a falcon ahead of you. It has been such a busy week, I completely forgot you were coming."

Akairya doubted the Lady had truly forgotten; her eyes were too shrewd to give off the impression of poor memory.

"Why don't you come in; there's a dragon's room in the back of the manor. Unfortunately, it's the only area of the building where Draykor can fit. It's comfortable enough for all of us to visit, however."

Without waiting for a reply, Calipsi turned on her heel and swept back up the stone steps and into the manor. A harried looking butler came hurrying out a few seconds later, and he motioned for them to follow him.

He led them around the sprawling manor to the back, where there was a dome shaped addition to the building. It was large enough that three Draykor's could have easily fit inside, although it was no taller than the peaked roof of the topmost floor of the manor. The butler strode straight for the massive doors of the dome and pulled a lever. With a tremble and a groan, the doors swung open. The butler bowed the company in, then shut the doors behind them.

It was richly decorated inside, with plush red carpet and beige stone walls adorned with intricate paintings and flickering sconces. A heavy brown curtain near the back hid something from view, and a deep bowl was carved into the floor in the center of the dome. Downy blankets were piled in the depression, and Akairya recognized it as a dragon bed. The Rider sleeping quarters in Kalisor had a handful of such beds.

Lady Calipsi was there to meet them. She sat at the single table, which was long enough to accommodate ten people. Cushioned chairs surrounded the table, and an array of dishes sat steaming among flickering candles and glasses of deep red wine.

"Your bed is behind that curtain," Calipsi told Akairya as she and Killian settled at the table. Jaxei jumped out of Akairya's hood and scampered to

Draykor, who was snuffling at the dragon bed. "I thought we could dine here, so your dragon isn't excluded."

"Thank you, that is gracious of you," Akairya replied. She was astounded that food was already prepared for them; they had only just arrived. Roasted fish, baked potatoes, steamed shrimp, and a variety of cheeses and vegetables were set out. Akairya's stomach growled in response to the delicious fragrances that wafted from the food.

"Please, dig in. I was just about to sit down for dinner before you arrived, and luckily the kitchens are in the next room. Setting the food here was no issue."

Killian and Akairya needed no further encouragement; they happily tucked into the meal. Another butler strode in through the only door with a large plate piled high with fish and a massive platter of raw meat. He set the dishes near the dragon bed and bowed to the room before exiting. Jaxei bounded to the fish and began wolfing it down while Draykor settled on his haunches and began to eat the meat.

Over the course of the meal Akairya gave Lady Calipsi a brief summary of herself. The Lady paled at the description of Yaeloa's demise, and shook her head with awe when Akairya told her how she found Draykor. She wept silently when Theandi's death was mentioned, and wiped her eyes delicately with her napkin.

"The princess was a soul full of life and kindness; she visited me a handful of times over the years. She really livened up the place, and my husband doted on her. May she forever rest in peace."

Akairya fought back a sudden rush of tears. She missed her friend dearly, and the ache only added to the melancholy she had been victim to since Yokar. Calipsi folded her napkin and placed it beside her empty plate, her blue eyes calculating as they swept over Akairya's face.

"You surely look the part you are meant to play," she said briskly. "You have a beautifully royal face, one with strength and iron will. You will be a force to reckon with, one day. Has the king selected a suitable husband for you yet?"

Akairya choked on her wine, taken aback. Killian froze and frowned at Calipsi.

"Wh-what do you mean?"

"Well, now that you are a Rider, you only answer to the royal family. You and I are on the same step of the hierarchy. However, you have the power to shift the country's fate into one that is less bleak than it currently is. Since you have no family that you know of, it is up to the king to approve your marriage, and as such, you will need someone who can match you both socially and powerfully. Maybe he'll engage you to one of the other Riders..." Calipsi trailed off, her face thoughtful. Akairya stared at her in horror.

"Why does it matter? I don't need to marry anyone!"

Calipsi laughed prettily and took a small sip of her wine. "Oh, my dear. I'm not saying you'll be married tomorrow! You probably won't even be married until after this blight is dealt with. Unless, of course, the king deems it necessary. I just like to think about this sort of thing, I'm a bit of a romantic."

Akairya had to hold back her opinion that Calipsi sounded anything but romantic. Killian's face had darkened, and he glared at the piece of fish he had been eating.

221

"I would like to wash off the journey's grime, Lady Calipsi. Would you be bothered if I excused myself?"

"None at all!" The lady replied, her eyes glittering. "I'll ring a butler in, he can help you get a bath prepared." She plucked a small bell off the table and rang it, its notes pure and impossibly loud. "Alchemist invention, such a handy little thing. The whole manor can hear when I ring, no matter where I am. I think they used some of the Air element when they created it."

The first butler from before came in.

"Kindly escort Killian to where he is to bathe and help him draw the water, please. Also, prepare a bath for the lovely Kairi. I'm sure she is absolutely craving cleanliness after being covered in grime for so long." The butler bowed, waited for Killian to stand, and led the way out of the dome.

"I would have loved to meet you at the last royal ball the king organized, but with my husband still at sea, I declined my invitation. I'm sure you bewitched many noblemen by the end of the night, hmm?" Calipsi asked conversationally.

"I was nearly assassinated," Akairya replied shortly. Calipsi winced.

"Ah, yes. The nobility are a flighty bunch."

Unsure of what to say to that, Akairya stayed silent.

Before long, a few maids arrived with steaming buckets of water. They dumped the water into a bronze tub that stood near the curtained bed and set aside a few plush towels before curtsying and quitting the dome. Once they left, Calipsi rose.

"Well, it was lovely to meet you. I shall leave you to bathe. I'm quite exhausted, I think I'll turn in for the night. If you require anything, simply ring this bell," she gestured at the small bell she had rung, "and help will come immediately. I look forward to seeing you in the morning."

She practically floated out of the dome.

Still slightly shaken by the topic of marriage, Akairya wandered over to the tub. The water gave off a flowery fragrance that enticed her, and she dipped her fingers in to check the temperature.

Dray, once the water cools a bit I'm going to bathe. Would you mind turning around so I could have some privacy?

I think I may head back to the city docks; the meat they gave me was delicious, but not enough to satisfy my hunger. I think I'd like some fish.

Akairya strode to the massive doors that led to the outside and examined the lever that was situated beside them. She pulled it experimentally and grunted in satisfaction when the doors opened. Draykor padded out of the dome, snuffled her hair as he passed, and soon took flight towards the city.

A few moments later she was blissfully soaking in the tub, the grime on her skin rinsing off and darkening the perfumed water. She sighed and closed her eyes, enjoying the delicious feeling of the heat loosening her tight muscles and relieving her aches. Jaxei was curled on the bed, which Akairya had revealed after drawing back the heavy curtain. She was looking forward to sinking among the soft blankets and plump pillows, and she felt quite at peace for the first time in a while.

Time dripped by as she soaked in the water, her eyes half closed. *How am I going to get the energy to get out?* She mused sleepily to herself. She lifted a hand to her burgundy hair and winced at the knots she felt. Sighing, she slipped her head under the water and scrubbed furiously. When she figured she was as clean as she was going to get, she stepped out of the tub reluctantly.

A brush sat near the pile of towels, and Akairya gratefully dried off and picked it up. She perched on the edge of the bed and began to slowly untangle her heavy mass of hair.

By the time she had the knots brushed out, her hair was mostly dry. She was just about to slip into the nightgown the maids had left when a rush of shock and humiliation bombarded her, causing her to gasp and stagger. Jaxei leaped up and growled, looking for whatever had harmed Akairya. The threat, however, was not in the room with them – it was wherever Draykor was.

Dray, what's going on? Akairya asked, mentally reaching out for her dragon. Another flood of emotions hit her, and this time anger made an appearance as well. She felt along her connection with Draykor and tried to see into his consciousness enough to get a glimpse of his surroundings, something she had been taught by Oren back in Kalisor. She caught a blurry image of a slimy dock lit by a single lantern before Draykor shut her out.

Do not come here – I can take care of myself. Please, stay at the manor. Draykor practically snarled in her mind before closing off from her completely. Shaken, Akairya simply stood, wheeling from the sudden absence of Draykor's presence. After a few seconds she sprang into action, dressed in the blouse and riding pants she had packed, and headed to the doors mere minutes after the emotions had first assailed her.

Jaxei trotted up to her, large eyes questioning.

"Sorry Jaxei, you have to stay here. I'm not sure what has happened to Dray, and I don't want you getting hurt more than you already are." Akairya gave her a pat before opening the doors and slipping out into the night.

The same two guards from before still stood vigil at the gates, their eyes glittering in the moonlight as she approached.

"Going so soon?" one asked, a smirk playing on his lips as he pointedly stared at the angular tips of her ears, which were peeking slightly out from under her mass of hair.

"I am meeting my dragon – we go for nightly flights, simply to practice some battle maneuvers." She replied impatiently. The guard raised an eyebrow.

"Why didn't you just go with him when he first flew off?"

"He wanted to eat first."

"Isn't it unhealthy, flying after a meal? Don't want your dragon to get any cr-"

"Look, I'd really appreciate it if you would just let me out. I won't be gone long." Akairya snapped. The second guard coughed in amusement before opening the gates just enough for her to slip through. He didn't move when she stepped out, and she winced as she slightly brushed against his armored chest. He grinned down at her, a grin she didn't return. Instead she shot him a venomous look before striding down the road.

"Don't go too far into the city, *milady*. Wouldn't want you to meet some…interesting people," the first guard called out. She clenched her teeth and ignored him.

When she was far enough away that she was sure the guards couldn't see her in the dark, she picked up a run that grew more desperate as her imagination took off on her. Did someone shoot him out of the sky? Did a Shadow dragon appear? Roraks? The possibilities were endless, and she raced down the smooth stone road, her breath ragged in her throat.

There was no guard standing at the narrow entrance into Seratea, so she met no resistance as she dashed into the organized cluster of buildings. Most of the houses along the street were still lit, but Akairya paid them no notice. There was a stitch in her side and her chest burned with exhaustion, but she pushed on. A dog barked at her as she passed, and a few men lounging outside one of the city's many taverns hooted after her.

She soon found herself on the main road near Mandolina's shop. Remembering that the main entrance to Seratea was to her right, she turned left towards the docks. As the shops and inns thinned out and became grimy warehouses, she slowed down to a quick walk, her eyes desperately searching for a dragon shape in the surrounding shadows.

She quickly came across the city's docks. Boats were clustered in haphazard groups alongside the wooden stretches, ships anchored a little down from where Akairya stood. She vaguely remembered a small fishing boat tied to the dock in the image from Draykor's mind, but nothing else except the single lantern. She studied the docks in front of her and noted that most of them boasted numerous lanterns, so she began to walk in the opposite direction of the ships.

She saw no sign of Draykor as she walked, and her heart clenched. Where *was* he?

A large warehouse loomed ahead, and a narrow strip of a dock with a single boat bordered its flank. Something large lay hunched at the base of the dock, and when it moved the dim light of the single lantern glinted off it.

"Dray!" Akairya gasped as she recognized her dragon. She dashed to his side and fell to her knees, furious tears welling in her eyes.

Her beloved dragon was tangled in a net made of thin steel wire, his wings cruelly bent against his body. He stared at her with eyes full of anger and disbelief. Their connection burst open once again, and Akairya winced at the sudden fear that shivered inside it.

I told you not to come! You haven't been able to wield the elements, you won't be able to protect yourself! I'm unable to use our power as well, I won't be any help!

I brought my sword, I'm not completely helpless. Oh Dray, what happened to you?

Never mind about me, go! Please! I'll figure this out alone.

Don't be ridicu-

She was cut off by a low whistle, its eerie tone sending chills up her spine. Before she could turn around, two pairs of hands cruelly grabbed each of her wrists.

"Ah, here she is. The lovely half-blood Rider." The man who held her rasped, his dull brown eyes raking Akairya's body. She shuddered from his perusal. "I think we should have fun with ya. Yar dragon is a little...tangled, so things will be much easier." He was a thick-set man, with mangy black hair that hung in greasy ropes to his shoulders.

Four other men who stood nearby were just as dirty, yet not nearly as broad. They all had the same cruel expressions in their eyes, and they were all staring hungrily at Akairya.

Fear clogged her throat as the man who had spoken roughly tied her wrists together. She had never learned how to protect herself from such men; citizens of Yaeloa ranged from rich to poor, but none she had known were inclined to rape or murder. Not like these five.

Once her wrists were secured, the man yanked her against his chest and rubbed his bearded cheek against hers. The rough hair grated against her skin, and she bit back a sob as the men snickered. Draykor thrashed underneath the netting, furious.

Fight! Don't let them touch you!

"Which one of us should play first, gentlemen?" the thick man asked. He pushed her away so she stood in the center of the group, her violet eyes shining with tears.

"Let's see...who had the first serving with the last girl?"

One of the men raised a hand, a leer on his thin face. The broad man nodded.

"Yar last, then. Who was after him?"

Akairya trembled as they figured out who would get her first, her eyes locked on Draykor's. As she sunk herself into his soulful gaze, she felt a sudden wave of shame. She was a Dragon Rider, bonded to one of the wisest species of the world. She shouldn't cower from such lowlifes!

Her fear, while still very much there, was joined by a sudden flame of anger. How *dare* they.

The men had finally reached a decision; the thick-set man had 'enjoyed' the last girl after everyone else, so it was his turn to be first. His muddy eyes once again swept up and down Akairya, and she gritted her teeth. When he grabbed for her, she leaped forward and knocked him soundly in the chin with her head.

The man howled in pain, and she fought a bout of dizziness as she bolted towards Draykor. Maybe she could slip off the chunk of steel wire around his muzzle with her teeth, then he could bite off the rope around her wrists...

Before she could reach her dragon, the man with the thin face cut her off and slapped her soundly across the face. She gasped and fell to the side, her shoulder hitting the stone of the dock hard. Draykor growled and thrashed against his bindings, desperate to free himself.

"Ya bloody whore! Got some fight in ya, hm? We'll just have to break ya like any feisty filly," the thin man said as he knelt beside her, his fingers caressing the bright red hand print on Akairya's cheek. The heavier man strode forward, cruel anger hardening his eyes as he rubbed his sore chin with one hand and roughly pulled her to her feet with the other, his grip painful on her upper arm. She bit her lip to stop from crying out, and shuddered as he yanked her against his foul smelling body with a snarl.

"All right, ya bitch. Time to break ya."

He jerked his hand and tore the sleeve of her blouse, a leer stretching his ugly face into one of a predator.

When her blouse ripped, her fear tore away and left behind a deep, cold fury that churned in the very marrow of her bones.

How *dare* they.

How dare they net her dragon like a dumb beast destined for slaughter? How dare they lay their filthy hands on her, breathe their wretched breaths on her skin, and rip the blouse someone had kindly given to her?

Enraged, Akairya's eyes burned a bright violet that shone with a primal, dangerous power. Her entire body trembled and was suddenly enveloped in a translucent purple light that was so subtle, so vague, that the men surrounding her barely noticed. But they did notice, and a sudden inexplicable terror gripped them as Akairya bared her teeth in a fierce smile and lifted her hands, the rope that had held her wrists frayed by the power. The heavy man let her blouse go and stumbled away, his greasy hair covering his face as he attempted to escape, his comrades also scattering, fighting to get away from the danger they couldn't comprehend.

Akairya's eyes glowed as they caught sight of the Spirit element encompassing each man in thin strands, the colour varying according to the person. The broad man in particular boasted strands that were sickly and disgustingly close to the flat black of the Shadow, the little purple left drowning in corruption. Without thinking, Akairya reached out with her power and trapped all five of the men by their very essences.

Two of the essences, the heavy set man's and the thin faced man's, felt slimy and diseased, and holding them with her own spirituality made Akairya feel nauseated. She made a ripping motion with her hands and the two men went limp, their lives severed from their bodies. The three remaining lives that she held, quite literally, in her hands were nowhere near as corrupted, and she let them go with a weary sigh. With their release went Akairya's hold on the Spirit element, but it didn't go far; it simply calmed and went to sleep inside her, like a guard dog whose job was complete.

She stumbled towards her dragon as the three men ran and left behind their dead. She fell heavily to her knees and worked at the wire that was tangled around Draykor.

Not killing all of them was…wise. Perhaps foolish, but it proves you aren't as terrible as they.

Did you feel what I did? While they were far from good, their souls weren't wholly evil like their comrades. It was an easy decision, especially after feeling the sickness that the two had in their souls.

I felt it. Draykor looked thoughtfully at the corpses. *The element has stayed with us, which is unlike the others. I wonder what that means?*

Akairya closed her eyes and felt the touch of the powerful element. It slumbered on. When she reopened her eyes, her gaze fell on her ripped blouse and she shuddered.

I feel defiled. I didn't know what to do, Dray. Not until the Spirit element awoke inside me. I was helpless, like you said.

Her dragon snorted. *You head butted the one right in the chin and nearly knocked the man out. I don't think that's helpless.*

Akairya managed to release Draykor from his bonds. He stood from the dock and shook himself before unfurling his wings with a great sigh.

It's late, we should be getting back.

Akairya agreed and hopped nimbly onto his bare back, the saddle stowed away in the dome on the manor.

They reached the estate in mere moments, and a stricken Killian ran to greet them.

"*There* you are! I came to discuss tomorrow's plans with you and you were gone, and the guards told me you had foolishly left on your own *without* Dray and I thought the very worst and-" he cut off as Akairya slipped off her dragon, his gray eyes locked on her torn and stained shirt.

"It's nothing, Killian. I-" she stopped when he raised a hand, his eyes now on her bruising cheek.

"What happened."

She opened her mouth, closed it, opened it again, and then gave up. *Dray, can you tell him please? I...can't.*

Shame burned in her chest as Draykor told Killian how he had been netted, how Akairya had come rushing to help him, and how she had nearly been raped by the five men who had captured him. Killian's eyes had gone as hard as steel, the colour drained from his face.

Then the Spirit element awoke inside her, and she...well, she killed two of them and left the rest.

"You didn't kill all five?" Killian said in amazement. Akairya shook her head.

"No. You didn't feel their essences, Killian. They didn't deserve death. They deserve punishment, but not death." She took a deep breath and felt a sudden welling of tears. "I was so scared."

Killian's eyes softened. He came forward and took her in his arms, his chin resting on the top of her head. She trembled and let the tears come, barely noticing Draykor walk away.

They stood like that for a long time, the moon slowly making its way down the dark sky that gradually took on a hint of dawn. Akairya pulled away first and took one of Killian's hands, his palms rough with calluses and his nails chipped and dirty from travel.

"Thank you, Killian," she whispered, shining violet eyes on his gray ones. "I mean it. I...don't really understand what I'm feeling, and I'm not sure what it means, but-" Killian dropped his eyes and pulled his hand from hers gently, his expression suddenly blank. Akairya looked at him questioningly.

"I am just a soldier, with no royal lineage or any sort of elemental strength. You are a Dragon Rider, the only one ever known to have the ability to wield all five of the elements. You also carry the name of the most powerful and influential woman in Alkairyn's history. I have no place in your life, other than as a guard," pain flamed in his eyes, but his jaw was set. "I will still protect you with my life, but that is all I can offer. I will not ask you to lower yourself to be with a man of my standing."

"Killian, no..." Akairya whispered, aghast.

"Don't, Kairi." His voice was ragged with emotion, and he turned and stalked towards the ivory gates of the estate.

CHAPTER NINETEEN

Akairya watched him leave through the gates, her heart heavy. She clenched her hands and looked at the ground, then kicked the nearest tuft of grass in frustration.

"It's for the absolute best, dear," Calipsi's smooth voice came from the manor's front doors. Akairya glanced up and found herself glaring at the woman.

"It's your fault he is being so thick headed. You're the one who talked about what type of marriage I should have. I don't give a shit about bloodlines and social standing. All I care about is the fact that I care about him."

"I understand, Kairi. However, this isn't all about you. Your marriage could easily influence Alkairyn's future, blight or no blight. There is no princess, remember."

Akairya stared at Lady Calipsi, shocked. "No Rider has ruled. Ever."

"Times can change."

Akairya shook her head and started towards the dome. She was suddenly bone-crushingly weary, and needed sleep. Calipsi didn't follow her.

Draykor was already curled in the dragon bed, but his eyes were open as she closed the doors and made her way to her large bed. Jaxei greeted her with a sleepy chitter before curling into a tighter ball at the foot of the bed. After Akairya changed into a soft cotton nightgown, she sunk into the downy blankets and sighed. Frustration, sorrow, fear, confusion, and many other emotions fought inside her as she closed her eyes. So much was happening to her, and she felt like she was standing on the edge of a ship's plank, looking down into angrily frothed waters full of hungry sea monsters. She had seen so much death and experienced so much trauma in such a short period of time, she didn't know how she was still sane.

It's because you are spiritually strong, Akairya, Draykor commented sleepily in response to her mind's turmoil. *You are no average woman.*

Dray? Why can't you use the elements?

Her dragon sighed. *My hold on the elements seem more...abrupt. I haven't been able to use them just randomly. I used Spirit that once, during Theandi's funeral, and then Fire at Durndel... I'm not sure why I can't use them as easily as other dragons.*

Just another question we'll have to ask the Elders.

Yes. Now try and get some sleep.

Akairya tried to obey, but it took some time for her to fall into the caress of sleep. She kept replaying the moment of the two men's deaths, done by her hand, and her hand alone.

She woke late the next morning to a maid setting the table with an array of breakfast dishes. Sweet rolls glazed in creamed honey, fluffy eggs dusted with paprika and cheese, and thick slices of bacon were set down alongside a round jug filled to the brim with cold milk. Akairya slipped out of bed when the maid left and quickly changed into a fresh blouse and pants, her stomach eager for the food.

Lady Calipsi joined her when Akairya was half way through her meal. Akairya barely glanced at the her, still upset with the part she had played in Killian's decision.

"Young Killian has yet to return, according to my guards. Any idea what he could be doing?" Calipsi asked conversationally. Akairya shrugged.

Draykor stepped out of his bed, stretched, and plodded over to the table. He curled a few feet away from the women and allowed Jaxei, who had just finished devouring some bacon and milk, to scamper along his back. The Squirlox playfully leaped on his head, squealed, then dashed to the tip of his tail, where she spun and dashed back to his head, her wounds clearly no longer bothering her.

The door leading into the manor opened, and Killian strode in wearing the same clothes from the night before. They were covered in grease and blood, and his expression was hard.

"You are filthy, Killian. What in the world were you doing?" Lady Calipsi demanded, affronted. Her rosebud mouth was pursed in disapproval.

"Never mind the dirt, are you all right?" Akairya asked in concern. Killian nodded.

"I'm fine. Just had some business in the city. Thought I would let you two know that I've returned, and that I need some sleep before we head to the dragon country. Lady Calipsi, would you be willing to have us under your roof for one more night?"

"I don't mind at all. Just go clean up and get some rest."

Akairya stood as Killian left.

"Well, I think I may go see that alchemist we met yesterday, now that I have a full free day. What do you think, Dray?"

We did promise her some answers.

"Please be careful in the city – even in the daylight there are dangers," Calipsi warned. Akairya nodded and left the dome, Draykor following behind her with Jaxei still on his head.

There were two new guards at the gates, and they were perfectly civil to Akairya. The one even inclined his head in a subtle bow as she passed, something that threw her completely.

People are so confusing. One person will be completely rude to me while the next acts like I'm royalty, she said to Draykor.

It's simple, really. Some people are intelligent, while others aren't.

Akairya snorted.

The sun was strong when they reached Seratea, and not a single wisp of fog cloaked the streets. The sky was a soft blue, barely marred by clouds, and a gentle breeze that carried the strong scent of fish blew between the city's buildings. People bustled about, and the main street was crowded with hastily erected stalls. Freshly caught fish lay in gleaming piles, as well as tubs of salt and oil and other manner of sea cuisine. People glanced at Akairya and Draykor curiously as they passed, but no one openly gaped except children.

Mandolina's shop door was propped open by a cracked cauldron, and Akairya could clearly hear the alchemist raspily singing a rowdy tune. The small boy, Irk, was laboriously stirring the contents of another cauldron, but he stopped when he caught sight of Akairya and her companions.

"Hello. Could you please tell Mandolina that Kairi is here to see her?" Akairya asked him with a gentle smile. He nodded and darted through a curtain of beads. A few moments later he returned, followed by the alchemist. The woman's blonde hair was even frizzier than before, and she grinned when she saw Akairya.

"Oh, excellent! I'm glad you kept your word and paid little 'ol me a visit! I wasn't too sure if you would, not after what your young man did."

Akairya frowned. "What do you mean? Who did what?"

"Why, Killian took it upon himself to brutally punish three of the city's greasiest men. Two were found dead before that, but Killian didn't go on his rampage until nearly an hour after the bodies were discovered."

Akairya went cold. "Did he kill the three men?" *He better not have, I spared them for a reason.*

"Oh, no. He simply maimed them a little. Scared them so much, I doubt they'll ever hurt another soul again. Chopped off a hand each, apparently. One of the witnesses said Killian coldly told them that 'they won't be able to grope any innocent woman fully again, now that they lost a hand each.' I wish I had seen it," Mandolina's eyes went dreamy. "Nothing is more satisfying than watching a good man get angry enough to punish some terrible men. I wonder what set him off?"

Akairya bit her lip. *They didn't deserve death. They deserve punishment, but not death.* That's what she had said to him, and it looked like he had taken it upon himself to give the men their sentences. She recalled the cold fury in his gray eyes when Draykor had first told him what had happened, and heard his emotionally torn voice telling her how he would still protect her with his life, even though he didn't think it proper for the two of them to have any sort of intimacy.

"Any idea how he found them?" she asked the alchemist, who shook her head.

"No. He apparently showed up in the tavern they were holing up in, asked the bartender a few questions, and then cornered the three of them and proceeded to chop off their hands. One ran, got in a warehouse, but Killian still got him."

"The guards weren't angry?"

"You joking? They were betting on whether or not he'd catch the runaway. The guards here love a good show, plus the three men are some of the lowliest lowlifes here."

Yet they still had some good in them. I felt it when I held their spirits. Akairya commented internally to Draykor. The dragon dipped his head in agreement.

Some people follow paths they are forced on.

"Anyway, enough gossip. I have some questions for you! I'll bring out some coffee, since I doubt your dragon would appreciate being stuck out here alone. My shop is too humble to fit a dragon." Mandolina ducked back behind her curtain of beads.

The conversation the two had over numerous cups of coffee lasted until the sunlight grew darker and spilled onto Seratea like melted gold. The two women sat on spindly chairs that Irk had fetched for them, and Draykor sat nearby with Jaxei perched on his head. While the road was busy with citizens walking past and going about their daily duties, it was strangely relaxing to sit outside and talk with another woman. Akairya grew incredibly fond of Mandy very quickly, the alchemist's no nonsense attitude masked a very kind soul who was utterly devoted to her work. She asked many questions about Akairya's bond with Draykor, and was fascinated with the mystery behind the entire situation.

"You must tell me what the Elders say! Come straight here after you are done on the island. There is nothing like an intriguing mystery to solve."

"Okay, only if you promise to never yank out Jaxei's fur again."

The Squirlox sniffed from atop Draykor, her tail stiff as she stared at Mandy. The alchemist chuckled and shrugged.

"Fair trade. You have a deal.

"I should probably get back to brewing my latest batch of potions – I told the man who ordered them that they would be ready by tomorrow evening, and at this rate they most certainly won't be. Thank you for remembering me and coming to chat, it's been lovely." Mandy stood from her chair and stretched before walking towards the door to her shop. "Oh, and don't give Killian that much of a hard time. His trying to stay away from you is just him attempting to be a good person. Give him time."

Akairya smiled vaguely and waved goodbye as she started to walk down the street. Draykor stuck close to her shoulder, and nudged her gently when she sighed.

She's right. Don't wallow, act normal and give him time.

I will. This whole thing is just so…confusing and strange. I've never felt like this before, and I am just

*learning how to navigate these emotions. I also think
he is an absolute moron.*

A merchant's stall that sat right before the side
street that led towards Lady Calipsi's estate was
fronted by a plump, balding man in flowing blue
robes. As Akairya, Draykor, and Jaxei passed his stall,
he hurried forward with a broad grin and brandished
a bronze amulet.

"My Rider! Someone such as you, even with all
your power, will have many enemies! This amulet,
forged with tongues of dragon flame, will help protect
you on your journey-"

"Oh, give it a rest, merchant. She isn't interested
in your trinkets," Killian's impatient voice cut the
man off. Akairya looked behind her and saw Killian
striding over from the side street, his face no longer
pale from exhaustion. The merchant's face dropped,
and with a sigh he let the amulet slide back onto the
stall's cluttered table. Akairya noted his robes were
frayed, and that even with his plumpness his cheeks
were gaunt. Once a rich man, now fallen on hard
times.

"Actually, I am interested in something. Not the
amulet, but a pretty chain that could fit around a
neck roughly this size?" She showed the man with her
hands. His eyes brightened and he turned to study his
wares before plucking out a finely braided chain of
white gold inlaid with miniscule pearls. He held it
aloft so that the setting sun would glitter on the metal
and smiled hopefully at Akairya. Killian crossed his
arms and didn't say a word.

"Perfect! I think I should have enough…" she
rummaged in her leather purse she kept tucked away
on her hip, its contents given to her by Telectus and

Oren before she had left the capital. She took out two gold coins, their faces carved with the symbol of the king, and placed them on the table. The merchant's eyes widened and he blinked rapidly before scooping up the coins and bowing, one hand stretched out to give her the chain.

"Thank you, milady. This is more than enough. Thank you."

She returned his thanks with a big smile and took the chain from him. She looked at Jaxei, who was primly washing one of her small paws on Draykor's back.

"Jaxei, would you be willing to wear this? To symbolize our friendship?"

The Squirlox set down her paw and studied the chain with large eyes. She chittered quietly before leaping off Draykor and onto Akairya's shoulder. She rubbed her head on the elf girl's chin.

"I'll take that as a yes," Akairya chuckled before slipping the chain onto Jaxei. It took a second to slide it over the creature's large ears, but soon it was settled on her neck and shone prettily against her chestnut fur. Akairya shrugged at Killian before waving farewell to the merchant, who was still bowing, and walked down the street towards Calipsi's estate. Arms still crossed, Killian trailed after her and Draykor.

"I didn't mean to seem pushy. Merchants are vultures, though. Especially in Seratea."

"I know. The poor man needed something to brighten his day. I think Jaxei is happy with her gift, anyway." The Squirlox twittered in agreement. "I take it you will be ready to head to Drakynold in the morning?"

"Yes. First light. The flight will take all day, maybe some of the night if we hit bad weather." His face paled at the prospect. Draykor butted Killian's shoulder playfully.

I'll take it easy on you! You'll learn to love flying.

Killian frowned at the dragon, unimpressed. "I'm more comfortable on a horse. Flying is just…" he shuddered and didn't complete the sentence.

The evening passed calmly. Killian and Akairya dined on herb dusted fish and scalloped potatoes with Lady Calipsi, this time in the estate's proper dining room. Draykor had decided to hunt for his dinner himself, away from the city docks.

The dining room was extravagant. The walls were painted a pearly blue and were adorned with intricately sculpted jade fish that caught the flickering candlelight. The floor was covered in a plush ivory carpet, and the long table where everyone was seated was carved from rosewood. Two butlers stood stiffly by the door.

"I had the maids pack each of you some food for your flight, as I am aware your supplies are running low. Are your cloaks water resistant?" Calipsi inquired as she primly cut her fish and brought a tiny piece to her mouth.

"Yes. We have everything we need, thank you," Killian answered her. Akairya nodded in agreement.

"Excellent. It was lovely having you here for the past two days. It gets absolutely monotonous while my husband is away. Any distraction is welcome."

The rest of the dinner was spent in silence; Akairya had nothing she really wanted to say, and Killian fell into a deep brood that cast a dark cloud over the table. Calipsi ate her fish slowly and sipped at her wine often, blue eyes on Akairya, who was worried the Lady was going to bring up the topic of marriage again.

Thankfully, she did no such thing, and soon everyone bid each other goodnight and went their separate ways to their beds.

Akairya again found sleep difficult. Tomorrow she would finally meet the Elders, and finally learn what the other two Riders knew and refused to tell her. Worry weighed on her, and she took a deep breath. Surely they wouldn't be angry at her for becoming a Rider the way she had?

She also found herself hoping that whatever she was going to learn was going to help her wipe out the blight entirely. Not only to salvage her country, but to avenge Theandi's brutal murder. The Shadow needed to be defeated, but she had no idea how. She still had no control over most of her elements, and the one she did feel the closest to was the most confusing of all.

The two deaths she had been responsible for sat on her mind as well. While they had deserved death, killing men bothered her a whole lot more than killing creatures in the wild for food. She had slain Roraks before too, but they were also different. While completely evil, the men had still been human.

Akairya took a long time to fall asleep, her mind troubled.

First light came too quickly, and Akairya's limbs were heavy with exhaustion as she rolled out of bed and fell into a heap by Draykor's feet. Her dragon had spent the last ten minutes trying to wake her, and his violet eyes were impatient as he used his nose to prod her onto her feet.

Hurry! We must be off at once if we want to get to Drakynold before dark. My saddle is beside my bed, Calipsi had it polished while we were out yesterday.

Akairya groggily dressed and made sure her sword was properly on her hip and her cloak properly tied before she stumbled to where the saddle was. She yawned as she picked it up and slung it near the base of Draykor's neck, and yawned again as she clumsily worked the buckles. She frowned jealously at Jaxei, who was still curled in a ball on the bed, sound asleep.

Killian strode in, fully dressed and ready, his saddle bags in one hand. He took in the sleeping Squirlox and Akairya's open saddle bag and chuckled.

"I see someone slept in."

She was sleeping so soundly, I felt bad and let her sleep for a little longer than we planned. Then trying to wake her up was a quest all on its own, Draykor informed him grumpily. Akairya shot him a look before stuffing her saddle bag and closing it. Jaxei blinked awake, stretched, then bounded straight to Draykor.

Calipsi swept in, followed by a maid carrying a tray of buttered bread and mugs of milk.

"I didn't order you a big breakfast because I figured you didn't have enough time, I hope you don't mind."

Akairya happily bit into her bread after thanking the maid, and gave her milk to Jaxei. Killian ate his in two bites, then raised an eyebrow at Akairya.

"Ready?"

"Yes."

After thanking Lady Calipsi for her hospitality and making sure their horses would be well taken care of while they were gone, the group traipsed through the estate's gates and turned west. After some time they came to a steep cliff that overlooked the ocean, its waters calm in the morning light. The sky, streaked with reds and oranges of sunrise, held a few small clouds, but nothing that threatened bad weather.

Akairya double-checked her dragon's saddle, unfolded an extra leather piece from underneath the seat that lengthened it enough for two riders, then nimbly leaped up. Jaxei was curled in the cloak of her hood, and Akairya hoped that Draykor wouldn't need to spin upside down for any reason during the flight.

After securing her legs and waist with the saddle's straps, she looked expectantly down at Killian, whose cheeks had gone gray.

"Th-there are enough straps for me, right?" he mumbled as he stared at the saddle. Akairya giggled and nodded. He gulped before clumsily taking her outstretched hand and throwing himself into the saddle behind her. His hands trembled as he found the extra straps and buckled them around himself. When he was done, he poked Akairya softly on the shoulder.

"Could you...do you think...would you mind double checking my straps? I...just want to make sure I'm secure," he rushed out. Akairya held back a chuckle, looked behind her with a serious face, and scanned his straps as best she could from where she was sitting.

"Looks good to me."

You two ready? Draykor asked impatiently. He swung his head around and looked at them with one eye. Jaxei moved into a comfortable position inside Akairya's hood.

"I'm ready. Killian?"

He barely mumbled his affirmation before Draykor unfurled his wings and jumped off the cliff.

CHAPTER TWENTY

Killian gave a strangled yell as Draykor plummeted towards the water, his blurred golden reflection becoming larger and larger as he gained speed. Finally, when he was only a few feet away from the ocean's surface, he gave two great beats of his wings and levelled out. He huffed in amusement as he struck north towards the dragon island.

Akairya winced as Killian's grip around her waist became painful. She patted one of his hands.

"Killian, you can loosen your grip. Dray was just having some fun with you." Jaxei's claws had dug into the back of her neck as well when her dragon leaped off the cliff, and she glared at the back of Draykor's head as she rubbed the scratches. Killian reluctantly eased his grip and took a deep breath.

"Damn dragon. I hate heights. Hate them," he mumbled.

Sorry. I couldn't resist.

Next time, do that when I don't have a Squirlox in my hood and a terrified soldier behind me, Akairya admonished. Draykor dipped his head as he flew on, but Akairya could still sense his amusement.

There was a cool bite to the air as they flew over the ocean, and Akairya shivered. The first snow was probably only a few weeks away, and she did not want to have to fly back over the ocean during the upcoming storms. She wondered how long they

248

would stay on the island, and stressed over the upcoming introductions.

The sea stretched out ahead of them like a massive turquoise blanket dotted with whorls and brushed with foam. The sky gradually brightened into a pale blue unmarked by clouds. If it wasn't for the cool autumn breeze that occasionally buffeted the company, it would have felt like summer.

The morning passed uneventfully. Killian stayed quiet, but his hold around Akairya became more relaxed as he grew more comfortable astride Draykor. The dragon beat his metallic wings smoothly, the silver membranes glinting from the reflections of light that glanced off the surface of the sea. His golden scales were almost painful to look at, so Akairya found herself looking out across the ocean. She was looking towards the far east when she saw something of interest.

"Is that a storm cloud?" she wondered aloud. She felt Killian shift behind her as he looked where she pointed.

Far in the distance sat a mass of black cloud, the sky around it stained by its darkness. She couldn't see much detail, but something about it churned her stomach.

"That's not a storm cloud. That's Tilaner Isle," Killian told her quietly. Draykor stared at the cloud as well.

Don't look at it. There is no reason we need to bother ourselves with that place at the moment.

Akairya ignored his advice and kept her eyes locked on the mass of darkness until hours later, when it faded from view. One day she would likely have to go there to fight against the Shadow, and for the very first time she was purely afraid. Her anger over Theandi's death and the fall of Yaeloa wasn't enough to convince her that she needed to step foot on that poisoned island, and she trembled as she imagined getting lost among that darkness. She took a breath and felt for the Spirit element, which still slumbered on. It pulsed gently, as if welcoming her questioning touch. Comforted it wasn't locked away like the other elements, she left it. She was tempted to call on Spirit and practice wielding it, but she had no idea where to start. She hoped the Elders would be able to help her grasp the power she was given.

About midday they passed a fleet of large ships, all burdened with nets stuffed with fish. Most of the ships had large nets trailing in the waters behind them, and Akairya could just glimpse wriggling fish underneath the surface of the water. The men on board the ships all looked up as Draykor passed, and some even raised hands in greeting.

"At least they are smart enough to know Draykor is no threat," Akairya commented drily. Killian laughed.

"He was still a black dragonling when we first met. I had some reason to be suspicious."

Jaxei poked her head out from Akairya's cloak, her pert nose twitching as she tasted the salty air. Killian cautiously took a hand off Akairya's waist and gently patted the Squirlox. She immediately pressed closer to his hand and half closed her eyes.

"Finally, I can touch her," Killian murmured.

"She's still a wild creature. I'm not surprised it took this long for her to warm up to you."

In time, a lump of land became visible ahead of them. Akairya breathed a sigh of relief; she could sense the growing exhaustion in her dragon; his wing beats weren't as strong as they had been in the morning.

How much longer until we reach the island, do you think? She asked Draykor. He perked his feathered ears towards the distant island, silver fur ruffling in the breeze.

At least another four hours, I would think. We should reach Drakynold early evening.

Akairya patted his scaled shoulder. She closed her eyes and felt along their connection, where Draykor's exhaustion was even more palpable. Without really knowing what she was doing, she felt along her own strength and sent some towards her dragon, who accepted the gift with a sigh. *Thank you, my Rider. I should be able to reach the island without a single doubt now.*

The closer they flew to the island, the more details they could pick out. Great jagged peaks of forested mountains stabbed the underbelly of the sky, and a rocky shore, the stones as white as the ones that made up Kalisor city, bordered the many slopes. The sea lapped at the unforgiving beach and crashed against jutting cliffs that stretched out from the mountains that stood in a rough circle. What lay inside the circle, Akairya had no idea. The colossal mountains, so close together, made the perfect shield against unwelcome eyes.

A dragon with bright blue scales took flight from the top of one of the peaks and flew towards them.

Please cease flight and hover where you are, brethren. I must ask a few questions before I can allow you into our home. The unmistakably female voice of the dragon reminded Akairya of the patter of rain against a pane of glass. Draykor stiffened as he hovered above the sea, his sudden fear reaching Akairya.

A female dragon. Akairya, I've never talked to a female dragon!

Relax, Dray. She's just a guard. No need to panic.

A female guard.

A guard nonetheless. Stay calm.

The dragon soon reached them. Her light green eyes curiously studied the company. She was only a little larger than Draykor, and much slimmer. She was elegantly built, with tiny ears and thin green spikes. Draykor trembled slightly.

What questions…answer, can we? He asked clumsily. The other dragon tilted her head, and her eyes flashed with amusement.

Well, who are you? I've never heard of a golden dragon. Nor one with a Rider…let alone two Riders and a Squirlox!

This is Draykor – I'm Akairya, his Rider. I discovered his egg waiting for me just over two months ago. The Squirlox is our friend, and this is Killian, High King Elric's best general. We are here to ask for guidance and answers to questions we were told the Elders would know.

The female dragon perked up at Akairya's name and stared at Draykor in amazement.

I'm a year old, and you are already so much larger than me! And Akairya…I have heard that name, and was told to keep an eye out for you. Please, follow me. My name is Olia.

They followed Olia over the remaining bit of sea and finally into Drakynold, the home of the dragons.

As they flew over the first few mountains the sun dipped toward the horizon, and its light darkened to a burnt orange that spilled over the treed slopes. A few other dragons, all different colours, caught sight of them and called out in greeting before returning to what they were doing. Akairya watched in fascination as a crimson and green dragon darted out from the sky and scooped up a fat pheasant, whose death screech echoed through the air.

They flew to the inner circle of the mountain ring, which turned out to be a large valley crossed by streams and rich with vegetation. Dragons were everywhere; flying above the valley, perched in large trees, catching fish in the streams, or simply lazing in the grass. The sun was behind the mountains, so the whole valley was shaded and cool. Akairya noted many caves dug into the sides of the mountain faces, and saw even more dragons at the entrances.

"Amazing," Killian whispered from behind her. Jaxei was perched out of Akairya's hood, chittering excitedly.

Olia led them to the mouth of the valley, which thinned into a slim path that led through the mountains. They flew over the path and followed its course into another valley, this one much smaller than the first. Akairya's mouth dropped at the spectacle in front of her.

At the end of the bowl shaped valley were five magnificent waterfalls that fed into a perfectly round lake, which in turn flowed into the many streams that cut into both valleys. At the top of each waterfall sat a massive flat stone large enough for a single dragon, and each stone was occupied by a dragon larger than any Akairya had seen before.

On the far west waterfall, its waters tinged a subtle blue, sat a massive turquoise dragon, who was currently looking at the dragon to her left, a deep red dragon who stood above the waterfall with water stained a pale crimson. The water of the fall to the far east flowed a very light green, and the emerald dragon who sat on his haunches above it stared at Akairya and Draykor with a keen intensity. The silver dragon on the fall beside him was stretching her broad wings, and Akairya was dazzled by the metallic sheen of her waterfall.

The center fall's water rushed a light violet, and the dragon who crowned it was slender yet powerfully built, with deep purple scales and violet eyes the exact shade of Akairya's and Draykor's. She dipped her head in greeting as Olia landed on the grassy bank of the deep lake. Its waters were strangely devoid of any colour. Draykor alighted behind her, and folded his wings with relief. Akairya nimbly undid her straps and slid off her dragon, eyes on the five Elders who were watching her closely.

Killian took a little more time to free himself, but jumped lightly off Draykor with a small grin.

Hello, my child. my fellow Spirit embracer. The central dragon spoke. *I have waited long to see you, and worried over your arrival for many years. We did not know how long it would take for you to return to us, but now that you have, we can get to work destroying the Shadow that has called your country home for far too long.*

My name is Lemori, and I am the Elder dragon of Spirit. I welcome you with all my heart, Akairya and Draykor. The violet dragon turned to the red dragon. *This is Yinang, the Elder dragon of Fire. The*

Elder dragon of Water is Kilani, of Earth is Brundor. She finally turned to the silver dragon, who was humming to herself with shining gray eyes. *And this strange creature is the Elder dragon of Air, Salinde.*

Akairya bowed, one hand clenched in a fist above her heart. Killian quickly followed her lead, and Draykor dipped his head.

Do not bow to us, my child. You are our equal, in more ways than one.

Bewildered, Akairya raised her head. *How?*

Because you are Akairya, Elf Queen reborn, the woman who created Alkairyn and its seven provinces over two hundred years ago.

CHAPTER TWENTY–ONE

Akairya nearly fell over in shock. Lemori had spoken in Draykor and Killian's minds as well, and both were staring at the Spirit Elder in disbelief. Jaxei, oblivious to what was going on, had crept out of Akairya's hood and was now perched on her shoulder, staring at the lake water in contemplation. The Elders of Earth, Fire, and Water were all watching the company gravely, but Salinde was nibbling at one of her front claws while still humming happily to herself.

I-I…what!? How? I don't understand how that is possible. I'm not even full elf! My father was a human hunter! Akairya's hands shook.

You aren't fully Akairya of old, no. Your old self had torn her soul from her material body many years ago, after the War of Elves. With mine and Yeilao's help, we placed the unbound soul in the waters of the Kito. There is much more to it than that, but I cannot explain it to you at present. You would not understand; your knowledge of the intricacies of Spirit is very limited. In time I will tell you. All you need to know now is that we intended for your birth and your bonding with Draykor. We planned for it. She studied Draykor intently, and snorted softly. *We did not know the two of you would become wielders of all elements, however. I'm unsure of what that means.*

Akairya was reeling. She remembered her first lesson with Yeilao, back in the library of Kalisor, when the Spirit elf had told her of the High Queen's mysterious disappearance. Yeilao had hinted she had known of Akairya's purpose, knew why she had discovered Draykor's egg…so did that mean she knew Akairya was *the* Akairya? Not to mention her father…he had named her after the High Queen, so did that mean he had known as well?

We may have the ability to wield all elements, but they have proven difficult to control. Akairya told the violet dragon. *For instance, I can only use Fire when I'm angry. I've yet to use Air or Earth. Plus, Draykor has only been able to use the elements twice. They barely come to him at all.* She glanced at Killian, who was looking at her with open amazement. *If I'm truly Akairya reincarnated, why do I not have her memories? Shouldn't I know about my past self, have some instincts with the Spirit element? The one time I used it, it overpowered me. I was barely able to keep a hold of myself.*

Lemori contemplated Akairya for a few moments. *Spirit is your greatest strength. Your very soul is connected with it in every way possible. Every living thing is a part of Spirit to an extent, but you and I, and the old elf Yeilao, were born with Spirit flowing in our veins. You especially have the power to heal the wounded land, which has been beaten down by the noxious Shadow. You do not yet know how to control this immense power, and I will help you with that.* The great dragon looked at her fellow Elders. Salinde winked at Akairya and gave a strange whistle that cut through the chilly mountain air like a blade. *This is purely speculation, because we have never had a wielder with the ability to wield Spirit and another element, let alone all five, but maybe you can barely control the other elements because you are so fused with Spirit? Anger directs your flame, sorrow controls your water. Emotions are a major part of spiritual power, so maybe once you learn to understand yourself and your emotions, your control over the elements will steady. Draykor, while you have some elemental power, it seems that the way the two of you were bonded has changed how the power is divided. Your Rider's soul is older and more adept with the elements than your own. I will hazard a guess and say that because Akairya has most of the power, you will never be able to wield the power as easily as her. You will simply have to work harder and just be content to use the elements when they decide to come to you.*

As for your memories, Akairya, they are likely hidden in the complex mysteries of Spirit that fill your soul. Plus, the old Akairya was a different person than you. You share the same soul, but you both have lived entirely different lives, and were raised in different times. I think…maybe if I…

Lemori opened her massive wings and glided down to the bank. Her purple body dwarfed Draykor, and he bowed his head in respect as she folded her wings and settled on her haunches beside him. Jaxei jumped off Akairya's shoulder and dashed up onto Draykor's head, where she sniffed the air and stared at the Elder.

I'm not entirely sure what this will do, but…it's worth a try. I'm going to attempt to pull out some of the old Akairya that is buried in your soul, Lemori warned Akairya before lowering her head and placing her slender muzzle on the crown of Akairya's head.

Girl and dragon stood there for a solid minute before anything happened. A bright violet light flashed through their bodies, and Killian yelled as Akairya slumped to the ground in a limp heap.

The weather was beautiful, and Akairya found it ironic. Such turmoil was taking place, yet the sky looked so peaceful.

A vast army stretched in organized ranks before her, each solider garbed in steel armor stamped with a half-moon inside a blazing sun, the symbol she had adopted when she had announced Kalisor as her country's capital. The sun symbolized light and strength, while the half-moon spoke of waning power and the inescapable run of time. Akairya wasn't daft, she had known her peaceful reign of Alkairyn wouldn't last forever. The half-moon was a small, insignificant tribute to that realization, and only she knew it.

This war against the elves had confirmed her suspicions. They didn't like one of their own ruling over a country of humans. They thought it unnatural. Not to mention Akairya was the first elf they knew of that could wield Spirit. So they aimed to put her down.

At first, Akairya had attempted to communicate with the elves. This is crazy, she had told them, war is not the answer.

They had ignored her.

So here she stood, on the newly built bridge of Kalisor city, with her army surrounding the lake and facing the land in front of them, ready for the attack that was sure to come. This was going to be the largest battle yet; all there had been so far were small

*skirmishes between tiny parties of Akairya's troops
and elven fighters. Now thousands of elves had set sail
from their home country, Ellivera, to storm the
capital. Akairya only knew of their movements
because of another young elf, a girl a few years
younger than herself, who had abandoned her race to
warn Akairya of what was coming.*

Yeilao, the second Spirit elf.

*Akairya would never forget the look of fear and
astonishment that had been on the other elf's face
when she had come into her element. Yeilao had
wept; she had believed she was one of the few elves
who would never feel the strength of elemental power.
Akairya wondered if her own power had awoken
Yeilao's. Watching the girl's hazel eyes change to
violet had been unsettling, and had brought back
memories of Akairya's own embrace of Spirit.*

*Akairya was brought back to the present when a
bugle echoed from where the elf army sat, some miles
from Kalisor. The peaks of the Jalkorin mountain
range stood behind the large enemy army, and the
steep hill that rose up near the lake hid the elves from
view. Akairya's patrols had pinpointed the army's
location earlier; once they moved out from camp, it
would take them roughly two hours to march to the
lake.*

*Another bugle sounded. Akairya clenched her
hands and closed her eyes. There would be needless
death today.*

Akairya gasped and opened her eyes. She blinked.
Killian, Draykor, Lemori, and Jaxei were all right
above her, staring at her in concern. She could just see

the other four Elders sitting on top of their respective waterfalls.

"What happened?" Killian demanded as he helped her sit up, brow knitted in concern. Akairya opened her mouth to reply, but the small movement rocked her and she found herself falling into the flood of another memory.

Blood covered most of the land that surrounded Kalisor Lake. Dead and dying were strewn all over the place, some in the steel armor of Akairya's troops, the rest in the boiled leather of the elves. Fires that had been started by elves proficient in the element hissed through pools of blood, melting pieces of sharp ice that had been thrown by Water elves.

Akairya stood near the southern edge of the lake, her once shining armor splattered with soil and blood. The thin blade she gripped in her right hand shook, and she took a deep breath to steady herself. Spirit was proving to be slippery to wield, and she knew why. Her heart was shattered.

So much death. She had plunged her blade in the hearts of countless elves, all of them just as determined to slit her throat as she was determined to end this war. She fought back a sob as she surveyed the torn battleground that stretched all along the lake. No elf had managed to cross the bridge into the city; the quadrant she had posted there was proving its worth. There were still hundreds of elves engaged with her thinning army all around the lake, and she didn't know how much longer her troops could hold off the enemy. There were just so many of them, and they had the elements on their side.

A sharp scream cut through the sounds of battle. Akairya turned towards it, her sword at the ready. A few yards away stood Yeilao, her blond hair snarled with blood and dirt and her spear broken in her hands. A tall male elf towered above her, his expression stormy. The ground he stood on trembled, and a couple of stones floated off the grass and hovered near Yeilao's head.

"How dare you betray your people? How dare you!" he screamed at Yeilao. He lifted his hands and motioned towards her. The stones flew towards her face, and she cried out once before she was knocked out, blood trickling from where the rocks had hit her. Grief tore across the male elf's face, but he whipped out a small dagger and moved to make the killing blow.

Time froze for Akairya. This wasn't right. This shouldn't be happening, she thought to herself. Elf killing elf, elements destroying the land, death all over the place…this simply wasn't right.

Something shifted inside her, and she grew oddly calm. Spirit lept into readiness inside her, and she closed her eyes for a moment as the element washed away her sorrow and replaced it with a clear knowledge.

Things should not have gone this way. She needed to fix it.

She moved her hands as if she was holding a bow and channeled Spirit towards the empty space between her palms. Seconds later a shimmering violet bow materialized, thrumming with a powerful energy. The elf who was about to slip his dagger into Yeilao's chest glanced up and froze, his eyes locked on the glowing bow in Akairya's hands. She notched an arrow that had flowed into existence from her mere thought.

"You have brought this on yourself. You elves attacked us without due cause, and you have given me no choice but to protect this land. You have no idea what is at stake here, absolutely none. I'm sorry, but you must die for your ignorance."

The elf sneered. "Without due cause? You have unnatural power! No one should have the strength you do! No one should wield Spirit! It's the soul of the land, you are using up the very thing you say you care about!"

"Your ignorance of Spirit grows clearer by the second. What I am is natural, it is the only thing keeping the soul beneath us steady."

"Lies!" The elf spat. Yeilao forgotten, he advanced slowly towards Akairya, dagger at the ready. The stones he had used before, some stained with Yeilao's blood, rose up from the ground once again to follow his careful movements.

Akairya breathed in and looked inside the elf, at the strands of Spirit that threaded together the person he was.

Most of the threads flowed pure, pulsing with a faint purple tinge that spoke of a good conscience. However some were stained dark, and spoke of anger and murderous intent. He had changed from the person he once was, and Akairya saw no choice but to loose her arrow into his heart, both for self-preservation and punishment for his ignorance. She did not have the time to cleanse him.

The arrow shot true, and cleanly sliced through the threads that held his soul to his body. He felt no pain, only release, and death took him in its soft embrace. His death brought a sharp pain to her, and she trembled from the loss of life she had caused.

Akairya turned from his corpse and noted with relief that Yeilao's threads still pulsed with strength. She would live.

The High Queen lowered the bow and looked towards the rest of the battle. Most of it was now taking place at the mouth of the bridge and on the other side of the lake, hidden from view by the island that floated in the middle, home to the new city that was still being constructed with the stone she had discovered on the island of dragons. A pang wounded her as she realized the city may never be completed.

She took a step, intending to make her way to the ongoing battle, but the sound of many heavy wingbeats made her stop. She looked up.

Coming from the north, dazzling in a variety of colours, was a massive group of dragons. The fighting ceased as the beasts drew nearer, their scales shining in the setting sun.

What were they doing here? Akairya wondered as they grew closer. When she had set sail and discovered their home, the beasts had avoided her and her crew, even when Akairya had begun taking some of the beautiful stone that made up their mountains.

Heading the group were five of the largest dragons, each a different colour. Akairya's eyes were drawn to the violet dragon, whose scales were the exact same shade of purple that made up the Spirit bow. She allowed the bow to dissipate, and watched as the dragons soared over the lake and lowered to the ground near where the High Queen stood.

Elf and human, their quarrel forgotten, muttered amongst themselves as the violet dragon folded her

wings, turned her purple gaze on Akairya, and sighed.
Akairya saw a keen intelligence in that gaze, and she
recognized the flow of the Spirit element in the
dragon's eyes. Shock shivered through the elf, and she
took a step towards the dragon, her hand outstretched
—

"Kairi!" Killian's voice cut through the memory.

Startled, Akairya noted that she was still sitting
up, supported by Killian's arm. She looked at Lemori,
and was struck by how little the dragon had changed
since she had interrupted the last battle of the War of
Elves.

"I...I just saw...I think I just watched Akairya's
memory of when you and many other dragons
stopped the war between the High Queen and elves."

Did you? Then it worked. For a moment I
thought I did more harm than good, but it seems that
I was able to pull out some of the old Akairya. How
are you feeling?

Akairya took a breath, smiled at Killian, then
stood up. Her legs trembled slightly, but she placed a
hand on Draykor's shoulder and steadied. *My head*
feels strange, and I'm a little shaken, but otherwise
I'm fine. She sure was a tough elf, wasn't she?

I respected the High Queen. She knew what was
good for her country, and sacrificed much.

I...saw. Some of it, anyway.

Akairya glanced at Killian. She noted the new
distance in his silver eyes, and her heart tightened.
Now that it was revealed that she was the reborn High
Queen, he would never allow himself to hope for a
life with her. She shook the thought off. That was his
decision, and she had other major issues to deal with.

Like controlling her elements and helping to destroy the poison that was slowly destroying her birthright.

We have some work to do, she said to Lemori, her jaw set. The Spirit Elder dipped her head in agreement.

That we do. She looked at Killian and tilted her head slightly. *I can't quite put my claw on it, but you...are vaguely familiar.*

Killian frowned. "That's odd...I've never been to Drakynold before today. Have you ever visited the king?"

I have not. No matter, I'm old and have met many. You should all get some much needed rest, I want to start Akairya's training tomorrow.

Olia led the company back towards the main valley, where she showed them the cave they were to call home while they were on the island. A sharp wind whistled through the trees of the mountains, and the sky was now a deep navy that grew closer to black by the second.

The cave was large enough for Draykor to fit and was surprisingly furnished; a stack of bedrolls sat near the back, and a deep fire pit complete with a hanging pot and pile of chopped wood was set on the perfectly smooth stone floor. A thin passageway led deeper into the mountain to some natural springs they could bathe in.

Olia dipped her head in farewell before flying off, her green and blue body swallowed by the growing night.

Killian and Akairya quickly went to work and soon had a bright fire crackling. The warmth of the flames washed through the cave, and Akairya blinked as a wave of exhaustion crashed into her. She yawned and pulled a bed roll out of the pile.

"Aren't you hungry?" Killian asked her as she untied her cloak, placed it over her pack, and, still in her travelling gear, slipped into the surprisingly comfortable roll. She yawned again and closed her eyes.

"No. I just need a good night's sleep. I'll eat a good breakfast in the morning."

She felt Jaxei press against her and curl into a ball, and she fell asleep before she heard Killian's reply.

CHAPTER TWENTY-TWO

Akairya struggled to feel even the smallest hint of anger, Yinang's orange gaze on her. It was late morning, and the autumn sun hung in the sky above the island of dragons. Its sharp light washed through the valley and highlighted the Fire Elder's cave. Draykor was off with the Air Elder, Salinde, and Killian was exploring the nooks and crannies of the expansive valley. Only Jaxei was still with Akairya, and she was fast asleep on Yinang's back.

Maybe the frustration of not feeling angry will, in turn, make you angry enough to wield a small flame, the big dragon chuckled in her mind. She sighed and kicked at the stone floor listlessly. She simply could not draw up enough anger to awaken the Fire element, even when she thought about Theandi's death and her near rape on Seratea's docks.

Yinang's tail whipped at her face, smacked her sharply on the cheek, and sent her sprawling onto the floor. Jaxei leaped off the dragon's back and yowled in protest, her brown eyes glaring at Yinang. The dragon ignored the Squirlox and watched as Akairya shook her head and stood up, frowning. His eyes flicked to her hands, where subtle signs of smoke whisked into the air and dissipated.

"Okay, ow. That wasn't really necessary," Akairya snapped. She rubbed her cheek gingerly.

Sure it was. Did you not use some of the element when you fell to the ground? I saw the smoke coming from your hands. Now try to hold on to whatever you felt when I hit you, and use it.

Her cheek still pulsing from the slap, Akairya took a breath and tried to pull back the quick anger that had flared up when Yinang struck her. It was like grasping at slippery pieces of soap; just when she thought she had it, the emotion escaped. She just wasn't angry enough.

This time Yinang's tail swept across the floor and knocked Akairya off her feet. She landed heavily on her hip, and with the pain came anger, which was closely followed by Fire's power. She clung to it desperately and fed it with memories of past fights with Roraks, most prominently the battle at Durndel village.

Flames flickered to life between her fingers, and she grinned at the rush of heat that enveloped her arms and hands.

Excellent. Now try and hold your anger and direct the flame into the shape of a perfect ball.

It wasn't so hard for Akairya to stay angry this time. Images of Roraks flashed in her mind, and she focused on the chaotic mass of fire she cradled in her hands. She narrowed her eyes and asked the element to form a flickering ball. It obeyed instantly, and she laughed in triumph at the glowing sphere.

A large shadow fell across the cave opening. Akairya lost her hold on fire and the ball winked out. Disappointed, she glanced up to see who had arrived.

Lemori hovered at the entrance. The two Elders nodded in greeting before Lemori turned to Akairya, her eyes calculating. *How goes your training?*

I managed to wield the Fire element for a short amount of time.

Yinang snorted in amusement. *She wasn't lying when she said she could only use Fire when angry; I had to knock her off her feet twice to make her mad enough.*

This is definitely an entirely new situation for us, Lemori commented. *Why don't you take a break from being angry and come with me? I'd like to teach you some things about Spirit. Tomorrow I hope to have Kilani work with you, since Water is the only other element you have managed to use.*

Akairya nodded. *I think learning more about the most important element is crucial. I'll gladly come with you. Should I call Draykor here so we can fly with you?*

No, that is not necessary. Salinde is showing your young dragon his home, and is teaching him some of our history. You will just have to brief him of your lessons later. You can hop on my back, I do not mind carrying you.

Akairya was suddenly afflicted with nerves. Riding Draykor was one thing, but getting on an incredibly powerful Elder was something else. Her knees shook slightly as Lemori landed in the cave and looked at her expectantly, her great wings only slightly tucked in. Akairya bit her lip, shook herself, then jumped up onto the dragon.

The Elder was much larger than Draykor, and Akairya almost misjudged her leap from Lemori's leg to her back. When she was astride, she let out a relieved breath and marveled at the difference. The Spirit dragon was surely bigger than Draykor, but her neck was more slender and her feathered ears more delicate. Her two horns that crowned her head were thin and elegantly twisted, unlike Draykor's.

As soon as Akairya was seated, Lemori jumped out of the cave and unfurled her violet wings completely. Akairya waved at Yinang, who had moved to the mouth of his cave, Jaxei perched on his head.

She marveled at the smooth wingbeats of the Spirit dragon. While Draykor was a much stronger flier than he had been back in Kalisor, Lemori's sure movements made him seem like a clumsy hatchling. She soared over the valley and pointed herself towards the tallest peak of the encircling range, where a wide cave entrance yawned in the rocky surface. She landed gently on the stone floor and tucked in her wings after Akairya leaped off.

We may as well begin immediately, Lemori stated. She settled on her haunches and gazed at Akairya, who sat gingerly on a boulder near the entrance. The elf girl felt incredibly nervous, and she hoped she wouldn't fail spectacularly at wielding the element of Spirit.

You said before that you have held the power of Spirit already.

Akairya nodded.

Then you have experienced the threads of soul that make up a person's self?

She nodded again.

You did not, by any chance, notice any other threads of significance?

This time Akairya frowned and shook her head. *What other threads would there be?* She asked.

Threads that make up the Spirit of the very land we call home. I can see and feel them when I focus, and of late they have become sickly. As you are aware, it is your fate to cleanse this sickness.

Forgive my impertinence, but why is it that you or Yeilao cannot do this? Why must it be me?

Because only your soul has touched the soul of the earth. Very few have managed such a feat. Akairya of old, and past rulers of kingdoms that have prospered and crumbled on the soil currently known as Alkairyn are the only ones to my knowledge. You two legged creatures have failed to note that only those with the ability to draw on the land's Spirit can keep the land healthy and the kingdom strong. When Akairya fought with the elves so many years ago, I finally took it upon myself to tell the High Queen this. She had already guessed that she was important, since it was because of her the land finally embraced the people that lived on it, but she was not aware that without a ruler such as her, one that could keep the spirit of the earth healthy, the kingdom would undoubtedly perish. When I told her this, she was mortally wounded. The Earth elf she had slain moments before I arrived had thrown a dagger right when she had loosed her Spirit arrow. She grew faint from loss of blood during our conversation. I had one of my Fire dragons breathe on her wound to close it, to give her enough time to meet with the Elf King and end the war with my help. Lemori's gaze had gone distant in the memory. Afterwards we attempted to see if Yeilao had the strength to tap into the Spirit of the land, but it was not to be. We then decided that Akairya would have to return, and as a token of our mutual decision, we decided that the new Akairya would be a Rider. We took her soul and placed it in *the Kito, the river that coursed through the forest that was home to Draykor's egg.*

Akairya blinked at the sudden onslaught of new information. So the High Queen *had* been dying all those years ago…she would have perished if she had not taken it upon herself to place her soul in the Kito. Still confused by how Lemori and Yeilao had taken the Elf Queen's soul and moved it to where it was now, the current Akairya closed her eyes and took a breath.

While I don't fully understand everything yet, there is one thing that seems out of place, she said to Lemori.

Which is what?

When I found Draykor's egg, it had been sealed in a stone etched with Dragonake. Dragon Riders were only just being introduced…how is it that a script that took many years to create, and only by Riders, ended up around the first gifted egg?

The stone had been placed around Draykor's egg when we first placed it in the Forest of Souls. The Rider script had been added years later, as a sort of explanation for future Riders. While there have been very few Riders since the end of the War of Elves, there has been enough that an explanation was required for the lone dragon egg sealed in a block of stone.

Lemori shifted her position to get more comfortable. *Enough of a history lesson. Since you have yet to grow into your power enough to see the threads of Spirit that make up the soul of the earth, we will start small.* She lifted her head and looked out of the cave. After a few moments Olia flew into view, a small cougar cub in her claws. The young dragon laid the cub gently on the floor of the cave, bowed her head to Lemori, then left just as quickly as she had come. The cougar sat where she had been placed and mewed softly, her amber eyes dim and her fur lank. Akairya's heart clenched when she saw how skinny the cub was; her ribs stuck out from under her coat, and she looked thoroughly dejected.

This cub's mother perished from a fight with a grizzly not long ago. As a result, this poor creature is currently in the throes of depression. The cat, barely glancing at her new surroundings, settled onto her belly and placed her head on her paws. *Today I'm going to teach you how to heal Spirit. Please take a hold of your element and immerse yourself in its strength.*

Akairya reached for the element. Almost immediately it embraced her questioning touch, and wrapped itself around her consciousness. She had been looking at the cub, and she gasped as she suddenly became aware of shining threads of violet Spirit that pulsed throughout the small creature. Some of the threads were darkened to a deep, unhealthy purple

Now I want you to focus on the threads. Look at the tarnished ones, and think of a rope and how you can work at a piece of it and pry it away from the main piece. The threads are like many ropes; pull away the rotted ones slowly and carefully. I'll begin for you, and then you can finish.

Akairya watched the cub's threads closely. There were only a few darkened threads, and the largest one suddenly shivered. After a moment it lifted slightly off the healthy thread adjacent to it.

Now focus on the thread I have begun to pry away. Feel for its stained presence and use your mind to pull it the rest of the way. Once it has been peeled away from the Spirit that is pure, rip it.

I did that once before, except on the entire soul…I killed two men that way.

Lemori looked at Akairya, her violet eyes suddenly serious. *Were their souls stained?*

Yes. Entirely. There were five men's lives that I had held quite literally in my hands…I let three of them go. The two I killed were too far gone, and I was too immersed in spiritual power to really control myself. Did I do wrong?

No. If they had been thoroughly corrupt, I am glad you ripped their souls. They will now be where they should be. Although it is a dangerous habit to get into; ending a life can easily stain a soul, whether or not it is justified. Always make sure you are convinced that the soul you are about to pull from its physical form is too far gone to save. This is why I am teaching you how to purify. Always attempt purification before ending a life. Always.

I will.

Now focus on the thread I have begun to work and finish helping the cub.

Akairya obediently looked back at the cat. She focused on the stained thread that was slowly moving back to its original place in the network of soul that made up the creature. She took a breath and clumsily grasped the thread with her spirituality, unconsciously lifting a hand and closing her fingers as if she were physically working at a real rope. Her skin glowed faintly with the power of Spirit, and she blinked as the primal essence of the cub flowed through her when she touched the stained piece of soul. Sorrow dripped from the thread, and Akairya's eyes shone with tears as she worked at lifting the thread even farther away. She finally managed to pry it off the rest of the threads, and gently ripped it. It dissolved immediately. The cub shook itself and blinked her large amber eyes.

Excellent. You already have a strong grasp of the element. You barely struggled with the thread, although it tired you. The more you dip into Spirit, the easier it will become to wield, and the stronger your connection. Soon you will begin to see the threads of the earth, and will feel the blemished threads of soul that feed the blight.

The cub had begun to bathe herself, and she was already much more alert. Akairya felt some pride in the young animal's improvement. She released her hold on Spirit, which quieted down immediately within her and faded from her skin. A shadow fell across her, and she looked up just in time to see Draykor land.

Dray! How was your lesson with Salinde?

Intriguing. I worked on some flying techniques and learned plenty of dragon lore. I tried to speak with you a bit ago, but you were too immersed in Spirit to hear me. I take it your lessons are going well?

Very. I helped this cub here.

The cougar in question was now curiously walking about the cave, twitching her nose while giving the two dragons and elf girl a wide berth. Akairya moved closer to her, but stopped when she yowled and swiped at her with a paw.

Remember, she is a wild cougar. Lemori chuckled. Akairya smiled sheepishly and backed away.

The Spirit Elder padded towards the cat, who was barely the size of one of her claws. *I'll take her back to the forest. I'll work with you some more tomorrow.*

Akairya wished Lemori farewell, then hopped on Draykor. Her dragon bent his neck and snuffled at one of her feet affectionately before spreading his wings and leaping into the air.

They returned to their cave, where Killian was cooking a pheasant over a fire.

"Just in time for a late lunch." Killian motioned towards the bird, which was wafting a delicious fragrance throughout the cave. Akairya sniffed in appreciation.

"You managed to hunt without me! You're starting to get it," she smiled.

"Well, I had some help. I made friends with a young Earth and Fire dragon who may or may not have killed the pheasant for me."

Akairya chuckled.

I haven't eaten yet today myself. I think I'll go and hunt. Reach out for me when you need me.

Okay, Dray.

Her dragon exited the cave quickly, leaving Killian and Akairya alone for the first time since the night he had pushed her away. Killian rubbed his neck and focused on cooking the bird while Akairya sat on her bedroll.

"Find anything interesting while you were out exploring?" she asked him.

"I met a lot of dragons. They are all incredibly friendly, and very curious about you and Dray."

"Are they really? Very few of them have approached us."

"Probably because they are intimidated. You wield the most elusive element while also being able to tap into the rest of them…Draykor may seem like a dragon too lofty for friendship."

"That is utterly ridiculous," Akairya responded heatedly. Killian glanced at her before looking away quickly.

"Not particularly. I can see where they are coming from."

Akairya shook her head and didn't reply. The pheasant was soon ready, and they ate in awkward silence.

The half elf found herself thinking about King Elric, Queen Leliana, Thoran, and Oren and Telectus. She hoped everyone was faring all right; she had left right after Theandi's funeral, the worst possible time to leave. She knew Oren was most likely on Ellivera speaking with the elves about possibly bolstering the current elf population on Alkairyn, and the king and Telectus were busy strengthening the army and planning on how to guard against the growing blight. Akairya wondered if Thoran had reached Kalisor safely, and if any more small villages had been taken by the Shadow Lord. She took a small bite of pheasant and sighed. So much relied on her. Her thoughts also turned to the Blood Hawk, and its odd invite. Maybe she would travel to the mysterious Twin Slabs after more training with the Elders. It had seemed as if the Blood Hawk had some much needed answers for her.

A falcon fluttered into the cave, a rolled up piece of parchment clutched in its claws. It alighted on Akairya's shoulder. Bemused, Akairya took the parchment and blinked as the bird immediately took off. Killian stared at the letter, which was stamped with the insignia of the High King.

"That can't be good news. King Elric told me he wouldn't send anything unless he absolutely needed us."

Concerned, Akairya broke the seal and unrolled the letter. She read it through once, and her eyes went wide. "Oren...he...no...I don't understand..." She passed the letter to Killian with a trembling hand. He took it and went pale as he read.

Kairi, Killian,

Please return to Kalisor – I am in dire need of your assistance. Oren has betrayed us, and has convinced the elves to turn their backs on us. I only have one Rider now, and desperately need two. The morale of the army has dropped considerably since the few elves that were here left, and Kairi's presence will only help. Please, make haste. I fear a repeat of the War of Elves may be imminent.

High King Elric

Underneath the hastily written letter was the king's signature and a stamp of his symbol.

"Oren? He was absolutely devoted to King Elric...what could have happened?"

"Maybe he was somehow taken by the Shadow, and the elves don't realize it?" Akairya suggested. Killian paced around the fire, his meal forgotten.

"That is possible. There are many infiltrators that carry the taint without turning into a Rorak; days before we left for here I had executed one. This isn't good. We won't be able to defend against both the elves *and* the Shadow."

"We need to leave."

Akairya reached out for Draykor, who was in the middle of eating his second goat. *The king has contacted us, and we need to go.* She quickly told him about the letter, and he was flying before she finished.

That bastard. The dragon growled. *I never would have thought him or Xandior would do such a thing.*

None of us did, Dray.

They were packed and ready to go in moments. Akairya was just buckling Draykor's saddle when Lemori landed in the cave.

Where are you going? she asked, her purple gaze taking in the bags and saddle. *We still have much to work on.*

I know, Lemori…but the king needs us. Akairya caught her up as well, and the Spirit dragon blew loudly out of her nose in astonishment.

There must be some mistake. Oren is an honourable elf, he was the one who had first told us that some of our young dragons had been taken by the Shadow. He would never betray the king or give in to the blight's poison.

I know, it's hard to believe. I desperately hope King Elric is mistaken, but if he isn't…he needs us. We have no choice; we have to go.

The great dragon shook her head and sighed. *You are correct. You do need to go. I only wish we had had more time. Return, if the time ever comes that you can.*

I will. I promise.

Killian bowed his farewell to the Elder before following Akairya onto Draykor's back. They were just about to take off when a chestnut blur darted into the cave and leaped onto Akairya's shoulder, chittering indignantly.

"Oh, Jaxei. Maybe you should stay here, I don't know what we are flying into."

The Squirlox nipped Akairya's ear before clambering into her cloak's hood and stubbornly curling up. The elf girl shrugged.

"Okay, Dray. We're ready."

Draykor spread his wings and was soon gliding over the valley. It wasn't long before he passed over the mountains and hit the sea, its waters rolling with a cold wind. The sky was mostly clear, but churning in the distance were some dark clouds that promised difficult flying.

Have you rested enough for this? We may hit a storm. Akairya asked her dragon as she studied the faraway clouds.

I'll be fine. I slept well, and ate plenty. I will get us back to Alkairyn.

The storm hit them hard. They saw it coming before it was on them; a sheet of whirling water and foam cutting brutally through the air. Killian's hold on Akairya's waist became iron tight. Jaxei burrowed deep into her hood, digging her claws into the thick fabric. Draykor's head was bowed against the strong wind and curtain of water, which had all of them soaked in seconds. Akairya tightened her hold on the saddle and leaned down against Draykor's neck.

Hold on. He said grimly.

His wings trembled as they pushed against the storm, golden scales and metallic membranes slick

281

with water. The sounds of crashing waves, roaring wind, and rumbles of thunder deafened Akairya, and she closed her eyes. She tried to have faith in her dragon's ability, and simply held on for dear life as he tilted and turned through the storm. In no time at all she felt numb, and wondered what would happen to the world if she died at sea.

After some time they were finally released from the storm's grip. The rain stopped, the clouds drifted away, and the wind died down to a gentle breeze. The storm left behind a tranquil night, with brightly winking stars and a full moon that painted the water with its ivory light. Draykor tiredly continued to carry them south, his endurance clearly wearing out. Akairya took a breath, reached into herself, and sent him most of her remaining energy like she had done before. He soaked it in gratefully and pushed on, and Akairya fell into a deep sleep with Killian still holding tightly to her, more to keep her on her dragon than for his own reassurance now that the storm had abated.

CHAPTER TWENTY-THREE

Akairya was standing on the banks of the Kito, her toes nearly touching the rushing waters of the river. Her cloak flapped in the wind that tore through the forest. Shivering, she looked up and started when she saw a woman standing in the middle of the channel. The woman wasn't submerged in the current; the hem of her dark green gown skimmed the surface and she stood proud and erect. Akairya cautiously touched the tips of her toes to the water and was met with a solid barrier. Encouraged, she stepped onto the flowing river and walked to meet the woman.

The stranger had wavy, deep red hair with hints of dark purple, identical to Akairya's. A shining circlet of white gold and diamonds was around her forehead, and her violet eyes spoke of a wisdom learned from sorrow. Their faces were quite different; the woman had a beautifully sharp face with pointed chin and ears, which told of Elvish heritage. Her lips where thin and her eyebrows were arched. Akairya's face was softer, her lips more lush, but the two of them mirrored each other in colour.

"Who are you?" Akairya asked when she reached the woman, who stood slightly taller than her.

"Come, don't ask such questions. You know the answer without me having to give it."

"*High Queen Akairya…why haven't we communicated before?*"

"*I'm not truly…communicating, in a sense. I'm simply an echo of the queen who had lived before, a remainder that was dredged up out of our soul when the Elder dragon brushed you with Spirit. I am glad our plan has worked…so far, at least. You still have much to do, child. How old are you?*"

"*Twenty-three.*"

"*So young. I was nearly thirty when I came into the element and awoke the kindness of the earth. I don't know how often I will be able to pull myself into your consciousness, or if I will ever be able to again, so listen closely.*" She stepped closer to Akairya and raised a hand to the younger's cheek. "*The fate of life rests with you. The disease will not be easily torn from the threads that make up our home. You will have to sacrifice all with the hand of another in order to erase the stain…*"

When Akairya awoke, Draykor was just landing outside the castle ruins they had slept in a short time ago, the beginnings of dawn creeping across the dark sky.

Why didn't you stop at Seratea, Dray? Look at you!

Her dragon's every muscle was trembling with fatigue, and he barely managed to stay upright as he tucked in his weary wings. His head drooped and he panted heavily as Akairya, Killian, and Jaxei leapt off.

I felt like it was necessary. The king desperately needs us, and stopping at Seratea would have taken too much time. I've shaved off two days of our journey, and if I get enough rest tonight and you all walk for a bit tomorrow, I'll be able to take us the rest of the way without too much trouble. He groaned as he walked slowly towards the ruins, his tail dragging behind him wearily. *I'm going to sleep now. I don't think I'll be able to take a watch, I'm sorry.*

Don't be. We'll manage.

Akairya watched her dragon slump to the ground underneath a section of broken roof, concern knitting her brow. She turned to Killian.

"I suppose we should set up camp. I'm happy to take the first watch."

"I'm not surprised, you slept the whole way after the storm," he replied with a small smile. He led the way to the camp they had used last time, the charred wood from before exactly as they had left it.

Soon they had a fire going and were munching on hardened biscuits Lady Calipsi had given them before they had left for Drakynold. Killian yawned as he fed Jaxei the last of his biscuit.

"I'm going to follow Dray's example and go to sleep. Wake me if anything happens."

Akairya nodded.

The night wore on, silent except for the crackling of the fire and Draykor's dragon snores. Jaxei was curled up in Akairya's lap, her large foxy ears drooping in sleep. The half elf patted her unconsciously as she gazed into the depths of the flames, sometimes looking up to study the camp for any signs of intruders.

You will have to sacrifice all with the hand of another in order to erase the stain.

What did that mean? Sacrifice all…as in the world? Akairya shook her head. That made no sense.

Sacrificing the world to save it simply did not work…the two cancelled each other out. As for the hand of another…

Her eyes flicked over to the sleeping Killian. Annoyed affection flooded through her. Stubborn fool, she thought to herself. Just because I have the soul of a queen doesn't mean we aren't a good match. She allowed herself the chance to study him.

His thick golden hair was flopped over his forehead, which softened his strong features somewhat. He had a strong nose, full lips, and high cheekbones, which were dusted with golden scruff he hadn't had the chance to shave off since they had left the dragon island in such a hurry.

Something cracked nearby, and Akairya froze. She stared in the direction of the sound, and was just about to rouse Killian when a Rorak leaped into the camp, thin sword high in the air. The creature swung its weapon at Akairya's face, and she rolled out of the way, tossing Jaxei in the process.

Killian woke to Akairya's yell and Jaxei's loud screeching. He exploded out of his bedroll and yanked his sword out of its sheath from where it sat against his bag, anger sharp on his face as the Rorak whipped back around and dashed towards Akairya. She had foolishly backed into a segment of broken wall and was trapped between two large boulders. She desperately grasped for an element, but in her confusion she couldn't focus on a single one. Her eyes followed the Rorak's blade as it swung towards her.

With a grunt of effort Killian reached them and caught the Rorak's sword with the tip of his. He disarmed it and kicked its feet from underneath it. It snarled, but promptly went silent when he knocked it out with a sharp jab to the head with his hilt. He didn't give the Rorak a second glance; instead he marched straight to Akairya and grabbed her chin, eyes sweeping across her in concern.

"Are you okay? Did it hurt you?" he demanded. Surprised, she shook her head. Letting go of her chin, he leaned his forehead against hers and sighed. His hands dropped to her waist. Her breath snagged in her throat and she froze as his face dipped closer. Warmth spread through her from where his hands touched her, and she leaned in to close the distance between them.

With a murmured curse, Killian let go of her and stepped back. He rubbed his face with one hand before turning to the unconscious Rorak. Akairya wrapped her arms around herself and watched as Killian hoisted the Rorak upright and leaned it against the wall. He pointed the tip of his blade at its throat, which reminded Akairya of when he had done the exact same thing a couple months ago in the Forest of Souls. A lot had changed since then.

They stood there for some time, waiting for the Rorak to come to. Draykor slept nearby. He hadn't stirred once during the attack, proving how exhausted he truly was. Jaxei was perched on the dragon's back and was staring at the Rorak while irritably twitching her tail. Akairya, slightly unsteady on her feet, willed the Rorak to wake.

Finally, the Rorak opened its beady eyes and snarled when it noticed Killian's sword. "You think you can get information out of me? My life is nothing! Nothing! I am just a pawn, a wisp of the Father's power...and I failed. The pawn has failed."

Before they could process what it said, it gave a guttural groan. Shadow seeped out of its skin and coalesced into a slimy rope, which then cut into the Rorak and killed it. Akairya gasped as the creature slumped to the ground a bloody mess, the Shadow curling into the air and shooting north. Killian shook his head in disgust.

"Pathetic things. I hope that's the only one around these parts. I wonder what its 'mission' was?"

"To kill me, is my guess."

Killian frowned and didn't reply. He motioned to her bedroll.

"Get some sleep. I'll watch until dawn, then we need to get moving."

She looked at him, her eyes questioning. He shook his head and looked away. "I can't, Kairi. I'm sorry."

Disappointed, she went to bed.

Draykor flew most of the way back to Kalisor. After a good rest he was back to full strength, and since he was continually growing larger by the day and was gaining stamina in the process, it was easier and easier for him to carry both Akairya and Killian.

On the morning of the third day since they had left Drakynold, they reached the capital. Its shining ivory and gold towers glimmered in the autumn sunshine, and the lake that surrounded the city's island was choppy from the cold wind that blew in from the Jalkorin mountains. Draykor landed a few feet from the gleaming bridge, which was strangely devoid of people and carts. Akairya and Killian jumped off while Jaxei stayed on the dragon. Her fur bristled as they strode onto the bridge and walked towards the large gates, her eyes narrowed. Akairya frowned at her and followed her gaze.

"What…" she mumbled. On either side of the gates stood an armored guard, like before, but above each soldier something was staked into the wall. Killian tensed and gripped his sword.

"Something isn't right," he said.

The guards lounged against the walls as the company drew closer, eyes hooded. Draykor realized what was staked on the wall first and growled in surprise. His nose flared and his eyes widened in alarm. *Those are heads.*

Akairya's heart dropped as she recognized the heads, both staked through the mouths onto the stone wall. High King Elric and Queen Leliana.

The wind picked up and lifted Leliana's white blonde hair, her dead eyes looking out across the bridge. Akairya clutched her stomach and heaved up her breakfast, sorrow and confusion rolling through her. Killian stood beside her, still as stone. His eyes were locked on King Elric's head.

"What is the meaning of this?" he asked in a low voice. Cold anger hardened his tone, and the guards slowly moved their hands to their weapons.

"A lot has changed since you left, *general.*" The man underneath Leliana sneered. Akairya blinked as she recognized Jilk's drawl. He turned his gaze onto her and lifted a lip in disgust. "And here's the spawn of the Shadow. The girl who tainted the royal family before flying off into the sunset with the army's best general. This is your fault, girl," he waved up at the heads. "The new High King would have spared them if they hadn't of taken you in." He laughed manically.

"Are you mad, Jilk? Look at you! You've clearly been tainted yourself! Kairi is trying to get rid of the Shadow, not help it, you fool!" Killian cried. He unsheathed his sword and moved in front of Akairya. Draykor moved as if to attack, but Killian waved him away. "Kairi, get on Dray and go. I'll deal with these two before they can ring the alarm. I'll meet you on the other side of the bridge. We can't stay-"

Before he could finish what he was saying, Jilk rushed him. Killian didn't have enough time to raise his blade to parry, and Akairya panicked as she saw Jilk's sword swing towards Killian's head. A fierce need to protect flashed through her, and she lifted her hands. The stone of the bridge trembled, knocking both guards and Killian off their feet.

Earth has answered you, Akairya! Draykor said. She looked at her hands in surprise as the element faded from her control. Was protectiveness even an emotion? She looked up as Killian jumped back to his feet and stabbed Jilk through the neck gap in his armor, the blade screeching as it scraped against the metal.

"You crazy idiot, you're too far gone to save."

The second guard, who had taken off his helment and who Akairya recognized as Brant, had never drawn his weapon. He watched impassively as Jilk fell, dead, in front of him.

"He deserved death more than you could know, Killian. I am only serving the usurper because I wish to live. Jilk, on the other hand, was so far gone in his crazy speculations he failed to see the truth in front of him."

"Why haven't you run?" Killian demanded. His blade dripped blood on the smooth white stone of the bridge, and Akairya willed away her nausea. Brant smiled tightly and lifted a hand. Encircling his wrist was a thin bracelet of Shadow, which pulsed and shivered against his armor.

"Because if I do, this will dart into my blood and either kill me or change me. I have no choice but to stay. You three, however-"

"Will also be staying." An achingly familiar voice floated through Kalisor's gates, and Akairya looked over. Killian groaned.

Thoran strode into view, cloaked and exhausted. His cheeks had sunk in since they had last seen him, and his normally kind brown eyes were hard and framed by dark circles. His brown hair was lank, and he walked slowly, as if held down by a great weight.

"Hello, my friends. I'm sorry...but I have no choice but to take the three of you prisoner."

"But...the letter...Oren?" Akairya stammered.

"I forced Elric to write the letter...before I killed him. Oren is not the traitor. I am."

"*Why?*"

Pain flashed across his face. "Because I have to be. My father...the one who took me in when I was left without parents..."

"Is this Shadow Lord." Killian finished for him, his expression cold. Thoran nodded.

"So, please, cooperate. I don't want to hurt you, but I will if I have to."

Tears welled in Akairya's eyes, and Thoran looked away. "Please don't cry, Kairi. Please."

"I considered you my *friend*. You even helped us kill Roraks! This doesn't add up..."

"He was gaining our trust, weren't you?"

Thoran sighed. "Partially. I really was being your friend. I didn't know what father needed me to do, all I knew was that I needed to be on the inside. He didn't command me to take over the capital until we saw him in Yokar."

Realization dawned on Akairya. "That's why he didn't attack you with Shadow...he didn't need to."

Thoran shrugged. He lifted a hand and made a few motions. Two thin bracelets of Shadow came into being, and before Killian or Akairya could react, they flew onto their wrists. Akairya gasped as she was cut off from her power. The sensation of Spirit, which she had grown used to, blinked out, and she trembled from the loss. Killian didn't even twitch an eyelid. He glared at Thoran, silver eyes hard as flint. Draykor was shackled just as quickly.

You will pay for this, Thoran. He growled.

"I already have, Dray."

CHAPTER TWENTY-FOUR

Jaxei yowled and launched herself off Draykor. She pelted towards Thoran with her teeth bared, ears flat against her head. Thoran blinked in surprise before waving his hand and placing a collar of Shadow around the Squirlox's neck, right on top of the chain Akairya had bought for her. The creature hissed but stopped, suddenly thrown by the lack of elemental power she had been born with.

"A Squirlox? I haven't seen one of these in years." Thoran commented. He knelt close to Jaxei and moved his hand as if to pet her on the back, which had only just healed. Jaxei snapped and Thoran jerked away. His face blank, he stood back up and motioned for Akairya, Killian, and Draykor to follow him through the gates. Brant had gone back to leaning against the wall, eyes on Jilk's body.

The city was nearly silent except for the occasional soldier. Everyone had cloistered themselves indoors. The market, while still bursting with colour, no longer wafted a hundred different fragrances. Only some merchants stood near their stalls, and even they wore dour expressions.

Grimy looking men prowled the streets that once boasted life and vitality. Some looked downright miserable, while others sneered with hate as Thoran, their new king, strode by, flanked by Akairya, Killian, and Draykor. Everyone Akairya saw wore a thin bracelet of Shadow.

Sorrow weighed on her as she followed Thoran through narrow side streets that cut through the city straight towards the castle. The noble estates they passed were either boarded up or guarded by surly men who watched the company pass by with hard eyes. Killian walked stiffly beside Akairya, anger vibrating off him.

She gasped when they finally reached the arched bridge that stood over the palace's moat. The beautiful garden of flowers she had admired only some time ago had wilted; the blooms were all faded into greys and charcoal, and their leaves were withered. Instead of the delicious floral perfume she had come to connect to the place, a sickly sweet smell of decay assailed her.

"My father doesn't particularly like flowers..." Thoran muttered when he realized what had upset her. He picked up his pace and led them quickly to the castle's golden doors. Someone had slashed the white insignia of sun and moon with black paint. The group traipsed quickly through the massive foyer and into the main hall of the castle.

Thoran swept through the palace without speaking. They approached the throne room doors in silence. Akairya looked for Jervos, the man who normally announced the entrance of everyone, but he was nowhere to be seen. Akairya was struck by a terrible thought; where was Yeilao? Did Thoran behead her too? Was her head staked somewhere else in the city? Shivering, she reluctantly followed Thoran through the doors and into the throne room, golden sunlight spilling through the glass wall and across the floor. The palace grounds that Akairya could see through the clear wall seemed unchanged, though she suspected the grapple trees had met the same fate as the flowers.

At the end of the room sat the three thrones, the middle one occupied by a dark mass that seethed with malignant power. Killian gripped Akairya's hand, worry in his silver eyes. Draykor growled low in his throat.

"Finally, we meet face to face," said a hoarse voice, one they had heard before. "I have desired to meet you after our chat in the village. What a happy chance that you have arrived before I left to return to my island. How excellent." Akairya stared as the Shadow in the throne shivered and molded into the shape of a man. The figure stood up and took a breath.

He was tall, taller than Killian by a good foot, but thin as a whip. He wore dull black leather armor that covered his muscled frame like a second skin. His flesh was the colour of thick smoke, with thin crimson markings that looked like warlock script. His eyes burned a deep red, and his thin black hair hung to his shoulders. Two large, serrated chakrams hung from his back, each ringed with Shadow and tinged with the glow of the Fire element. He caught Akairya's eye and grinned maliciously, his teeth surprisingly white and straight.

"You are quite lovely in person, my dear. I can see why my son is so reluctant to harm you." He clasped his hands behind his back, just beneath the chakrams. "I have yet to figure out what your purpose is, however. You hold sway over the Spirit element and that can prove meddlesome. Thoran claims he can keep you under control, so for now I'll keep you pure. If you put one toe out of line, however…be assured I will slip some Shadow into your blood faster than you could think."

His voice, while conversational, held a subtle violence that terrified Akairya. She was supposed to destroy *him*?

"You, now…" The Shadow Lord glanced at Killian. "I could use you. You would make an excellent soldier, once you've been fed some of my power. What do you say?"

Killian bared his teeth. "I'd rather not."

The Lord shrugged. "Suit yourself. In time you will either die or become a Rorak, so I don't really care at the moment. If you weren't a good friend of Thoran's, I would simply force you. I'm being quite generous." He shifted his gaze to Draykor. "The dragon, however, I *will* take. A beast that can wield all five elements…he will be the perfect mount for me."

Before Akairya could protest, the Lord raised his hands and a line of Shadow shot towards Draykor, who roared in surprise. Akairya gasped in pain and fell to her knees as her mind was invaded by rolling darkness and the poisoned essence of the Shadow.

It was silent. She could feel the softness of a plump pillow underneath her head and the weight of a thick blanket on top of her. Her head ached with the memory of the onslaught of Shadow, and her eyes snapped open in panic. *Dray.*

"You're beautiful, you know that?" Thoran's voice floated to her from the corner of the room, the same one Akairya had slept in when she had first arrived in Kalisor city. He was sitting in the armchair, his hands folded on his lap. The shadows under his eyes had deepened, and his cheeks were sallow.

"Where's Draykor? Is he okay?"

"I believe so. When my father threw Shadow at him, the Spirit element somehow shielded him from its poison. Not easily, but it did. Father was enraged, but I managed to calm him down and convinced him to leave you be. We have the capital, and are slowly gaining enough forces to march through the country, so he is quite agreeable right now. You're lucky."

"*Lucky*? You've shackled us! You're keeping us prisoner, and you murdered the royal family! How is this *lucky*?"

"You're not dead," he replied flatly. Akairya glared at him.

"Why haven't you just shackled the entire country? I'm sure that would be the easiest route to take," she suggested drily.

"The blight is a huge force, yes, but its power only stretches so much. Most of it is being channeled into new Roraks and it's keeping enough people prisoner to keep my father happy."

"Why are you telling me this? It could be considered a weakness, and I'm your enemy." When she said enemy, he flinched. He shrugged and didn't answer her question, but he didn't need to. It was clear he was confident she had no way to overthrow him.

"I'm not your enemy, Kairi," he said softly. Akairya snorted.

"You have an odd way of thinking, Thoran. Of course you are my enemy. Anything drenched in the stink of Shadow is my enemy. Where's Dray?" She couldn't reach him through their connection.

"Still in the throne room. I'll take you to him."

He stood and walked out the door, his steps even more weary than before. Akairya followed, slightly unsteady on her feet.

"Where is Killian?"

"Right here," Killian joined them in the hall outside the room, his golden hair in disarray from running his hands through it in agitation. He motioned to Thoran. "This bastard wouldn't allow me in the room with you."

"Stubborn fool," Thoran muttered. Akairya and Killian both ignored him.

The three of them made their way to the throne room, Akairya taking the lead. When she reached the doors, she picked up her pace and practically ran inside.

Draykor was curled on the rich carpet. Yeilao stood near him, looking even more ancient than before. Her ivory hair was unkept and her wrinkled face pale. A bracelet of Shadow pulsed on her wrist, and it was many times larger than any other Akairya had seen thus far. She cried out in relief and hugged the elf lightly.

"Oh, child. Why did you return here?" the old elf rasped. Tears shone in her tired violet eyes, and she took a breath. "No matter, what's done is done."

"Is Draykor all right?"

"Yes, but he won't be able to protect himself from another attack like that. We're lucky the Lord decided against taking him. The Shadow shook his very soul, and his defenses are weakened. It will take many months before his spiritual power is back to full strength."

"How do you know this?"

Yeilao's eyes flicked to Thoran, who still stood at the doors. Killian had followed Akairya and was standing nearby. "It takes a lot of energy, and a lot of practice, but if you are determined, it is possible to break the Shadow that binds our power. I cannot break my bonds simply because Thoran doubled mine and I do not have the energy, so I can only use trickles of my strength. I was able to glimpse your dragon's soul threads and saw some of the damage." The elf's voice was barely louder than a breath.

This new information caused Akairya's heart to beat faster, but she kept her face composed. "You mean it is possible for me to free myself?" she whispered. Yeilao nodded. Hope surged through Akairya's chest, and she glanced at Killian. He smiled.

"Your Highness, dinner is served." A meek girl with mousy hair had appeared near Thoran, her cotton servant dress stained and dotted with small holes.

"Thank you, Trysti. We'll be there in a moment." He motioned for Killian, Akairya, and Yeilao to come. "Draykor looks like he'll sleep for some time. Let's go eat."

Dinner was sparse, and no one spoke as they took sips of thin potato and leek soup. Thoran kept his eyes on his bowl and barely ate anything. Akairya took the opportunity to study his face. With his once round cheeks concaved and his eyes lined with exhaustion, the kind looking man now looked hard and broken under a great weight. She didn't know if it was the Shadow's poison changing his appearance, or something else.

Once everyone else had finished eating, he waved for the servants to take the dishes. He then leaned his elbows on the table and looked at each of them in turn.

"As is obvious, you are now prisoners. With the Shadow bracelets around your wrists, elemental power is blocked. For those without elemental power," he raised an eyebrow at Killian, "the bracelets simply act out consequences. For instance, if either of you attempt to cross the bridge leading out of the city, the Shadow will slip into your blood and either kill you or poison you into Roraks. Attack me, it will outright kill you. You are free to wander the city, but Kairi...I'd rather you didn't. The people on the streets now are far less kind than they were a short time ago. A half elf, Rider or not, would be the perfect prey. If you do wish to walk in the city, either ask me or Killian to accompany you."

Killian sat stiffly as Thoran spoke, but he held his tongue. He gripped the edge of the table with shaking hands, his knuckles white.

"I'm curious...why haven't you simply turned all of the citizens you have prisoner into Roraks? Doesn't the Lord need his army bolstered?" Akairya asked. Thoran looked at his hands.

"I asked him to spare those who cooperated with us. Many escaped in the chaos that followed when Telectus burst out of the palace and bellowed the news that I had killed Elric and taken the throne, which I am honestly relieved about. Less lives were lost. Most of the nobility have left, and those who remain rarely leave their estates. They do not know I have managed to save their lives. I know it looks like it, but I am not my father. I am simply a man locked in a life that was not my choosing. I'm surprised he has allowed me to keep the citizens left pure, but he has…and I'm not going to look a gift horse in the mouth."

No one had any response to that.

"Where are the other two Riders?" Akairya inquired.

"Oren is still in Ellivera, I believe. Telectus…" Thoran shrugged. Akairya frowned, but didn't push the subject. She had a sinking feeling that Telectus was either dead or poisoned by Shadow.

The first few days of imprisonment were uneventful, as the Lord had returned to Tilaner Isle. Killian and Akairya took to the arena where Oren had given Akairya her first glimpse of an elemental weapon. They spent much of their time sparring and watching Draykor practice aerial maneuvers over the dying crop of grapple trees, the sickly sweet smell of the rotting fruit thick in the air.

When she wasn't sparring with Killian, Akairya cloistered herself in the castle's library with Yeilao. They spoke quietly about what Akairya had learned on Drakynold. She told the older elf about Lemori pulling out some of the old memories that had been buried in her soul.

"You saw me as a young elf, eh? I remember that day…the elf who had knocked me out and ultimately killed the old Akairya was my lover before I betrayed my race," Yeilao mused as she prodded the fireplace they sat by with a poker. Akairya stared.

"That…must have been difficult to go through."

301

"It still wounds my heart. I loved him very much, even after I had decided to take Akairya's side. When he attacked me, my heart fractured in such a way it still hasn't healed. It's a miracle I can still use my element at all."

"I can only imagine."

"Yes, well. I'm glad you are finally aware of who you are. I so desired to tell you when you were here, but it was always the plan to send you to Lemori. She is the only other living being who can tap into the earth's soul, although she can only do so much. She is a wild creature, no matter how wise, and as such the Spirit of the land would become wilder and more difficult for people to live off of if she tapped into it. I can see the threads of Spirit that make up our home, but I can't touch them. Their power is simply too great."

"I hope I can find the strength to do what I need-" Akairya stopped abruptly as the library door swung open, revealing Thoran. He walked slowly towards them, his hands holding a small bouquet of the strange flowers that used to grow in abundance outside the castle.

"Um, here…" He muttered as he handed them over to Akairya. She took them and inhaled their sweet fragrance. She brushed a thumb over the petals of a yellow bloom, its silky surface coated with silver hair.

"I thought your father killed all of them?"

"I saved a few before he poisoned them. I thought you would like to have a couple."

She stared at him, unsure of what to say. "They are lovely."

An awkward silence fell over them, interrupted only by the sharp crackling of the fire. Yeilao stared into the flames, a slight frown creasing her ivory brow.

"Well, I'll leave you two be," Thoran mumbled before turning on his heel and nearly running out the door. Akairya watched him leave and shook her head. She glared at the bracelet of Shadow that ringed her wrist and caused the gnawing emptiness of power inside her.

"I never thought that he was one of the Shadow. I feel so…" she trailed off as she hunted for the right word.

"I believe betrayed is the term you are looking for, and I couldn't agree more. He always seemed like such a kind soul."

"The strange thing is, I don't think his kindness was ever an act. It was so genuine."

"It's amazing how convincing evil can be," Yeilao stated bluntly. Akairya didn't say anything. She thought of how tired Thoran looked, and how sickly.

"I think this is killing him," she muttered.

"Good. After what he's done…"

Akairya left the library a few minutes later, confused by the sudden irritation that Yeilao's attitude gave her. The old elf was right, Thoran was a traitor and the enemy. Then why did Akairya feel like giving up on him was wrong?

She made her way through the castle, deep in thought, not really paying attention to where her steps took her. When she finally snapped back to herself, she was on the ground floor of the palace, near the back doors that led to the grounds. The thick wooden door that opened to the dungeons was just a few feet away. She stared at the door in sudden speculation.

Would there be any prisoners down there? She found herself wanting to see if Thoran had filled the cells, or if he simply killed any who fought against his kingship.

Her mind made, she opened the door. Stairs led down into a deep darkness, and a touch of cool air breathed on her face . She hesitated, then began the descent.

The stone steps took her quite far down. When she reached the landing, her hand brushed against something. She flinched, but realized it was simply a table. Her eyes, accustomed to the dark, could just barely discern a few objects laid out on the surface. She recognized the shape of a lantern, and after feeling around she discovered flint and steel.

She soon had the lantern lit, and blinked as the warm light illuminated her surroundings. A slim passageway stretched away from her in one direction, cells bordering each side. She began to walk, lantern held aloft so she could see inside the small prisons.

The first few were empty. They held ragged bedrolls and chipped chamber pots, but no prisoners. She continued on. Her light fell into the next cell, and a raspy moan of surprise stopped her short. She hurried closer to the cell and peered inside.

She clapped a hand to her mouth. A man, dressed in noble attire now ripped and stained, was slumped against the back wall, hands up to block the light. The sharp stench of human waste assailed her, and she gagged.

"Please, have mercy, put out the light," the man wheezed. His voice snagged her memory, and she frowned. She placed the lantern down the passage a few feet away from the cell so the light wasn't so hard on the prisoner's eyes. He sighed and lowered his hands, eyes squinting.

Akairya gasped. Although it was hard to tell through the tangled beard that covered his face, she recognized Lord Reinald, the man who had attempted to assassinate her during the ball. The man who had thought her a pawn of the blight.

"W-who are you?" he asked timidly.

"Akairya," she whispered. Reinald went stiff, then his shoulders drooped and he looked at the ground.

"Ah," was all he said.

Akairya studied the man who Killian had said was once the most prestigious of Kalisor's nobility. His short time in the dungeons had taken its toll on him. His hair was grown out and greasy, and his bones jutted out against his skin.

"Do you...know what has taken place?" she inquired. He looked up at her and nodded. His eyes dropped to her wrist, where her Shadow bracelet writhed, and he shuddered.

"I am so sorry I thought you were a traitor to us. Thoran has been down once or twice, and...I know what he has done," his eyes, though feverish, were quite sane. "I see you are also imprisoned, and that tells me all I need to know. I was a fool at the ball. An utter fool."

Akairya barely heard him. Seeing him reminded her of how Thoran had saved her from Reinald, how he had tackled the noble to the ground before another arrow could be loosed. Was that because he truly

305

cared for her, or was it because it helped him live his lie?

"Are you going to save us, Lady Rider?" Reinald whispered. Akairya started.

Save. If she could break her bonds, like Yeilao said she could, maybe she could save Thoran. Maybe the kind man she had thought she knew was still there, pushed to the side by the Shadow's influence. Was it possible? Would she even have the strength?

Mind whirling, she turned to leave.

"Wait! Please! Don't leave me here. They stopped feeding me. I don't want to die here!" Reinald's voice increased in pitch as his desperation grew. He struggled to stand, limbs trembling from the effort. "I know I deserved punishment for what I tried to do to you, but please…I know now I was wrong."

"One moment," Akairya told him. She rushed back to the table, her eyes searching for the cell keys. They were hanging off a peg above the table, and she snatched them. She returned to Reinald's cell.

"Oh thank you, thank you, thank you," he murmured as she bent to the task of finding the correct key for his cell's lock. After a few attempts she managed to find it, and she threw open the door.

"What's going on?" Akairya jumped as Thoran's voice cut through the dungeon. Reinald groaned and sat back down on his bedroll, defeated. Akairya crossed her arms as Thoran approached, frowning. She took in his sick features with a critical eye. Was he dying because he fought against the poison he was forced to wield?

"I'm freeing Reinald," she said.

"He tried to kill you, Akairya, in case you've forgotten."

"I'm aware. But he's realized he made a mistake. Surely he can go free if the person he attempted to kill has forgiven him."

Thoran turned to look at Reinald, who watched them with wide eyes. He shrugged and waved a rope of Shadow towards the emancipated man, which curled around his wrist. Reinald gasped at its oily touch

"He can go. Don't try to leave the city, however. That bracelet will kill you if you do."

Reinald nodded and stood. Thoran moved aside, and the once-lord inched past and left as quickly as his weak legs would allow.

"That was good of you," Akairya commented. Thoran looked at her questioningly. She didn't say anything else, simply studied his dull brown eyes with her violet gaze.

"I only did it because you wanted it."

Akairya remained silent. Thoran sighed and nodded his head to her before turning and leaving. She waited some time before she left as well, her heart troubled.

After leaving the dungeons, she made her way towards the Rider Quarters, where Draykor was. He was taking care of Jaxei, who was not taking kindly to the shackles on her power. She had lost plenty of weight and her chestnut fur no longer gleamed with health; it hung lank off her body and had darkened to a sick brown. Akairya worried over her Squirlox, and she decided she would attempt to overpower her own bracelet and help the ill creature. If she couldn't help her, then there would be no point in her trying to save Thoran. If she decided to.

Draykor was curled outside the large Riders
Quarters, Jaxei sleeping on his back. He blinked his
violet eyes as Akairya walked up and blew some air
out of his nose in greeting.

How is she? The elf girl asked him.

Same as yesterday. She didn't eat anything again.

*I'm going to try something. It will likely fail, but
I have to try.*

She closed her eyes and reached for Spirit. She
collided almost instantly against a mental block that
bruised her consciousness, but she shook it off and
continued to push. Sweat beaded on her forehead as
she pressed against the block, which gave no signs of
collapsing. It felt oily against her inner self, but she
persevered and pushed even harder.

She pushed and heaved against the block, her
energy rapidly dwindling as the cage around her
power stayed maddeningly solid. She gritted her teeth
and perservered. Finally, right as she began to feel like
she was going to fall unconscious, it cracked slightly
within her, and a trickle of the Spirit element spilled
through into her power. Panting heavily, Akairya
opened her eyes and narrowed them at Jaxei. She was
able to see the Squirlox's threads, but they were
incredibly opaque. She noticed that one thread was
purely black, and that it sat on top of the other
threads in a way that hinted it didn't belong there.
Akairya guessed that it came from Jaxei's Shadow
collar, and wasn't a part of the creature's soul at all.
She took another breath and, clutching desperately to
the little bit of element she had in her grasp, slowly
picked at the dark thread.

Time moved sluggishly as Akairya labored.
Draykor watched in alarmed concern as her face grew

paler by the second, but he didn't dare move and ruin her concentration on the sleeping Squirlox. His tail twitched as his Rider grew visibly weaker, the sap of her strength clearly proving to be too much.

Finally Akairya sighed in satisfaction and let go of the element, which slipped back behind the cracked mental block. She had done it. When she had managed to pry the black thread away from the healthy ones, it had simply faded away and had not required her to rip it. She assumed it was because the thread had not been a fragment of soul, it had only been a part of the Shadow collar. Sure enough, when Akairya looked at Jaxei's neck, the collar had vanished.

We'll have to keep her away from Thoran, she commented tiredly. Draykor nodded.

Go inside and rest, you look dead on your feet.

Akairya didn't need any further encouragement. She stumbled into the Rider Quarters, walked past the empty rooms that used to be home to Oren and Telectus, and soon fell into her bed. Sleep claimed her in seconds.

After that, Akairya felt stronger. The crack in her block had stayed, and she knew that she could reach the Spirit element if she truly wanted to. While its full power was still locked away behind the strength of the Shadow bracelet, the fact that she could still feel a breath of the element gave Akairya some much needed hope. Jaxei had made a full recovery, and Draykor was tasked with hiding her from Thoran whenever he came around. Killian was just as ecstatic as Akairya was about the breakthrough.

"This is excellent," he said the morning after Akairya had first healed the Squirlox. They were sitting in wooden chairs outside the Riders Quarters, their cheeks flushed from the crisp air that tasted of the coming winter. Itaye, unharmed and fully healed from his past injury, sat regally on Killian's shoulder, one leg wrapped by a Shadow bracelet. "Maybe you'll have the strength to break Draykor's bonds next, and then yours. Once you are both free you can escape."

"I want to break yours and Yeilao's as well…and I want to try and heal Thoran."

Killian stared at Akairya as if she were insane.

"Thoran was never a good person, Kairi. He is too far gone to save. He doesn't deserve it."

"I think you are wrong. Look at him! He looks absolutely diseased…I believe he truly is a good person, just twisted in the bonds of the Shadow because he had been unlucky enough to be picked up by the cursed Lord when he was an infant."

Killian shook his head. "You are too important to the fate of our country to kill yourself over a lost soul."

"Isn't that why I have this power? To heal?"

"Yes. To heal the *land.* Not Thoran."

Akairya sighed. "Please, Killian. I know you still care about Thoran too. I can see the pain you feel whenever he is near. You used to be so close…you know this wasn't his choice. He's dying, and I want to try and save him."

"Fine. But if you manage to break your bonds, promise me you'll escape if things go wrong. He is still a part of the Shadow, and even if his kindness is still there, the poison can still take control."

"I promise."

They fell silent. Draykor was playing with an exuberant Jaxei a few feet away. The Squirlox would dash all over his golden body as he rolled and attempted to toss her, but she was too agile to be thrown easily. She chittered excitedly, her large eyes bright. Akairya smiled. At least she had been able to help her.

CHAPTER TWENTY-FIVE

At dinner the next evening, Thoran was especially awkward. He knocked over his goblet of wine twice, and could barely get his food on his fork. After a few minutes of clumsily attempting to eat, he finally gave up and stared at Akairya.

"Tomorrow I would like to take you to the Garden of Illumination," he said briskly. Akairya blinked in surprise. Yeilao dropped her fork, the clatter masking Killian's mumbled curse.

"Um, okay...I have been meaning to visit there."

"Then it's settled. I'll meet you in the foyer tomorrow morning."

It wasn't until later that night, when Akairya was lying in bed, that she remembered Killian once telling her how he would like to take her to the Garden of Illumination. That felt so long ago, and she felt a small pang of disappointment that she had to go with Thoran. She and Killian had grown even closer the past week, since they spent nearly every day in each other's company. Killian's soldiers had all escaped or had been killed when High King Elric had been beheaded, so the barracks were just as empty as the Riders Quarters. They only had each other and Draykor for friendly companionship, and as a result Akairya felt their relationship solidifying.

Thoran led the way over the palace's bridge and into the city. Akairya tried to ignore the powerful scent of sick flowers that hit her the moment she passed the greyed blooms; she thought of the few healthy ones Thoran had saved for her. While she was still confused over the gesture, she had kept them, and had placed them in a small vase. They were in her lodgings inside the Rider's Quarters, and she was determined to keep them alive

She kept close to Thoran as they left the castle behind. He wore his black cloak against the onslaught of cold that cut through the city, and it billowed behind him as he walked purposefully towards the garden. Akairya trailed along behind him, shivering in her emerald green cloak that Yeilao had wordlessly handed to her the night before. Her travelling cloak desperately needed repairs.

The city streets were empty, and Thoran and Akairya's footsteps echoed through them. The gleaming white walls and golden roofs of the buildings soaked in the crisp light of early morning. A few falcons, all shackled by Shadow bracelets, flitted above them, carrying rolled up letters.

The Garden of Illumination was a sprawling garden of glass and crystal that was located beside the Shining Estates, the neighborhood of the higher classes. It was encircled by a tall wall of frosted glass etched with intricate designs of flowers and vines. Bright gates of crystal, already wide open to admit visitors, winked in the sun. The sandy stone of the city streets shifted into smooth white marble once one was in the garden, and the only live vegetation inside was thick green grass dotted with tiny white flowers. The rest of the garden was made of warped glass and crystal, all in the shapes of bushes, flowers, trees, fountains, and benches. Lanterns and chimes were strung along the thin paths that led throughout the garden, ready for when night fell across the city.

"It's beautiful," Akairya breathed as she took in the gleaming sight. She walked slowly along one of the paths, drinking in the cool beauty.

"It's called the Garden of Illumination because of how it reflects light, and how it 'illuminates' passion," Thoran told her. He clumsily reached for her hand, a subtle flush staining his sunken cheeks. Akairya suddenly realized the meaning behind Thoran's desire to bring her to the garden, and she looked at him in horror. He noticed her expression and his already pale complexion drained of colour, his blush gone.

"You didn't understand the implication before, did you?" he murmured. She shook her head.

"Not even when Killian once mentioned he'd like to take you here, back when we first arrived in the city?"

"How could I have known? I've never been here before," she replied softly. A light wind tumbled through the garden, tinkling the chimes. The pure tones fell sweetly on Akairya's ears, but her heart had gone cold. "I'm sorry, Thoran…but I can't…"

"It's because of Killian, isn't it?" Thoran snapped. His brown eyes had curdled to a near black that echoed the stain of the blight. Akairya winced at his tone.

"It's not just because of him!" she cried. "I couldn't ever look past what you have done! You are a part of the *Shadow*, the very thing that tore apart my home, poisoned my country, and killed so many, including Theandi! Oh, *oh.*" She swayed as she truly understood the depth of Thoran's betrayal. "You were a part of Theandi's death. You helped kill her."

"No! Kairi, I had nothing to do with her death! That was all my father, not me-"

"And the king? The queen? Countless citizens? What about them?" Her eyes shone with tears and agony. Thoran's pained expression shifted into a blank stare.

"I see how you think of me, and I'm sorry for it. I had hoped...thought..." His hands shook. "I was a fool for thinking you could ever want me, or save me from my fate. My deepest apologies." He bowed before he turned on his heel and walked out of the garden, leaving behind a distraught Akairya. She stared after him, his words ringing in her ears. *Save me from my fate.* Could she? Should she even bother to try?

I needed this, Akairya said to Draykor as the two of them soared above the city. *Flying takes me away from everything...below. While the blight is still there, Thoran's betrayal still real, and the future still unknown...flying with you helps me forget for a little while.*

Draykor sighed. *I know. Me too. Have you been working with Spirit?*

Yes, as much as I can. I think I'm getting a stronger grasp on it, and I may be able to break my bonds completely soon. Then I can break yours and Killian's and maybe tear Thoran away from his father's clutches.

If that's even possible. Don't hope too much, Akairya. It will only hurt all the more if Thoran cannot be saved.

Akairya gazed out across the choppy waters of the Kalisor lake and fought back her fear. So much depended on her. Too much.

Look! A Shadow dragon! Draykor alerted her, his golden head facing the figure of a large dragon, its scales a flat black. Akairya narrowed her eyes; someone was riding it.

The pair drew closer, and Akairya recognized the peppered hair of Telectus. "Oh, no," she whispered.

Saverign's white eyes, once a beautiful azure, stared at Draykor as he banked and hovered a few feet away. Telectus, his complexion splotchy and his green eyes now black like a Rorak's, sneered at her. "Well, if it isn't our newest Rider. The Lord sent me to check up on his son, and what a chance! I get to see you again."

Akairya met his gaze with pained defiance. A sudden thought occurred to her: "If you have been with this Shadow Lord on Tilaner Isle...why doesn't he know what I am? You knew before I left for the Elders."

"What are you talking about?" Telectus sneered.

Draykor tilted his head and gazed at the Shadowed Rider. *It looks as if his embrace of the Shadow took some of his memory.*

That's...incredibly lucky.

A shout from below caught their attention. They looked down to see Thoran standing near the grove of dead grapple trees, waving.

"Ah, the young lord." Telectus said. Saverign turned to fly down to Thoran. As he passed near Draykor, his head snaked out and nipped the younger dragon on the leg. Draykor roared in surprise and pain, nearly unseating Akairya as he twisted in midair.

Before he could retaliate, Saverign and Telectus had flown away.

*That...I...*Draykor trailed off as he bent his neck to lick the blood off his wound. Akairya patted him on the shoulder, sorrow heavy in her chest. Telectus had once been so kind, so full of life, and Saverign used to be so wise and calm...the blight had taken yet two more lives from them.

I hope Oren hasn't...

I don't think he has. Thoran himself said that he and Xandior were still on Ellivera. He probably doesn't even know that the king is dead. It hasn't been very long.

Killian was telling me that news of the royal family's demise is spreading fast now that escapees have reached refuge. He was talking to Brant, who managed to receive falcon mail before a tendril of Shadow killed the bird. The letter came from a fellow soldier, who had reached Terndion, the capital of Morkrain, just a short time ago. He said the Duke has been able to keep the city and its few surrounding villages free from Roraks so far. The people of Alkairyn are becoming more aware, and Morkrain's Duke is doing his utmost to rally an army.

Morkrain is in the upper corner of the country, right? Quite near Tilaner Isle?

Yes, but the province has the advantage of mountains. The entire landscape is mountain and forest. Not easy terrain for Roraks to sneak up on the capital, especially since the people born there know the land incredibly well.

I suppose.

Akairya glanced down at where Thoran stood with Telectus and Saverign. The poisoned duo were just taking flight back towards Tilaner Isle, and Thoran stood watching as they drew further away. His body language screamed exhaustion and sorrow, and Akairya couldn't help but feel a pang of sympathy. What must it be like, chained to a father so steeped in evil? Thoran didn't look up at her and Draykor. He turned and walked towards the castle, his head bowed.

There's Killian. Shall I land? Draykor motioned with his muzzle towards where Killian stood, his hand lifted in greeting.

Yes. Maybe he'd like a duel. I feel the need for some exercise.

"How was the Garden of Illumination?" Killian asked nonchalantly as he handed Akairya her sword. She took it, sighed, and kicked at the sandy floor of the arena.

"Awful. I didn't realize what it…signified, him taking me there."

"He didn't try anything, did he?" Killian's expression looked dangerous. Akairya shook her head and gave her blade a few practice swings.

"No. He blamed you for me not returning his affections, though."

Killian nearly dropped his weapon. "Me?"

"Yes."

Instead of asking more questions, he simply launched into the duel. Akairya gasped and barely knocked his blade away. Annoyed, she gritted her teeth and threw herself into the fight.

They moved rapidly across the arena floor, sand flying, their swords constantly grating against each other. They were both covered in sweat in a manner of seconds.

Akairya, so completely focused on Killian's movements, missed when the look in his silver eyes shifted. She blinked when he smoothly disarmed her and placed his blade against her throat. She stood there, arms limp by her sides, eyes flashing defiantly. He stared at her.

"You know what? I don't care anymore," he growled before throwing aside his sword and catching her by the waist. Before she knew what was happening, he had her pressed against the arena wall and was roughly kissing her.

Finally, she thought to herself as she whole heartedly returned the embrace. It was far from gentle, but she didn't care. Bottled up passion bubbled up to the surface, and she reacted with instinct.

"*No!*" an enraged voice exploded from the arena door, and Akairya and Killian jumped apart. They both looked over, and Akairya paled.

Thoran stood seething, his expression murderous. Smoky clouds of Shadow writhed around his figure, thickening as his rage grew. His eyes were thoroughly black, and his cheeks had gone gray. His entire body shook with anger.

"Thoran-"

"Silence, you *whore*," he snapped. Killian stiffened and picked his blade out of the sand.

"Don't you dare call her that."

"What are you going to do? Kill me? You know the bracelet will end you before you could land a blow." Thoran gave a high pitched laugh. "Actually, do it. Please."

Killian's jaw clenched, but he didn't lift his sword. Thoran laughed again, then whipped a lash of Shadow towards Akairya. It slapped cruelly against her cheek and sent her sprawling. Her head smashed against the wall and she nearly passed out. Dizzy, she tried to stand as Killian threw himself at Thoran in rage.

Panic clutched her chest, and without really knowing how, she had the Earth element in her grasp; its power had ripped through the Shadow bracelet with blunt force. Rooted to the spot and suddenly feeling steadier than before, she lifted her hands and focused on each grain of sand that obeyed her command. She demanded them into a solid wall in front of Killian, who slammed into it seconds before he reached Thoran. Dumbstruck, he turned and stared at her. Relieved he wasn't dead, she dropped the wall of sand and felt the Earth element slip away, back behind the Shadow's block.

Thoran stood frozen, his eyes still stained black. His cheeks weren't as gray, however, and the cloud of Shadow had dissipated.

"How did you do that? You're shackled."

"I d-don't know…I thought Killian was going to die, and-"

"Silence." He said the word coldly, and Shadow once again surrounded him. "Why couldn't you feel such emotion towards me? Am I that loathsome? I *told* you I have no choice but to obey my father. If I rebel against him, the Shadow he planted in my blood will kill me. Is that what you want?" His voice grew rougher as he went on, and he bared his teeth before shoving his hands in front of him, causing a wave of Shadow to roll towards Akairya. She tried to dart out of the way, but not before it knocked her on her back. For the second time that day her head collided against the arena wall, and the last thing she saw before she passed out was Thoran falling to his knees, face in his hands as he sobbed.

CHAPTER TWENTY-SIX

Akairya woke in her cot in the Riders Quarters. Killian sat on the edge of the mattress holding her hand, and Draykor was curled in his dragon bed, violet eyes on her face. She lifted a hand to her aching head and groaned.

"Good, you're still alive," she said weakly to Killian. He shrugged.

"I didn't try to attack Thoran after he knocked you out. He...well, he looked absolutely dejected and it threw me."

"I told you he is still him...just twisted out of his control."

Doesn't excuse what he did. Draykor commented. His tone was hard, and his tail twitched in irritation. Jaxei, who was curled up beside him, watched it move.

"Where is he now?" she asked as she slowly sat up. Killian watched her carefully for signs of dizziness. When she gave none, he answered her question.

"He bolted out of the arena and back to the castle. Is your head okay?"

"It's sore, but I'm fine otherwise." The image of Thoran crumpling to the ground in despair haunted her. She threw off her covers. "I think I'm going to go talk to him."

Are you insane? He knocked you out! He is not stable enough for you to talk to.

"I agree with Dray. You should stay in bed and rest."

Akairya glared at both of them. "I'm fine, alright? Dray, just stay focused on me and alert Killian if I need help."

"I'm coming with-"

"No, you are *not*. I wish to speak with Thoran alone."

Killian and her dragon grudgingly let her go, although they made her promise to break off conversation with Thoran if he showed even the slightest hint of agitation.

She made her way to the castle, the chilly evening air sharp against her skin. Its touch lifted her completely out of the stupor that had lingered from being unconscious. Winter was nearly upon them, and its cold grasp would soon include dark skies and blankets of snow.

It took her some time to reach the ivory and gold castle, its stone walls washed with evening light. She stepped into the warm interior and stopped, suddenly unsure.

The sconces that hung throughout the halls of the palace were already lit, ready for when evening gave way to night. No one was nearby. The halls were eerily empty, devoid of the life that used to be rampant before the fall of the royal family.

Her eyes flicked through any rooms with open doors as she walked quickly through the castle. She came across one or two maids dusting, but no Thoran. The kitchens, boasting only one dejected cook, were fragrant with cooking meat and roasting potatoes, reminding Akairya that she hadn't eaten in quite some time. Ignoring her hunger, she took a flight of stairs to the second floor after the cook pointed her in that direction.

After a few more minutes of searching, Akairya came across one of the castle's many balconies, its large glass doors swung open to admit the cool air. Thoran stood leaning against the railing, his tired eyes looking out across the city.

"Hi," Akairya greeted him softly. He glanced at her, blinked in surprise, and turned his gaze back towards the city.

"What are you doing here?" he asked. "Surely you have nothing you want to say to me. Not after...what I did."

"It's killing you, isn't it?" She mumbled. Thoran stared at her. He frowned, his shoulders sagging.

"Yes. It is."

"You're a good man, and the Shadow is pure evil. Why haven't you tried to fight it off?"

Thoran gave a bitter laugh. "Father would never allow me freedom. He may have kept me relatively free from the taint for most of my life, but now he makes sure more and more of it is fed into me as his power grows. I'm his minion, through and through."

"How did he even get you?"

"He found me as a babe, nestled in my dead mother's arms. She had been travelling to Erconya, and bandits struck her wagon and killed her. They would have killed me if the Shadow Lord hadn't killed them first and took me in."

"So he adopted you."

"Yes, and raised me in Lakayol. I never truly understood the pure evil that lived in him when I was a child. He had also kidnapped a woman, and forced her to take care of me. Her name was Ina, and I remember her having long brown hair that smelled of cinnamon. I grew very attached to Ina, and she to me. She never blamed me for her kidnapping, and I thought of her as my mother. Father didn't like such affection. He had only wanted her to keep me healthy when he was away, so as punishment, he killed her with the Shadow in front of my eyes when I was six years old."

"That's..that's awful!" Akairya cried, her heart wounded for Thoran, who was gripping the railing tightly. He shrugged.

"You would think that I would have changed after that, would have become more cruel and cold towards people. But I didn't. It simply isn't in my nature. After Ina's death, I fell into a deep depression that delighted my father. 'Such dark emotions only feed the blight!' he would tell me. Without Ina, I had no one. Only Roraks, a handful of warlocks, and the Lord." He kept his eyes averted from Akairya. "Six year old me craved a parent, so I turned to the Lord. I began to call him father, and threw myself into pleasing him. He grew attached to me in his own evil way, and told me of his hopes to destroy the land and create his own kingdom, one festering with Shadow and crawling with creatures stuffed with twisted, evil souls. I don't know what he is, or how he was created, but he is powerful, and even though I no longer feel like pleasing him, I have no choice. The Shadow he has blended into me drives me now. I have no independent will. I am the minion he wanted when he first plucked me out of my mother's cold embrace."

Thoran fell silent. He was trembling, and tears shone in his eyes. A light wind blew across the balcony and ruffled his hair, and Akairya laid a comforting hand on his arm.

"Before I knew who you truly were, I thought of you as a kind man. You were the first to treat me with complete respect when you and Killian discovered me in the forest with Dray, and you always had this sweet aura around you. Your kindness is genuine Thoran. It's why the Shadow inside you is slowly killing you instead of simply turning you into an evil version of yourself, like it did to Telectus and Saverign. Your very soul is fighting against the poison."

Thoran sighed heavily and bowed his head. "Even if that's true, it doesn't erase the past. I could have killed you earlier. The Shadow inside me churns into such a fury so quickly, I have no hope of being able to control myself. I'm scared, Kairi." His voice broke on her nickname. "When I first saw you, I noticed a goodness in you that I had unconsciously thirsted for. My life has only been a withered mimicry of what it could have been if the Shadow Lord had never taken me in and chose me as his surrogate son."

"I...I think I might be able to help you," she whispered, her heart suddenly pounding. She was putting a lot at risk at telling Thoran this, and she wasn't entirely sure if she was making a mistake or not. She threw all caution to the wind and told him anyway. "I've been able to reach the Spirit element, even with the Shadow bracelet. I was able to dispel Jaxei's collar, and I am hoping that maybe I can help free you as well."

Thoran had gone absolutely still, and his once trembling hands were now frozen on the railing. Regret immediately washed through her, and she felt suddenly dizzy as the implication of what she had done hit her.

"You think...you can save me?" Thoran finally said, his voice hoarse. Nervous, she nodded. She blinked as he straightened and stared at her, his eyes bright with a fierce hope.

He stepped forward and wrapped her in a tight hug. "Thank you, Kairi. For even wanting to try."

Flustered, Akairya patted him awkwardly on the back. Relief made her knees weak; things could have gone a completely different way, and she felt incredibly lucky that they hadn't.

"I want to give you something," Thoran said when he stepped back. He reached into the folds of his cloak and pulled out a thin golden chain, a small charm hanging from it. The charm was delicately molded in the shape of a running horse. Two letters were etched in sloping script on the horse's barrel: H and F.

"This was apparently on me when father found me, and he never took it from me. I have no idea what the letters stand for, but I think it signifies whatever family I had before my mother's death and my...adoption. I would have tried to use this to figure out where I came from, but...well, I honestly see no point." He brushed the tiny horse charm lovingly with his thumb before holding it out to Akairya. "Now I want you to have it. You still wish to help me and be my friend, even after everything, so I want to give you something in return."

"Oh, Thoran...I couldn't possibly, this must mean so much to you-"

"Which is exactly why I want you to have it. Stop arguing and take it. Please."

She took it, and didn't know what to say, so she awkwardly stood there. After a few minutes of silence, Thoran rocked back on his heels.

"When will you want to try and…help me?" he asked.

"As soon as possible. I don't like you knowing, to be honest. The Shadow inside you may awaken and change your mind for you, or somehow alert the Lord."

"Yes. Let's do it now."

"Now?"

"Now. In the throne room. I have always had some of the taint in me, but Father poisoned me even deeper after the beheadings of the king and queen in the throne room. I'd like to be freed in the same room I was wholly chained in."

"Okay. I'll tell Dray to meet us there. I may need his support."

Draykor and Killian strode into the throne room to meet up with Akairya and Thoran. Akairya was standing near the expanse of window, staring out at nothing, her burgundy hair highlighted by the rich light of late evening. Thoran was pacing near one of the thrones, his hands tightly clasped behind his back. He stiffened when he saw Killian but said nothing.

Draykor joined Akairya by the window and snuffled her shoulder. *Be careful, my Rider. Freeing Jaxei took a lot out of you…I can't imagine how taxing this will be.*

I know. I'm going to try and break my bracelet first, so I have full power again. It's still fractured, and I've been worsening the fracture since I first helped Jaxei. I like to think I've gained some endurance.

Akairya closed her eyes and placed a hand on her dragon's golden muzzle. She drew herself inwards and felt along the ever present block that kept her from her power, its small fracture allowing slight breaths of elemental strength to reach her. She reached her mental fingers through the tiny cracks and tried to pry at them, hoping beyond hope she could break a large enough hole for Spirit to flow through. As she worked, she called the element. She could feel it, just on the other side of the block, reaching for her. Sweat broke out on her forehead, and she was soon out of breath. Killian, Thoran, and Draykor all watched her in concern as she struggled.

A whisper of something dark breathed through the crack in the block, and she shivered as it slid along her mind.

Why fight this? It inquired. *Just embrace it. These shackles can become your armor, your newfound strength.*

Shut up, she snapped. A surge of strength rushed through her, and she thanked her dragon for his gift as her own energy began to decline.

It is not wise to refuse such an offer. The whisper became a loud, angry voice, and Akairya suddenly found it hard to breathe. The voice had become an invisible hand, and gripped her throat with its fingers. She gasped and fell to her knees. Draykor growled and lent more of his strength, his scaled leg pressed against her side in encouragement. She soaked in the energy and shoved against the block, her jaw aching as she clenched her teeth, her windpipe still at the mercy of the unseen hand.

"Can't you just...take the bracelet off for her?" Killian asked Thoran through gritted teeth. Thoran shook his head.

"No. I don't have the strength or the ability. I can create the bracelets easily enough because the Shadow is willing to imprison, but it would fight me every inch of the way if I tried to take it away from someone."

Killian opened his mouth to reply, but Akairya cried out in satisfaction before he could say anything. She had broken through, and Spirit rushed through her as soon as the block crumbled, no longer able to hold out against the element. She panted from the exertion and adrenaline that accompanied the element, her violet eyes once again bright with power. No longer choked by the invisible hand, she stood, looked at her dragon, and delved into Spirit so she could see the threads that made up all living souls.

Tears filled her eyes as she saw how much weaker Draykor's threads were since the Shadow assault. They still shone with pure light, but the purple was faded. Yeilao's diagnosis had been correct; it would take some time before Draykor's spiritual strength was back to where it had been before the Lord had attacked him. Angry, she ripped the ebony strand that lay on top of his soul threads, and his bracelet immediately blinked out of existence.

Much better. I can feel our elements again, he said happily. *I can try to immerse myself in Spirit, but I won't be much help in breaking or pulling apart poisoned threads. I'm still quite weak, and I don't know if the element will work for me.*

I know. I will manage. Akairya assured him. She felt much stronger now that she was free from the bracelet, and had full confidence in her spiritual ability, even though she was still quite ignorant of the complex workings of the element. She turned to Killian, who was grinning from ear to ear. She returned his grin and broke his bracelet thread as easily as a brittle branch.

"I knew I needed to keep an eye on you, my son."

Thoran's face drained of the little colour it had, and he looked at his chest in horror as some Shadow seeped out and wrapped itself around him. He shivered in disgust as it pulsed darkly against his body.

"I returned with Telectus, and good thing I did. Not only are you a traitor, but you are utterly oblivious to my movements."

"He's not fully here, Akairya," Thoran shouted to her. She blinked at his use of her full name. "He's only partially here – his full self is still on Tilaner. He must have placed some of his personal Shadow in Telectus and then switched to me." He choked on the last word; the Shadow had tightened visibly around him.

"That's enough. I may not be fully present, but I still have power here. I could slaughter you, just as easily as I slaughtered Ina." The Lord's voice was hard, and Akairya winced as the Shadow tightened around Thoran even more. She gritted her teeth and asked for the Spirit element to come to her once again. It responded immediately, and her spiritual vision flickered back. As soon as it did, the Lord's Shadow dove back into Thoran, who shuddered from the poison that shot into his system.

Determined, she reached for the blackened threads that twisted through the few violet ones that made up Thoran's soul. They were blended impossibly together, and the Shadow that pulsed through him sickened her to her very core. She fought the urge to throw up as her grip slipped along the slimy strands of malignant fury, which were fighting to stain the little bit of purity that was the true Thoran. One particularly large thread jerked towards her, and she gasped as its diseased aura slapped against her own soul.

Her hold on Thoran's Spirit snapped, and Akairya fell, accidentally biting her tongue from the force of the fall. Warm blood filled her mouth, and she choked in dismay. Thoran moaned, the Shadow visible just under his skin.

"I-I can't get a grip on him, I can't drive it away!" Akairya cried, her chest heavy with failure. Some blood trickled down her chin. "It's too strong!"

The Shadow is too much a part of him, Draykor murmured. *It's impossible to save him. The Shadow will kill him if he doesn't embrace it.*

Draykor must have spoken in Thoran's mind as well, since he opened his now fully black eyes and stared at Akairya. "I'd rather die than be stained like this forever," he snarled. A sob tore from Akairya's throat, and she struggled to her feet and stepped closer to him.

"No! Stay away, Akairya, please." His eyes, once such a soft brown, were full of pain and roiling darkness. She stopped with her hand reaching towards him, her heart ripping apart.

Thoran took a deep breath and then screamed, all of his strength aimed towards pushing the Shadow away. Its flat darkness seeped out of his skin but didn't dissipate; instead it thickened into black ropes and entangled him. Drops of blood fell from where the Shadow touched him, and his expression grew more agonized. Panting, he gave Akairya one last, crooked smile.

"Destroy the Shadow, Kairi. Rid Alkairyn of its filth."

Before she could reply, the Shadow ropes tightened its grip and his body crumpled from the pressure. Killian leaped to Akairya and pressed her face against his chest so she didn't have to see the blood pour from the gruesome rips on Thoran, whose life finally snapped as his body was torn apart. The Shadow then billowed into a dark cloud, seething with dark intent.

"Now it's time to finish what I started with the dragon," the Lord said as the Shadow prepared itself. Realization dawned on Akairya, and she pulled away from Killian and darted to Draykor.

"We need to fly! Now!" She screamed as she jumped onto her dragon's back. She whirled to see where Killian was. "Come on!"

Killian shook his head. "No, Dray will fly faster with only you. Go!"

Draykor needed no further encouragement. With a roar, he launched himself at the glass wall and broke through it with ease, his metallic wings glinting with the failing sunlight and his violet eyes fierce with determination. Akairya clung desperately to his neck and closed her eyes as shards of glass rained down on them. Then they were outside, and Draykor was flying east as fast as his wings allowed.

Chapter Twenty-Seven

The cold evening air cut across Akairya's skin as her dragon flew away from the castle. She was luckily wearing the deep green cloak Yeilao had given her, but the chill still seeped into her bones and caused her teeth to chatter. She dared to glance behind them, and moaned in disbelief.

The cloud of Shadow, impossibly bloated, was just behind them, its deep darkness swallowing the light of the dying sun and greying the air around it. It wasn't fast enough to overtake them, but it matched their speed. Draykor would have to keep up his harsh pace or else fall prey to the living poison.

Akairya thought of her sword, sitting in its scabbard in the Riders Quarters. She had nothing with her but the clothes on her back, and she felt utterly hopeless.

Hopelessness soon turned into fury. The Lord had no right to destroy the land, kill people she loved, and chase her and her dragon. No right at all.

Her anger awoke the ever passionate Fire element, and she grimly allowed two large fireballs to flame into existence in her palms. Gripping Draykor with her legs, she turned and took a breath before throwing the fire right at the churning nebula of Shadow.

The blight froze for a second, but then widened, like a huge jaw ready for its next bite. The two balls of blazing power were swallowed effortlessly, and winked out as they were inhaled by the cloud.

Akairya nearly wept from the failure. *Fire did nothing to it. We'll just have to out-fly it.*

I don't know how long I'll be able to last, Draykor admitted. His wingbeats were strong for the moment, but the pace was brutal.

I'll lend you energy whenever you find yourself growing tired, okay? That should help.

It's the only choice we have.

They had already flown over the expanse of grassland that made up most of Ariniya, and were now soaring over a rugged landscape studded with thick shrubbery and tall trees. Pools of stagnant water dotted the land; they had reached the swampy expanse of Darton, the province directly east of Ariniya. A place where not many could live because of the mysterious creatures that called the swamp home. Akairya shivered as the sun finally sank beneath the horizon and plunged the land into twilight. Far ahead of them churned thick storm clouds, pregnant with the year's first snowfall.

The cloud of Shadow kept to their heels all through the night. Akairya was forced to dole out her energy to Draykor in small portions, which were barely enough to keep the dragon from losing the pace and falling into the embrace of the Shadow Lord. Both Rider and dragon were desperate, and both knew that Draykor wouldn't be able to withstand another assault on his spiritual essence. As a result, they flew on without a clue as to when the Shadow Lord would give up the chase…if he ever did.

A great roar sounded from behind them. Looking back, Akairya blinked when she saw that the cloud had paused in its chase. A few seconds later she knew why; Telectus and Saverign had arrived.

Um, Dray...we have a problem...

Saverign roared again as he sped towards them, massive black wings blocking out the stars.

"Let's see how you fare against two of your teachers, shall we?" The Lord's voice echoed around them. Akairya trembled as Telectus raised his hands and a ball of steaming water coalesced into existence. He sneered at her before throwing it, droplets glinting in the moonlight.

Draykor dove out of the way, and Akairya gripped with her knees as her dragon rolled out of the way of a second water sphere that came at them seconds after the first. Telectus threw ball after ball, his grim smile never wavering.

"Telectus, stop!" Akairya cried. "Don't let the blight control you!"

"Control me?" her former mentor laughed. "I willingly gave myself to the Lord. Do you have any idea of what kind of *power* he has promised me?"

"This isn't you! The Telectus I know never cared about power, only about his country, his *kingdom!* Don't you remember?"

"I remember being weak!" he snarled. He threw another sphere while twisting his free hand. A thin tornado screamed into existence, and Draykor flew right into it when he dodged the water. While not powerful enough to do any damage, it knocked Draykor off balance and Akairya was thrown off his back.

She screamed as she fell towards the swampy ground below, cloak flapping wildly around her. Draykor tucked his wings against his body and pelted down to catch her, front claws reaching out. He scooped her out of her fall, but was then hit by one of Telectus's spheres. He roared in agony.

As her dragon's pain flashed through her, Akairya gritted her teeth. She needed to protect him.

Earth rumbled inside her, and she snatched its power. She growled and thought about the mud that stretched for miles below them. The mud responded to her control, and some of it squeezed together to form two solid spears. She willed the mud spears to harden into compact dirt, then lifted her hands and pointed to Saverign.

Before the bigger dragon realized what she was doing, the two massive spears found their mark in each of his wings, slicing through the delicate membrane that had once been blue. The Shadow dragon shrieked, and fell heavily out of the sky.

The Shadow Lord's writhing cloud of poison froze in shock. With some difficulty, Akairya wearily climbed from Draykor's claws to his back.

The cloud moved back into action, and Draykor immediately turned and once again fled.

Akairya fell forward on Draykor and rested her cheek on his scaled neck. She fought to stay conscious. She knew that if she fell asleep, Draykor would lose any energy he had left and would drop out of the sky like a bird hit with a stone.

Her half closed eyes stared vacantly towards the ground, where the many bodies of murky water glimmered in the moonlight. She caught sight of random twinkling lights, and dimly remembered the tales her father used to tell her of the swamp fey, tiny creatures who beckoned unwary travelers into their muddy abodes by waving their fingers tipped with light. She wondered if Saverign and Telectus were dead.

Dawn crept across the sky as Akairya gave Draykor the last bit of her energy, which barely affected him. The Shadow was still behind them, as menacing as ever. As the sky grew steadily brighter, the clouds Akairya had seen before were finally above them, and soft flakes of snow began to descend. A large mountain stood ahead of them, steep slopes already garbed in thick blankets of snow. Draykor shifted and made straight for the mountain.

I'm not going to make it, my Rider, he told Akairya, his voice heavy with fatigue. *I'm going to let the Shadow take me.*

No! You can't! Dray, I need you-

I know. But I am weak. My wings feel like they are going to fall from my body any second, and my chest is burning. It'll be up to you to save me, Akairya.

I don't know how! Look what happened with Thoran!

I have full faith in you.

Akairya screamed as Draykor's flying slowed and the twisting cloud of blight was upon them. The Shadow Lord's bodiless laughter echoed around her as she and Draykor were wrapped in Shadow. The presence of the poison was heavy on her mind and soul, and she cried out as the seething evil of the cloud dove at her and her dragon. She reached for Spirit in utter panic, and was immediately swathed in the element.

It was what saved her. The Shadow soaked into Draykor as the dragon reached the mountain and slammed onto a wide shelf of stone and snow, but it simply bounced off Akairya as Spirit blocked its entry. It felt as if her soul had hardened into an impossibly strong armor, and it barely shuddered as the blight pushed brutally against it.

"What *are* you?" The Lord's voice snapped as he failed to poison Akairya.

Draykor, however, roared in pain as the Shadow hit him without mercy, staining his golden scales to black and erasing the purple of his eyes. Akairya felt his mind snap, and she nearly vomited as his conscience became cloaked in poison. She tumbled off his back, fell into a deep drift of snow, and watched in horror as his soul threads darkened into the sick strands of Shadow. She mentally grabbed hold of the last pure thread, the largest one, and stroked it. She ran her spiritual power over the strand and followed it to where it ended at Draykor's mind. Without really knowing what she was doing, she gently twisted it. Her dragon stopped moving and sighed, then fell into a slumber too deep to ever wake from naturally. The Lord cursed her. Then everything was silent. She knew that the Lord was gone, since his only connection was with the Shadow that was now fast asleep inside her dragon.

Snow was falling in earnest now. A lithe shape, nearly invisible amongst the whirling eddies of ivory flakes, stepped forward from where it had been hiding behind a massive tree. It looked at Akairya with blue eyes full of wild wisdom; its thick white coat rippled from the biting wind that tore around the mountain. One ear was twisted towards Draykor, who lay like a frozen ebony statue.

Hot tears blurred Akairya's vision as she turned from the wolf and stared at her beloved dragon. His now black scales were a sharp contrast against the snow. Their connection, while still there, cut into her with its malevolence. It was subtle because she had forced his Spirit to sleep, but its dark touch still drove like a knife into her mind.

With a broken sob, she threw herself at Draykor's head and wept. She cried for Thoran, whose naturally kind soul had been torn apart by the life he had been forced to live. She cried for the slain royal family, especially for Theandi, who had joyously adopted Akairya as a sister the moment the half elf had walked into the castle, confused and filthy. She sobbed for Killian, who had given her his heart and had no idea that now it was she who could never be with him, not now that she was bonded with a dragon poisoned by the very thing they fought against. She cried for the loss of Telectus' goodness and Saverign's wisdom, and lastly she wept for Draykor, her playful yet unbelievably serious dragon, who looked to be lost to her forever.

Her tears finally dried, and she rubbed her eyes free from the frozen remnants that clung to her lashes. The passion of weeping had kept the chill at bay, but now that she had calmed somewhat she noticed the cold. Her hands, ungloved, ached from the cutting wind. She looked up and saw that the wolf had remained, stolidly standing in the storm that was just beginning to recede. Its eyes beckoned her, and when she stood, it turned and began to walk away. She hesitated. As she deliberated on whether or not she should follow, the Blood Hawk's dark voice echoed through her mind; *when you cannot find answers to questions, not even from the Elder dragons, travel to the Twin Slabs. I will meet you there, no matter when you arrive.*

She definitely had questions that had no answers. She needed to find the Twin Slabs, and find out what the Blood Hawk could give her that could help her with Draykor's diseased mind. Saving her dragon and ending the blight that had taken him from her was her absolute priority.

Her mind made up, she glanced at Draykor. He slept his poisoned sleep, drifts of snow already building up against him. She whispered a promise that she would find a way to save him, and followed the wolf into the swirling snow.

End of the first half of
THE FRACTURED SOUL

ABOUT THE AUTHOR

When Abrianna Leaming was only eight years old, she 'wrote' her first book and created imaginary worlds and scenarios that actually quite worried her family. "Will she ever be able to tell what is fantasy and not fantasy?" They asked themselves. Luckily, she simply grew up into what we call a writer. *Akairya* is her first novel, and she lives in Chilliwack, British Columbia, where she rides horses and plays too many video games.

Made in the USA
Columbia, SC
10 May 2017